In Appreciation

Love and gratitude always and forever to husband Larry. Larry read this novel—numerous times--with eagle eyes, and without complaining. I don't know what I did to deserve him? I must also thank granddaughter Cody and Daughters Rene and Andrea for their love and encouragement. Rene and Andrea offered so many wise suggestions, as did my sis Alice Kay, sister-in-law Cheryl Semerad, editors Deb Wheeler and Barbara Warren. I must also thank Carol Missildine for loving this book and not wanting it to end and James Anderson for the lovely blurb and encouragement. Any errors you find are entirely mine.

Chapter One

Diary of Carrie Sue Justice

Monday, February 16, 1987

A chair—scraping the floor like fingernails on blackboard—jolted me out of my daydream and back to our staff meeting. I usually take notes during these weekly meetings. I've been known to fill half a reporter's pad with my scribbles, but this morning my lovestruck brain refused to focus on work. I should have known better, but even if I'd been able to focus, I couldn't have predicted the trauma to come.

Darla Denton grabbed her tote from the mahogany conference table and pointed to the starburst clock on the wall. "It's five past ten. If I don't leave now, I'll be late for my appointment."

Marcus ran a hand through his dark hair. "I have one more thing to say, Wonder Woman." We all called Darla "Wonder Woman," due to her ability to sell ads for the Southern Journal and her likeness to actress Lynda Carter.

My eyes feasted on Marcus, *handsome*, in a heather-grey suit and blue tie. His navy eyes captured my baby blues. He hiked up one side of his top lip in a smile that could make dark clouds disappear. "I've proposed to Carrie."

Lindsey Jernigan, the features editor, stood and picked off lint from her green suit. "Proposed?"She reminded me of a young Jacqueline Kennedy Onassis. Lindsey faced me and squinted her brown eyes, her version of x-ray vision. "Oh, wow, Carrie Sue. Did you accept?"

My heart hammered. Marcus didn't tell me he was going to announce our engagement during our staff meeting.

Lindsey grabbed my left hand to examine the diamond and ruby ring. "Gorgeous. Does this mean engagement and marriage?"

My burning face must have looked as red as the rubies. "Doesn't it usually?"

Thomas Anderson wrapped me in a tight hug. He smelled of *Old Spice* and reminded me of actor Jimmy Stewart in the movie *Rear Window* "Congratulations to both of you."

Thomas taught journalism at Georgia State, my alma mater, until he retired a few years ago. Retirement didn't suit him, so he joined our staff part time.

He draped an arm around his wife Lisa, twenty years his junior. "You're not surprised. Are you, sweetie?"

Lisa, the office secretary and circulation manager, pushed back her flaxen hair and pulled me into a gardenia-perfumed hug. Her blue eyes filled with tears. "This is wonderful news. I wish your Mom and Dad could be here."

I tried to bite back my tears, but they leaked out as I stuttered, "I'd...I'd like...like to think... they're here in spirit." I could almost hear Mom say, *"Remember to pause and allow your brain to process what you want to say before you speak."*

Jackie Steiner shot me a green stare. "Seriously? You've got to be kidding. Didn't you just get a divorce from what's his face?" Jackie and I were around the same age, but she looked like a teen in her frayed blue jeans, oversized sweater and honey-blonde hair bound in a ponytail. Marcus had recently hired Jackie, a new grad from Georgia State.

I bristled at her candor, though she spoke the truth and had the guts to say it, which I usually welcomed, but not at that moment.

Lisa, our peacekeeper, stepped in to mediate. "Carrie Sue knows marrying Kyle was a big mistake. We all make mistakes. Let's focus on the here and now. I'm more interested in knowing how, when and where Marcus proposed."

"He took me to the Sun Dial Restaurant on Valentine's Day."

Lisa clasped her hands together. "An Atlanta landmark, perfect. Did he get down on one knee?"

Marcus smiled and nodded. "I did, but Carrie Sue made me wait. She didn't answer right away."

I sighed. "I was too shocked to speak."

As everyone laughed and jabbered, my mind flashed back to the night Marcus proposed. He wore a tux. I wore a flashy-red sequined dress and let my bushy blonde hair fly wild and free. A rare situation for me. In my job as a crime reporter, I dress much more conservatively. Our waitress said I looked like Barbie. Not one of my goals, but I thanked her for trying to flatter me.

Marcus and I ate a full course dinner, drank champagne and shared a baked Alaska before he kneeled and opened a black velvet box.

"Will you marry me?" His deep voice resonated through the crowded restaurant.

The blood drained from my head. My tongue froze.

A woman at a nearby table yelled, "Give him an answer!"

Marcus' eyes twinkled in the candlelight as he continued to kneel, all 6-feet, 5 inches of him, patiently waiting.

Marcus drew me back to the moment when he said, "I hope I didn't embarrass you, Carrie. I just wanted to share our happy news. If no one else has anything to add, let's adjourn." He motioned to me. "If your column is ready, I can edit it now."

Thankful for the retreat, I grabbed my little Tandy computer from my desk and followed him to his office. He was closing the door when Lisa stuck her head in. "Marcus, you have an urgent call on line one."

He answered the phone in his forceful baritone. "Marcus Handley." After a moment, he grimaced, gulped and dropped down in his chair. "You're alive? Oh god, Susan. What happened to you?"

I knew of only one Susan in Marcus's life: his late wife, Susan Silverman. She was killed in a helicopter crash during the Vietnam War, he'd said. He was piloting B-52s at the time, and Susan was riding in a copter, near where he'd been ordered to drop his bombs. She was a war correspondent back then, and he had no idea she was in the path of his napalm, which burned her beyond recognition, he'd said. He still suffered from excruciating guilt and nightmares.

Marcus massaged his eyes and listened quietly for a few minutes. When he finally spoke again, his voice cracked. "How terrible. When are you leaving the Manila hospital?"

I moved closer, straining to hear the caller. Marcus held the receiver—almost buried in his large hand—tightly against his ear.

"Ahem," he cleared his throat. "When do you expect to fly to California?" He listened silently for a few more minutes. "Okay, take it easy. Get some rest and feel better. I'll see you soon." His eyes locked with mine for a moment. Then he quickly looked away. "Me, too, Susan."

My heart hurt. Did she tell him she loved him, and did he respond with, *"Me, too?"*

After he hung up, I wrapped my arms around him and pressed my cheek to his chest. I could hear his heart thrashing. He smelled clammy like an injured pet.

He cushioned my face in his hands. "Susan is alive."

"What, what are you saying, Marcus?"

"I thought my wife was dead, but she's alive."

"That doesn't make sense, Marcus. You said Susan was killed in a helicopter crash. How could she be alive?"

He groaned. "We thought we'd recovered what was left of her body. We found her identification and the identification of the pilot. Susan was inside the copter when it took off, according to everyone who saw her before she left." He sucked in a breath. "She was planning to free Virginia Fischer. It was a secret mission, and I didn't know about it. Virginia was one of her friends from college. After college, Virginia worked with the CIA and was captured by the Vietcong. I don't have all the details yet." His frown deepened as his eyes locked with mine. "Susan is at a hospital in Manila. She's flying to California. She suffered head injuries and lost her memory for a time, or at least that's what she said."

I stroked his face. "Are you saying she had amnesia?"

Marcus shrugged. "I'm unsure of the medical diagnosis."

"Marcus, if she survived the crash, I'm confused as to why you didn't receive word she survived?"

He heaved a sigh. "She was captured and imprisoned. No one came forward with new information."

"Someone should have notified you. The official report from our government stated all the prisoners of war had been returned. Those missing were believed to be dead. Isn't that what our government claimed?"

"This was a secret mission and with the CIA involvement, I'm not surprised I didn't hear anything."

"Are you sure it was Susan you spoke to just now?"

"Yes."

"You're absolutely sure the woman you spoke to was Susan?"

"She and I grew up together. Yes, I'm certain."

I longed to ask him other questions, but I doubted he'd be able to answer them, or maybe I feared the answers. How would he respond if I asked him: "Do you still want to marry me?" Would he hesitate, or not answer at all, or say no?

My body ached with grief. Marcus looked grief stricken, too. This puzzled me. He now knew he wasn't responsible for his wife's death. She was alive.

His eyes shifted from side to side, a signal he was processing information. What would he decide? Marcus disliked uncertainty. He needed to be in control. He made quick decisions. But this was not like deciding to cover one news story over another. This was his life, his future, our future, Susan's future.

I grabbed my chest to ease the stabbing pain—like a knife in my heart. The Marcus I knew would never desert his wife in her time of need. His integrity wouldn't allow him to divorce her. He'd known and loved her longer than he'd known and loved me, but I refused to doubt his love for me. Our love was like the song: *How Deep Is the Ocean? How High Is the Sky*? He'd played that song for me on his piano this weekend, as a serenade to our love, and even though I loved him deeper than the ocean and higher than the sky, I knew he would do what he thought was right, even if it broke both our hearts, and as this unbearable truth sunk in, I convulsed into sobs. Nothing was certain now, only heartache.

Marcus pulled me close and stroked my hair. "I'm sorry, Carrie. I'm not handling this well. I love you. Never forget that."

Chapter Two

When Marcus and I passed the reception desk, Lisa looked up from her phone conversation and placed a hand over the receiver. "Are y'all leaving?"

I gave her a wobbly wave. "Yes."

Lisa frowned. "When will you be back?"

"I'm not sure, Lisa. I'll call you later and let you know."

I followed Marcus out. He marched like a sluggish soldier down the front steps of the old three-story Victorian house Mom and Dad had transformed into a successful newspaper business.

Marcus had modernized all the equipment after he'd bought the business. He wanted the best, and as I considered his demand for perfection, I began to feel defective.

When we reached the sidewalk, he stopped and stared up at the gray sky. "Guam," he whispered.

I could smell a dank odor—rain falling on asphalt. A flash of lightning slashed a purple cloud, followed by distant thunder. "Why Guam, Marcus? What happened in Guam?" I touched his arm to bring him back to me.

"I flew missions out of Anderson Air Force Base."

"I've read something about that base. It concerned air crews tracking and entering typhoons."

Marcus nodded. "Right, the Fifty-Fourth Weather Reconnaissance Squadron. During the Vietnam War, they provided cloud-seeding along the Ho Chi Minh Trail."

"What is cloud-seeding?" I genuinely wanted to know, but I also hoped my question would break his funk and mine.

"Cloud-seeding is when a pilot flies above the clouds and shoots flares containing substances like dry ice and certain types of salt into the coldest portions of the clouds. This encourages water droplets to grow and form rain."

As he spoke, his trembling right hand dug into the pocket of his suit and pulled out a ball of keys.

I grabbed the keys from him. "Let me drive, Marcus." He was in no shape to get behind the wheel.

I'd driven his Jeep Cherokee before. It was a standard shift, similar to my Triumph Spitfire—sidelined since the day I came home early to find Kyle, my sleaze-bag ex, bedding another woman. For two months, the Spitfire had been parked at Tyrone Thompson's shop for repairs.

I preferred driving an automatic like the Cadillac I inherited from Mom, but the Caddy was parked at my house. Marcus had picked me up for our Saturday night date. We'd spent the weekend at his place. In my lovey-dovey state, I'd forgotten about my wheels.

As I cranked up his Jeep, I longed to ask Marcus what Susan's return meant for us. But he had already turned away and was staring out his passenger window at the grey, gloomy day.

I drove in a painful silence all the way to the old Georgian Colonial he'd restored. He often left his Jeep parked at the Southern Journal and jogged the three miles to and from his home. He'd shower in the apartment above the offices, where he kept an array of clothing. He had many predictable habits, which I'd come to know and love, but he still remained a mystery to me.

I pulled up in his drive. Killed the engine. He jumped out and came around to open my door. His stern—soldier at attention—face showed no emotion as we walked inside his house.

I collapsed on his sleigh bed, where I'd enjoyed the greatest sex of my life. He picked up the black phone from the corner desk of his bedroom to call his travel agent. He would be flying from Atlanta to Santa Ana, California. Santa Ana wasn't far from his mother's house in Irvine, he explained.

"How long will you be away, Marcus?"

He squinted at my question, as if it confused him. "I'll ask Thomas to fill in for me until whenever."

"I'll call Thomas and Lisa, Marcus. You have enough to think about. I'll tell them you had an emergency. I won't go into detail. I'll just say it's a personal family matter."

He sucked in a breath. "Thank you."

"Susan's return should be a big news story, Marcus. How should we cover it?"

He glared at me, as if I'd asked him to lie down in front of a speeding train. I ached like I'd been run over by one as I remembered the 8 x 10 photo of Susan he kept in his office drawer. She resembled a blonde movie star.

"I didn't notice anything on the wire," he said, referring to the Associated Press service. He still called it "the wire," even though AP was now transmitted to his desktop computer. "With the CIA involvement, we need to be careful about covering Susan's return. Also, we have to be mindful of Virginia's parents. I'm sure they're still hoping and praying she's alive, but from what Susan said, Virginia died in the copter crash." He picked up the phone and punched in a number. "We'll discuss this later, okay?"

I listened as he talked to his Mom. He recited his flights and arrival time. I wanted to go with him, but I was afraid of flying, a fear I developed after I lost my parents to a plane crash. I refused to believe they were dead, until their wedding rings were found in the wreckage.

Would Marcus have asked me to go if he didn't know of my fear? I thought not. He had enough to worry about, and I'd be another complication, like a thorn in his side he couldn't expel or hide.

I gulped deep breaths and fisted my hands to keep from grabbing him and holding on for dear life. Every nerve in my body pulsated in terror as my separation anxiety grew. I wanted to cry out, *please don't go. I can't lose you, too.*

Marcus hung up from his mom and said, "She's talked to Susan already."

"What about Susan's parents, Marcus? Will you be calling them?" My voice sounded eerily calm to my ears, though I could feel my body shutting down and dying inside, similar to when I lost my parents. During that tragic time, I sank into a deep depression. I had no energy or desire to run a newspaper business, so I sold it all—the business and the building—to Marcus. Dad trusted him, and Marcus seemed like the logical person to take over. *"He's an old soul,"* Dad used to say.

"Susan's mother died young of breast cancer," Marcus said. "Ted, her father, remarried when Susan was twelve. Susan didn't mesh with Elizabeth, the new wife. Elizabeth never wanted children. Mom was more of a mother to Susan than Elizabeth. I'm sure Susan will speak with her dad at some point, if she hasn't already. Mom said he's very ill. He suffered a stroke recently and has some form of dementia." He stared off; his eyes unfocused.

"I'll drive you to the airport, Marcus." I wanted to spend as much time with him as possible.

"That won't be necessary, Carrie. I'll take a cab."

He placed the call for a taxi, then walked over and stroked my cheek. "I know this is terrible for you, baby. I'm sorry. I want you to take it easy today, okay? Be good to yourself. I'd love for you to stay here. Take a Jacuzzi, read, relax, do whatever you need to feel better."

"I love the Jacuzzi, but I'm not in the mood now." We'd taken two sexy hot tubs over the weekend while drinking the Dom Perignon he'd ordered to celebrate our engagement. But how could he possibly think I would be able to relax when my world was crashing around me, and he, the love of my life, belonged to someone else?

"Okay, but promise me you'll stay safe, Carrie."

"I wish you wouldn't obsess about my safety." This had been a sore point for us, but I often excused him, thinking his controlling nature stemmed from his terrible guilt as a result of what happened to Susan. But now he knew Susan was alive.

"Don't worry about me, Marcus. I'm a survivor."

He sat on the bed beside me. His eyes glistened with tears. Marcus had the ability to conceal his emotions, but I could feel his body trembling, on the brink of a breakdown.

He wrapped his arms around me and covered my mouth in a deep kiss, as if this would be the last kiss we'd share.

I stroked his powerful chest and blabbed about how much I loved and needed him.

"Ah, baby, I love you and need you, too."

He slipped his hand inside my skirt. My body tingled hot for him and I lost control. I unzipped his fly—longing to free his swollen loins and soothe mine. But then the rude doorbell rang.

"Dammit," he groaned.

"My thoughts exactly."

He walked to the bedroom window and pulled back the blue draperies to peer out at the driveway. "Cab's here. I didn't expect it this soon." He adjusted his erection and zipped up before grabbing his suitcase. "I'm sorry, baby. I'll call you when I arrive."

"I probably won't be here, Marcus."

He squinted at me and pursed his lips. "Will you be at your house?"

"I'm not sure. I need to check on Freemont and spend some time with him. If I'm not at Freemont's, I should be at my house. I've seen him only twice since he left the hospital. We've talked on the phone daily, but I should have visited him more often. No excuse for my neglect. He's only a mile from me, as you know, and we are as close as siblings." My mind flashed back to the first time Freemont referred to himself as my 'black brother.' We grew up together and he'd been my closest friend for as long as I can remember.

Marcus smiled, but his dark eyes appeared sad. "He's like a brother to you, isn't he?"

"Yes, he likes to say, he's my 'black brother.'" I closed my eyes to hide my tears.

"Maybe you should write a column about the amazing history you and Freemont share."

"I'm still thinking about doing that." Marcus had recommended this before, but fear made me hesitate. Some of the narrow-minded, prejudiced folks in our community might react violently if they knew my double great-grandfather George probably sired Freemont's great-grandmother Georgia. My Granny Justice researched the relationship between George and Georgia's black mother, and it's all in her journal. During the 1800s, my double great-grandmother Charlotte—married to George—willed Freemont's great-grandmother Georgia—of mixed race—her freedom, along with an acre of property and a small house. Thanks to Granny's tireless research, Freemont's ancestors were able to claim their property.

Marcus wrapped his arms around me in a tight hug. "Tell Freemont we'll get those Klan fuckers eventually."

"I hope it's soon. Those bastards almost killed him. I still can't believe no arrests have been made. We've found enough evidence. Freemont's security cameras showed the license plate on the green truck carrying those criminals. Unfortunately, their pointed white hoods covered their cowardly faces. Cain Powers still owns that truck."

"Yes, but he happens to be the dad of Detective Nev Powers and those good ole boys at the College Station Police Department rally around their own. The dad and Nev covered their asses when they reported the truck was stolen during the Klan march in College Station."

"I know that Marcus, but Freemont shot one of the Klansmen. Blood stains were found in the getaway truck, and Mr. Powers had a bloody bandage on his arm. That GBI friend of yours thought it looked suspicious and asked Powers about it."

"But as you know, the father claimed he was injured in a hunting accident, and Nev verified his dad's story. They've both lawyered up now. I'm confident we'll get them eventually." He motioned to the cab driver to give him a moment. "I've got to go, sorry. Promise me you'll take care of yourself, and don't try to stir the hornet's nest."

I nodded—more to appease him than agree. Gray clouds had blanketed the sky. I felt a sprinkle of rain and inhaled the earthy smell of wet grass.

As the cabby got out and placed Marcus' luggage in the trunk, I pulled Marcus aside and whispered. "I wish I could have taken you to the airport." I shivered and hugged myself. "I've developed a dislike for cabs since the night that yellow cab tailed us to the Pot Aux Roses restaurant. A similar cab followed you on your way to pick me up from my house that night. Remember?"

Marcus sighed. "Oh Carrie, I don't have time to talk about this now. As to taking me to the airport, I didn't want you to drive out there and get stuck in Atlanta traffic when you're this upset. You're suffering as much as I am." He kissed my lips lightly. "Everything will work out. Trust me."

I started to tell Marcus about the note I'd found stuck in my door the same night of the taxi mystery. That happened two months ago and I should have told him already. I suspected Neeley Nelson may have left the note. "You'll be sorry, bitch," sounded like something she'd write. No coincidence we ran into Neeley at the restaurant. She flirted with Marcus right in front of me. Nelson used to model for *Penthouse* magazine, until she had a "come to Jesus moment." Or so she said. She moved to College Station after she accepted a position as the executive director for the Chamber of Commerce. God only knew what kind of commerce she had going on now.

I forced all those crazy, dark thoughts away and threw Marcus a kiss as he left in the cab. Then I walked inside and called the office.

"Southern Journal," Lisa drawled. "How may I help you?"

"Hi Lisa, Marcus had to fly to California. He wanted me to let you know. Please ask Thomas to help out until Marcus returns."

"Okay, absolutely, I will. Why did Marcus have to leave in such a hurry?"

"It's personal, and I'm not at liberty to say. I'm sure he'll share the details when he can."

"He looked terrible when he walked out. He usually tells me where he's going. You looked like you'd been crying, Carrie Sue. What's going on? Did it have something to do with that woman who called? She refused to give her name. I knew it wasn't his mother. I'd recognize her voice."

I paced the master bedroom, cradling the phone and pulling the twisted, black cord as far as it would go. I caught site of my sad image in the armoire mirror. My long hair stuck out in a wiry mess. The purple suit I'd ordered from a catalogue dwarfed my frame. Its shoulder pads looked like dislocated tits.

"You're like a daughter to me, Carrie Sue."

Lisa was unable to have children. She had endometriosis in her 30s and decided to have a hysterectomy before she married Thomas. Thomas had a son—Jacob—from a previous marriage. Tragically, Jacob was killed in the Vietnam War.

"You're one of the most compassionate people I've ever known, Lisa. You've always given wise advice. I wish I'd listened to you about Kyle."

"I knew he wasn't right for you. He was your professor for heaven's sakes. A professor shouldn't date one of his students."

"My mistake."

"You were naïve and trusted him."

I sighed. "You're right. I had to learn the hard way. Freemont also warned me, but I didn't listen."

"Freemont is such a good guy. He went through a horrible time after his mama passed, but he still tried to be there for you, didn't he? I've been so worried about that man."

My stomach knotted with guilt. "I should have visited with him more often. He's a great guy, the greatest. I don't know what I'd do without his friendship."

Lisa huffed. "Listen, Carrie Sue, you're wise and strong. You need to believe that. If your parents were alive, they'd tell you not to let anything defeat you or bury your spirit. You're young. You're beautiful. You're smart. You're talented. You've got the whole world at your fingertips and a wonderful future ahead."

As I listened to Lisa, I licked the salty tears off my lips. Had she listened in on the phone call from Susan? Lisa had a tendency to do that. I wanted to ask her. But why offend or embarrass her? "Thank you for the pep talk, Lisa. Don't worry. I'm going to be okay and so is Marcus. Dad and Mom thought the world of you, and so do I. And even though Marcus may not always say how much he appreciates you, I know he does."

Lisa sniffled. "Where are you now, Carrie Sue?"

I couldn't tell her I was at Marcus' house. She'd drive over, and I had no desire for a pity party.

"I'm getting ready to head to Freemont's house. I need to check on him."

Lisa continued to talk, as if reluctant to say goodbye. I eventually had to lie and tell her Freemont was expecting me soon, or I never would have gotten her off the phone.

After we said goodbye, I paced through the house and sobbed. Marcus wanted us to live here after we got married. The rooms are a lovely mix of vintage and contemporary furniture, blues, reds, whites, greys, browns and blacks. This weekend he kept a fire going in the living room hearth, and when we weren't making love, bathing in the Jacuzzi, cooking, eating or talking, he'd entertained me by playing love songs on his grand piano.

I sat down at the piano and banged out *Chopsticks* in a futile effort to feel closer to him and lift my spirits. Then I washed my face and squirted drops in my eyes to ease the burning and redness. I stripped out of the depressing purple suit and put on my favorite blue jeans and grey sweater. Marcus had cleared out a portion of his walk-in closet for my clothes, but I'd stored only a few things in there. I didn't want to crowd him out of his own closet, and when I told him this, he said, "I'll renovate one of the bedrooms to create a larger closet for you." Would he trash those plans now that his wife had returned from the dead?

Oh, how I feared the answer to that question as I picked up the phone to call Freemont.

He answered on the second ring, "Jackson Laundry."

"Hi, it's Carrie Sue. Can I come over?"

"Sure. Come on. I got your message from yesterday. I guess congrats are in order."

"We'll talk when I get there, Free. How are you feeling?"

"I'm hanging in. But I'm not so sure about you. You don't sound too joyful."

Chapter Three

When I arrived at Freemont's house, his white laundry van was gone. In its place, was a silver, Dodge Colt. Then I remembered he'd hired someone to make his deliveries until he fully recovered from his shoulder injury. But he didn't say who.

As I stared at the Dodge Colt, it hit me. I knew the owner. Why wouldn't Freemont want me to know? Why did he avoid my question?

This confused me as I sat in the quietude of the Jeep and watched the rain. The remnants of the burned cross were still visible in his yard. Despite the desecration, I could see his grass had been mowed recently, his shrubs neatly clipped. How had he managed to do all of this, plus run his laundry business, and keep up with his college studies? An amazing man, that Freemont Jackson.

No one would have guessed this house was once a slave's quarters. Mama Jackson had expanded and renovated the place, and Freemont had widened the front porch. No professional wood-worker could have done a better job.

He'd added two cane rockers and a clay pot that held a rose bush. It reminded me of the roses I'd planted beside my front steps near the veranda. They'd survived. Despite my brown thumb that I'd accused Freemont of jinxing me with. I even wrote a column about the jinx. I didn't mention Freemont by name, but several readers identified him as the person who'd yanked up my tiny peach tree that resulted in my brown thumb. *"I have no memory of killing your little sprig," he'd said in his defense. "I couldn't have been more than six at the time. As to giving you a brown thumb, I don't have that kind of power. I wish I was that powerful, but I'm not."*

Thinking of our playful banter, I felt a groundswell of gratitude. Our close friendship continued to thrive. No disagreement could separate us. Our bond was stronger and heartier than the blanket of rose bushes, separating my property from his. And they were pretty damn hearty. During the spring and summer, these roses create a breathtaking display of red, pink, orange, yellow and white. The Jacque Cartier's had been thriving since the 1800s. According to Granny Justice's journal, they provided a method for Freemont's ancestors, Georgia and Simon, to hide secret messages. Simon had left a map for Georgia that allowed her to escape my ancestors' plantation, Granny wrote. Georgia and Simon eventually married in Philadelphia.

Soon after my "jinx" column was published, a reader sent me yellow rose bushes and instructed me to plant them as a challenge to prove I no longer had a brown thumb. Rather than plant them with the others, I put the new roses next to the front steps to my veranda, and despite the jinx and cold weather, they'd survived. Freemont and I had promised to leave messages in the new roses to continue the tradition, but we'd slacked off lately, due mostly to my neglect and Freemont's injury.

Freemont startled me out of my reverie when he opened my car door. "What's wrong, Carrie Sue? Why are you out here lollygagging? Afraid you'll melt?" He held a large umbrella in his right hand. His damaged left arm rested in a black sling. He'd undergone several surgeries to repair the damage caused by a hollow-point bullet, but looking at him at that moment, he appeared invincible, 6-foot 6 and 300 pounds of mostly muscle, in blue jeans, cowboy boots and a brown flannel shirt, the color of his skin.

I hopped out of the Jeep and hugged him, careful to avoid his injuries. "I'm not sweet enough to melt." I smiled impishly. "How's your arm and shoulder?"

"Worse than when Madman Bowman broke my tailbone." He was referring to massive tackle, Richard Bowman, who sidelined Free during a high school football game. Free could have played for UGA, but he turned down the scholarship, due to his mama's weak heart. Every time Free would get hurt, she'd have to pop a nitroglycerine tablet. Eventually her soft heart gave out, despite his sacrifice.

"Oh, no, can't be that bad," I said, as he walked me into his house.

"Have you ever known me to lie?"

I backed up to his blazing fireplace. "I refuse to answer on the grounds that it may incriminate me."

Freemont smiled, but his brown eyes showed concern. "Could I offer you anything, Carrie Sue? I got our favorite meal from Papa's Chicken and Burgers. I haven't felt much like cooking. If you were hoping for home-cooked veggies, you're out of luck."

I smiled at his generosity. Even with his incapacitated arm, he was offering me food. "I should be fixing you something to eat or at the very least, I should have brought you something. I've been neglectful lately. I'm sorry."

Freemont plopped down on his brown leather couch. He'd recently redecorated his home with new furnishings. Two matching chairs faced the couch. A large red rug, bordered with diamond shapes of orange, green, blue and brown covered most of the hardwood floor in the living room.

He frowned and shook his head. "Okay, enough small talk. Stop the pretense. What's going on with you? Your message said you and Marcus were getting ready to tie the knot. Are you afraid the knot's goin' to be too tight?"

Tears spilled out as I told Freemont about Susan. "Please don't tell a soul, Free. Okay?"

He walked over and wrapped a giant right arm around my shoulders. "Not my business to tell." He opened an ottoman and pulled out a box of Kleenex. "I'm sorry, honey. I really am."

I took a tissue and wiped my eyes and face. "It's like losing Mom and Dad all over again."

"Yeah, Mama used to say the more loved ones you lose, the more your heart hurts. Heartache compounds every time you lose someone, adding up to more suffering than you think you can stand, Mama said."

I nodded, missing Mama J more than ever. "Are you saying you think I've lost Marcus for good, Free? I have this dreadful feeling it's over for us."

"No, I don't think you've lost him. Marcus asked you to marry him, and it's obvious he loves you. You've changed him. He used to be grumpy as hell and looked like the Sunday school version of Jesus till he got rid of that beard and had his hair cut."

"Without the hair and beard, Lisa says he's a combination of Elvis Presley and Patrick Swayze, only taller. But in my opinion no one can compare to Marcus. I loved him from the moment I saw him."

"That may be, but you used to complain about his cantankerous perfectionism. You once said you could bring in an article that Hemingway wrote and he'd probably criticize it. All he talked about was work."

"He's still a workaholic."

"Right. Well, you're kind of a workaholic, too, so you have that in common. But the main thing is, Marcus is much happier now, and I think you're the reason why. You're like a woman who's found her great love, and he's like a man who's found his great love. Great loves don't come along every day. A great love may not come around in a lifetime. When you find one, you don't want to let it go. You'd be crazy to let it go. Right?"

"Right."

"That's not to say he didn't love his wife, but he's been at the Southern Journal for how many years now?"

"Seven."

"And he lost his wife when?"

"During the war, I'm not sure of the exact year. I don't think he's told me that. The war ended in seventy-five, I think. Then he worked with his dad until he died. His dad owned a string of newspapers. I may have mentioned that already."

Freemont nodded. "Okay, let's say Susan has been gone from his life for ten years. That's a long time to mourn, and I've never heard of him dating anyone other than you."

"He probably wouldn't have gotten involved with me if I hadn't stayed in the office apartment after I caught Kyle cheating."

He waved me off. "Yeah, I know the whole hullabaloo, but have you ever thought it was kismet. I don't know if you believe in that, but I do. I think the timing must have been right. He was having work done on his house, which caused him to be staying in the other bedroom. Then one thing led to another, and nature took its course."

"I was on the rebound and acted like a hussy."

Freemont turned my chin to face him. "Oh, come on now. You can't force a big, obstinate man like Marcus to do something he doesn't want to do."

"In the beginning, he said he didn't want to get involved. He thought it would interfere with our working relationship. He didn't want to take advantage of me, but I was the one taking advantage." I gulped and sobbed.

Freemont handed me another tissue.

I blew my nose. "I convinced him we needed each other. I was shameless. Now he knows his wife's not dead, and he may not want me anymore."

"Honey, I'm sure Marcus doesn't see things that way. You need to have a little faith in yourself. You need to trust Marcus and the commitment he made to you. He's known you for many years. He knows the kind of person you are. There's no question he loves you. Anyone who isn't blind can see it. You shouldn't doubt that love. At one time he loved his wife, or thought he did, but he was younger back then. He's older and wiser now, and he's changed. He's fallen for you."

I nodded and listened. I wanted to believe my friend.

"In time, you might even feel empathy toward his wife. But you'll need plenty of patience, and patience is not your strong suit. Marcus can't desert her right off the bat. He wouldn't be the man you fell in love with if he did, but he's an honest, straight up guy. He's bound to tell her about you. Even before he tells her, she's bound to sense something. The question is: will she let him go without a fight?"

"If I were her, Free, I damn sure wouldn't let him go without a fight."

Chapter Four

After we talked, and I cried my tears out, I cooked the peas and butterbeans Freemont had put up in the freezer. He hovered over me and gave instructions, like Mama J used to hover over him while teaching him how to cook. He handed me an iron skillet to fry the cornbread on top of the stove, as Mama J had done, but when I attempted to flip the bread over, it split in two pieces.

I placed the broken pan bread on a plate. "I mutilated it, Free."

"Don't fret. It'll be good regardless."

As I placed the torn pan bread on top of the Lazy Susan table, I had to admit it looked good, along with the cold slaw, mashed potatoes and gravy, bucket of fried chicken, bowls of peas and butterbeans and biscuits.

In the fridge, I found a bottle of chardonnay with the gold label, Handley Wineries. "Since you've stopped taking your pain meds, Free, we might as well indulge." I popped the cork.

"Marcus gave me that bottle."

"It's from his family's vineyard."

Freemont lifted his eyebrows in surprise. "His family owns a vineyard? He didn't tell me that. Where's it located?"

"Somewhere near Whittier, California. My dad told me about the vineyard when he first hired Marcus, but Marcus never breathed a word about it until recently when he gave me a bottle of this very same Chardonnay."

I filled two glasses and took a sip of mine before I handed a glass to Freemont. He sniffed the wine and smiled impishly. "I'm not much of a wine connoisseur. I'm more of a sweet tea kind of guy." He took a sip, and smacked his lips together. "Okay."

I laughed at his attempt to imitate a sommelier, but too soon our conversation turned serious. Perhaps the wine had allowed Freemont to let his guard down and vent his frustration.

"The Sheriff's department in College Station, and all the powers that be, moved like lightning to arrest and indict four black boys for shooting a white boy, but in my case, nothing."

"I know, Free. I'm angry, too, or as Mama J used to say, 'fit to be tied, but not mental enough for a straitjacket.'"

Freemont crossed his eyes and made a silly face, his interpretation of crazy. Then he flicked his bottom lip with an index finger. I would have laughed if I hadn't noticed his heavy eyelids, revealing his fatigue.

"You go rest, Free. Let me clean up. You've been doing laundry all day, studying for exams and God knows what else."

I expected him to protest, but he said, "You got that right. I'm too pooped to pop. And I still need to toss some clothes in the dryer."

From the kitchen, he walked through a breezeway at the back of the house to the laundry building. Freemont actually designed and built this structure—separate from their home—for Mama J. The building contained two large rooms. A commercial-sized washer and dryer and a dry-cleaning machine were located in one room. The other room held the clean garments. Some were folded as customers had requested, and others were placed on hangers.

After he left, I cleaned up the kitchen and filled our wine glasses with the last of the chardonnay, then carried the glasses to the living room. A moment later, Freemont came in, holding up a cassette tape. "You remember when Mama used to sing at AME Christian?" He was referring to the church his ancestors started, located about four miles away, behind Justice Academy, which Granny Justice started. She doubted the public-school system would integrate as required by law. She purposely built the school close to AME Christian Church. Mama J was in the church choir and often sang beautiful solos. "Soulful like Aretha Franklin and Gladys Knight," Mom used to say.

"How could anyone forget your Mama's singing? I remember when Shandra Mason asked your mama why she was wasting her talent doing other folks' laundry when she could be a famous singer, and Mama J said, 'We're all famous in the eyes of the Lord, Shandra.' Mom and Dad loved to hear Mama J sing."

Freemont smiled. "And I remember how your folks would drag you to church, kicking and screaming."

"I don't have a memory of kicking and screaming, but I may have whined some."

Freemont laughed. "You did more than whine."

"Mom and Dad liked to go to AME Christian whenever your mama sang. Other times we'd go to the Synagogue, since Mom was raised Jewish. Dad claimed he was ecumenical. He usually went where Mom wanted."

Freemont walked over to his mahogany entertainment center. "I was going through Mama's things and found this." He popped the cassette in the stereo.

A rhythmic piano and humming choir filled the room. Then Mama J's rich voice rang out: "You got to walk that lonesome valley. You got to walk it by yourself. Nobody else's goin' to walk it for you. You got to walk it by yourself."

Freemont smiled and closed his eyes. When the song ended, he rewound the tape and started singing with Mama J in his strong baritone.

On the third replay, I tried to harmonize. I thought we sounded pretty darn good, but I was slightly inebriated by that time and may not have been impartial.

After we finished singing with Mama J, Freemont popped another cassette into his stereo player. "Mama loved this one, too."

We listened to Gladys Knight and the Pips perform Midnight Train to Georgia, while dancing around and singing with them. I cracked up as Freemont, even with his injured arm, moved and pranced like one of the Pips.

After the food, wine, music and singing, I leaned my head against the back of Freemont's leather sofa and closed my eyes. Merciful sleep soon claimed me.

A harsh, honking noise snapped me awake. I turned to see Freemont, sitting beside me, asleep on the couch, with a square pillow tucked under his head. Mama J used to say,

"That boy could sleep standing up. A bomb could go off, and he wouldn't hear it."

I nudged him several times without response. Then shouted his name.

His eyes popped open. He glared at me as if I'd threatened to shoot him. "What going on?"

"Someone's honking outside."

He jumped up and walked to his monitor, located near the front door. Jeff Daniels, a former CIA agent, had installed the monitor and security system soon after he'd installed mine. My system didn't have a fancy video monitor like Freemont's, which he was quick to point out. Our playful rivalry had been going on since childhood.

His monitor showed his white van in the driveway, rain pouring down. Freemont grabbed his umbrella, opened the front door and walked out.

I watched through the monitor as he opened the driver's door. Dora Lee Thompson emerged, looking like actress Demi Moore in the movie *Saint Elmo's fire*. She had on jeans, a black leather jacket and black boots. She used to work for Police Chief Barnum, but quit soon after Freemont got shot.

When I first heard about Dora Lee leaving the sheriff's department, I thought Barnum may have forced her out. She'd given me some police transcripts without Barnum knowing. I'd kept her identity private, but I wondered if Barnum or his detective Nev Powers may have suspected I'd gotten the transcripts from Dora Lee. We'd published them verbatim on the front page of the Southern Journal to show Tatum Brookins was innocent of the crime for which he'd been arrested and indicted.

As Dora Lee walked into Freemont's house, I greeted her with a hug. "Freemont didn't tell me you were working for him."

Dora Lee and Freemont had been friends for a while, but nothing serious, he'd said. He couldn't get involved with anyone until he'd finished his education and realized his goal of becoming a teacher.

Dora Lee's pink lips smiled at Freemont as she handed him the keys to his van. "He needed help. I needed a job."

Freemont placed his folded umbrella inside the cylindrical stand beside the front door. "Have you eaten, Dora Lee? There's plenty of supper left. We'll be glad to warm you a plate."

"Aw, thank you, Freemont. I wish I could stay. But Mama's been with Tiffany all day, and I need to get back."

Tiffany was Dora Lee's four-year-old daughter. As a single, divorced mom, Dora Lee struggled to provide for Tiffany. Freemont understood her struggles. A single mom had raised him.

"But don't worry about me. I've already eaten. I had a Big Mac and fries earlier."

She withdrew three checks from the pocket of her jacket. "These are from the Johnsons, Masons and Ms. Franklin. They said thank you for being patient on the payment." She handed the checks to Freemont, and he thanked her.

Mama Jackson had always been lenient with customers who struggled financially. She'd keep doing their laundry even if they couldn't afford to pay on time. "Cleanliness is next to Godliness," Mama J used to say. "Everyone needs clean clothes. Can't earn respect if you don't look neat and clean."

Freemont had continued her tradition. Knowing him, I suspected he paid Dora Lee more than she made at the sheriff's office. He had inherited a substantial sum after his mama died. She'd worked hard and saved and she'd taken out a hefty life insurance policy. If something happened to her, she wanted to make sure Freemont could follow his dreams and not work himself to death in the laundry business as she had. But he continued to work hard, despite his inheritance.

Dora Lee winked at Freemont. "I hear congratulations are in order, Carrie Sue."

She grabbed my left hand and studied my engagement ring. "My, my, that's absolutely gorgeous. It may be the most gorgeous ring I've ever seen, lucky lady."

I shot Freemont a warning look, committing him to silence. "Thank you, Dora Lee."

She walked to the fireplace and rubbed her gloved hands together. "I'll be so glad when warm weather gets here, and you won't hear me complaining when summer comes. I can't wait. I love the heat. And speaking of heat, I have a little gossip to share." She smiled wickedly. "Y'all will love this. Guess who I saw today?"

I didn't know how to answer. She could have seen anyone.

Freemont walked over to the fireplace, threw two logs on the fire and speared them with an iron poker. I waited for him to respond to Dora Lee. When he didn't, she answered her own question.

"Detective Nev Powers was getting it on with Neeley Nelson. He was leaning in the window of her pink Porsche and kissing her like there was no tomorrow. Then he jumped in his cruiser and followed her to her house. I followed them, but don't worry, they didn't see me. I kept a good distance."

Freemont's eyebrows shot up. "Dora Lee, you were in a white van with Jackson Laundry as big as day written on the side. And you're claiming they didn't see you?"

"I'm positive they didn't, Freemont. I was way across the street when they pulled out of the station. It was too late for lunch and too early for supper. They had hanky-panky all over their faces. Nev lives with his parents, so I knew they weren't going there. And he's too cheap to rent a hotel room. He wouldn't go to a motel anyway. Someone might see him, and you know how vain he is, so guess where they went?"

"Her place," I said. Neeley wasn't married and neither was Nev. As far as I was concerned, they could hanky-panky all they wanted. But the news surprised me. Neeley Nelson had been chasing after Marcus since she'd moved to College Station.

"Bingo, Carrie Sue, bingo. They went to her house and stayed a long, long time, most of the afternoon. I whizzed by again around three or so. His cruiser was right where he'd parked it. They were in there for a long, long, long time."

I'd been taught not to judge and frankly, I had no business judging anyone. I'd started an affair with Marcus before I'd divorced Kyle. Kyle had cheated on me many times with many women. Still some strict religious folks might say I'd committed adultery, but I couldn't help myself. I loved Marcus with my whole being, and when we were together, I felt closer to Mom and Dad. My love for Marcus included every type of love, Eros being the most prominent. "I don't care how much they diddle, Dora Lee, although it's interesting and a bit surprising. I wouldn't have put those two together."

Freemont yawned and stretched, a signal he wanted to rush this conversation along.

"Me neither, Carrie Sue. But they deserve each other. Nev is hateful, and I'm convinced he and his daddy were part of that Klan group that hurt Freemont. That's why I quit working for the Chief, not that he had anything to do with it, mind you, but I couldn't stand to look at Nev's hateful face and be subjected to his sexual innuendos. And if you ask me, Neeley Nelson is just like him. She talks down to people. Nobody likes her, not even the people at the Chamber. She thinks she's the hottest thing walking. First time I saw her, I thought she was gorgeous with all that red hair and a body to die for, but it didn't take me long to see the ugly on the inside." Dora Lee sighed. "And maybe I shouldn't tell you this, Carrie Sue. But she hates you. I've heard it from several people. I'm not going to say who, and I don't want to repeat what was said. I didn't believe it. As far as I'm concerned, what she said about you was a pack of lies."

My stomach knotted. "Thanks for the heads up, Dora Lee. She hates me because she has a crush on Marcus."

Lisa once told me she thought Neeley Nelson stalked Marcus, and if so, she knew I'd spent the night at the Southern Journal during the time Marcus was staying there. When she saw us at the Pot Aux Roses restaurant, she smirked and asked about Kyle and wanted to know where he was, as if to imply I had no business, as a married woman, dining out in a romantic restaurant with a man other than my husband. But had Neeley left that nasty note at my door? I still didn't know the answer to that.

"You're probably right, Carrie Sue. She's jealous. I hope I haven't made you feel bad. I wanted to let you know. You need to be on guard. You should caution Marcus, too."

The phone rang. Freemont walked to the kitchen to answer it.

My heart hammered, thinking it was Marcus. But it turned out to be one of Freemont's customers. As he talked to the caller, Dora Lee drove the van around to the back.

Soon after Freemont hung up the phone, I helped him and Dora Lee transfer the dirty clothes to the laundry building. The rain poured down, but we were sheltered by the breezeway.

After we finished unloading, Dora Lee said she'd be back tomorrow morning at nine. Freemont—a gentleman to the core—held an umbrella over her all the way to her Dodge Colt, while I retreated inside to the fireplace.

When I heard the phone ring again, I answered, "Jackson Laundry."

"Are you working for Freemont now?" Marcus said.

My heart pounded at the sound of his voice. "I thought I'd try something new while my fiancé's away." A flippant response, intended to conceal my worry, exhaustion and insecurity.

"I miss you, b-baby." He slurred his words, and I could tell he'd been drinking. But who was I to judge? I'd consumed at least three glasses of wine that night.

Marcus had once confessed he sometimes needed a few shots of Jack to lull him to sleep, but his need to self-medicate with the booze had diminished since we'd become a couple, and I didn't think of him as an alcoholic. He could drink a few glasses of wine or champagne and stop. I'd interviewed several alcoholics who said, "One is too many and a thousand is not enough," and in my opinion, Marcus didn't have that illness. He imbibed booze to reduce his pain, stress and guilt.

"I miss you, too, Marcus. How was your trip?"

"Numbing."

"I'm glad you arrived safely."

"How are y-you, b-baby?"

"In limbo."

"I-I would have called earlier. I've been putting out fires." Marcus was over articulating his words, trying not to slur. "We had a crisis."

"What kind of crisis?" I could hear Marcus breathing heavily.

"Mom let it slip to one her friends about Susan's return. This friend—her name is Anita—works for one of the newspapers Dad used to own. I may have mentioned we sold those papers to TNA after Dad died. Anita works as a stringer for TNA. I tried to mitigate the damage by calling Anita and asking her to keep the story under wraps, but she'd already released it to one of the reporters. And ... now ...we need to run a story in the Southern Journal. It'll be in the next issue. I'm calling Thomas and sending him what he'll need."

"You told me your family sold your newspaper business, but I didn't know a multinational conglomerate like TNA had purchased it."

What other secrets had he kept from me? Why did he agree to the sale? He could have replaced his dad as publisher, rather than accept Dad's offer to take over the Southern Journal. After Dad died, Marcus spent a bundle, buying our newspaper business and the Victorian building housing it. *Why?*

"Will the article in our paper include the local angle of your relationship with Susan?"

"Ahem," Marcus cleared his throat. "I haven't made up my mind what to include. We need time to sort through this. I talked with Susan tonight, but I haven't told her about us yet. She's very ill." He moaned. "I'm sorry, Carrie, I wish I could reassure you. What are your thoughts?"

I stood with my mouth open, in shock, unable to speak. "*Wait for your mouth to catch up with your mind*," Mom's words echoed in my brain.

Freemont walked in, knitted his eyebrows at me, and mouthed, "Who is that?"

"Carrie, are you still there?" Marcus asked.

"I'm here. I was thinking about what you said."

"This is rough on you, I know."

"It's rough on both of us, Marcus. Tougher on you, I'm sure."

I listened to his throated sounds, gulps and moans, and I thought he might be crying.

"Oh, Marcus, I wish I could be there with you."

"I wish you were here, too."

"Is Susan there?"

"No, she's arriving tomorrow night."

Why had he left Atlanta so soon, if Susan wasn't arriving till tomorrow night? We could have spent more time together and made love. I gritted my teeth to prevent my thoughts from spilling out.

"What if Susan is barraged with photographers when she gets off the plane, Marcus?"

"I've notified airport officials. We're going onboard and wheeling her out into a van to protect her from all of that."

"Is she in a wheelchair?"

"She's extremely ill. I'll call you tomorrow night and we can talk more about this, okay?"

A knot—concrete hard—formed in my stomach, but I knew this wasn't the time to unload my emotional stress on him. "Okay."

"Are you staying at Freemont's tonight?"

"Yes, probably, I need the comradery. It's comforting. Dora Lee came by. She's working for Freemont now." I repeated the gossip Dora Lee shared, then rambled. "Can you believe Nev and Neeley are coupling now? And according to Dora Lee, Neeley despises me, which isn't surprising."

"I need to call Jeff Daniels and have him guard Freemont's house tonight," Marcus said.

"Does Dora Lee's news frighten you?"

"I was planning to call Jeff anyway."

"Don't call him on account of us. We'll be okay, Marcus. Don't worry. Freemont has a state-of-the-art security system."

"He had that same system the night he was shot."

"His security system worked fine, but unfortunately, Freemont lost his temper and grabbed his gun."

"He had every right to protect himself and his property."

Marcus and I had often disagreed on this subject. Freemont should have called 911. Then he could have escaped out back and come over to my house. He ran faster than anyone I knew. Instead, he grabbed a pistol and confronted those idiots. I didn't even know he owned a gun. Mama Jackson despised guns. She refused to have one in her house, but Freemont had obviously rejected her nonviolent approach.

THE RAIN POUNDED FREEMONT'S roof like galloping elephants. He'd gone to bed hours before, and I hadn't heard a peep out of him since. Only Freemont could sleep through this racket.

"As soon as his head hits the pillow, he's asleep," Mama J used to say.

He'd invited me to stay in his guest room, but no way could I rest with a storm raging outside. I paced his living room as my mind kept rehashing the conversation with Marcus. I wanted to talk, but I didn't have the heart to wake Freemont. He was lying on his back in his king-sized bed, snoring up his own storm.

His security monitor showed the magnolia trees and rose bushes gyrating in the wind. One of the porch rockers had toppled over.

I jumped when I heard a loud pop. Then, darkness shrouded the room. The monitor turned black. I smelled smoke and grabbed the phone to call the fire department. But got no dial tone. *Damn*.

Through the picture window in the living room, I saw lightning snake through the sky. I've been afraid of lightning ever since an elementary school classmate was struck and killed by lightning as she ran from the playground to escape a thunder storm.

Despite my fear, I watched the torrential rain. Earth-shattering thunder followed one lightning flash after another. When I spotted a van, parked on the street, next to the curb, my heart jumped in my throat. *No one but a stalking lunatic would be out in this horrible weather.*

Chapter Five

Tuesday, February 17, 1987

A loud pop snapped me awake. I threw off the afghan I'd wrapped up in and searched for Freemont. He wasn't in the bedroom, and he hadn't made his bed. Unusual for him. His mother trained him from a young age to make his bed first thing in the morning, but he'd either lost the habit or something had distracted him from his duties. The lights were on in the kitchen, meaning the power had been restored, but the security monitor still looked black. Where the hell was Freemont?

I heard another pop coming from outside. I drew back the cream-colored curtains covering the picture window and saw Freemont on the porch with his right arm stretched out, a pistol in his hand. When he fired this time, my ears rang.

Jeff Daniels, Marcus' CIA friend and electronics expert—stood next to him with a pistol pointed in the same direction. They both fired at a line of bottles on the porch railing.

I flung open the door. "What the hell are y'all doing? It's too early to be making such a god-awful racket. Please stop. My ears are going deaf."

They stared at me as if I'd flown in from another planet. I'd fallen asleep in my blue jeans and grey sweater and hadn't combed my hair, washed my face or brushed my teeth yet, and may have appeared extra-terrestrial.

Freemont had on a black sweat suit with his left arm in a black sling. Jeff had on jeans, a blue sweater, a black leather jacket and running shoes. His tombstone gray eyes overwhelmed his long, narrow face. His short gray hair framed his head like a bathing cap. Next to Freemont, Jeff appeared small and thin.

Freemont's honey-brown eyes gleamed, his mischievous look. "We're target practicing, Carrie Sue. I'm sorry we disturbed you. We had one heck of a storm last night, didn't we?"

I sucked in the cool air tinged with gun power. An orange sunrise bled through gray clouds. "It knocked out your security system. I don't know how you slept through it."

Freemont smiled, showing the gap between his front teeth. "I guess that makes me an exceptional guy."

I harrumphed. Jeff nodded and glared at me with eyes as somber as the clouds.

"Jeff's been out here all night, Carrie Sue. We've been waiting for you to get up, so he can fix my system."

I slammed the door, ran to the bathroom. In the mirror above the sink, I studied my pitiful self. Dark circles encased my eyes. My hair stuck out in all directions. If Mama J were here, she'd have said I'd been "rode hard and hung up wet."

I found a bottle of aspirin in the medicine cabinet and swallowed two with a swig of faucet water. My body ached and my skin itched. I should have slept in the Atlanta Braves tee-shirt I carried in my tote. It would have been more comforting than the jeans and sweater. Dad bought the shirt April 15, 1974, the night Hank Aaron surpassed Babe Ruth's home run record in the fourth inning against the Los Angeles Dodgers.

As I remembered that night, I heard an intrusive knock. "Carrie Sue, you in there?"

"No, Freemont. I flushed myself down the commode."

"Okay, I got your point. You're pissed. But listen, this is important. Jeff wants to know if you want him to check out your security system. I think it'd be wise."

I groaned. "Can you give me a frigging moment?"

"What was that? I can't hear you."

I cracked open the door. "Can he wait for me to pee and pull myself together?"

Freemont smiled. "Probably."

"And I need a bath. I'm a mess."

"True, but I wasn't going to mention it."

"Next thing I know you'll be telling me I smell."

Freemont smirked. "Out of kindness, I wasn't going to mention that either."

I flung open the door and poked him in the stomach.

"Oh, careful now. Just cause you're in a funk is no excuse to attack your black brother."

"Why did Jeff come over here. Did Marcus call him?"

"Yeah, that's what he said."

"Who suggested the target practice?"

"That was Jeff's idea. He told me next time I'm attacked, fire at their stomachs."

"I don't want to hear it, Freemont."

"Okay, enough said. Why don't you take a shower and try to feel better?"

"I need to go home and change."

"I think I have something you can wear. It's an outfit I bought Mama. Still has the tag on. She said it was too small, and neither one of us exchanged it. It's red. Red was her favorite color. You're welcome to wear it, might be a bit roomy on your skinny self, but it's pretty soft, made of velour." His wide smile looked exactly like his mama's.

I returned his wide smile, revealing the gap between my front teeth, like Mama J's gap and Freemont's. Freemont has often said our teeth gaps prove we're related. "I'd be honored. Thank you. How're you feeling?"

"Better, I slept well."

Unbelievable. I shook my head. "That thunder last night could have awakened the dead. I'm surprised you didn't hear me screaming."

"No matter what happens in my life, Carrie Sue, I can sleep."

"Yes, I know and that worries me." I closed the door then turned on the shower. The warm spray relieved my aching muscles. I lingered in there longer than I should have, enjoying the hot shower and saying a prayer of gratitude, which my Mom and Dad drilled in me. "*Be grateful and give thanks. So many people don't have the luxuries we take for granted,*" they'd say.

Freemont knocked again to say he'd placed the outfit on a stool near the bathroom door. I dried off, slipped it on and pulled my wet hair into a ponytail. By the time I walked out of the bathroom, I thought I might be able to muster enough energy to face the day.

I found Jeff pacing the living room. He'd already repaired Freemont's security system, he'd said, and Freemont had gone to the laundry area to load up the van for Dora Lee.

I smelled the aroma of coffee brewing and told Jeff I wanted to grab a cup before we left for my house.

He nodded, but said nothing until I returned to the living room. "I'll drive you over, Carrie. Let's leave Marcus' Jeep for Freemont. He doesn't fit well in that Dodge Dart. Marcus's Jeep is bullet proof, as is my van."

"I've heard of mobsters and military officials owning armored vehicles, but why would Marcus need a bullet proof car? He never told me his jeep was bullet proof."

Jeff shrugged without explaining as he led me to his Chevy van. I waited as he opened the front-passenger door and removed a large, square case from the front passenger's seat.

The van had a small television screen imbedded in the console. Beside the screen, were walkie-talkies—similar to those I'd seen in police cars. He even had a reel-to-reel recording device and all kinds of buttons and gadgets. A true, spy mobile.

He had retired from the CIA, and shouldn't require all of this equipment in his line of work as a security specialist. Unless he still worked as a spy.

My knowledge of the CIA was limited to novels, James Bond movies and hearsay. Dad and Mom once took me to see a rerun of *Dr. No*, with Sean Connery, the first James

Bond. The movie was originally released around 1962, Mom said, the year after I was born.

Dad loved the Ian Fleming British spy books that led to the making of the Bond movies. Connery, as other Bonds, appeared debonair, handsome, and impeccably attired, not at all like Jeff.

I tried to imagine Jeff wearing a formal suit with cuff links, but couldn't picture it, although his strong, calloused hands looked capable of strangling a fierce enemy.

"Did Marcus talk to you about Susan last night, Jeff?" I flashed a smile in my attempt to be charming. "I might have to write a story about her, which will be difficult, due to my relationship with Marcus, but I'd like to try to understand her if possible. I can't figure out why a news correspondent like Susan would get involved with the CIA. Do you know anything about that?"

He shook his head. "No, nothing specific, but I can give you some general background." He shot me a cold stare. "Whatever I say must be off the record, you understand?"

"Yes, Jeff, of course, I understand. I'd never reveal you as a source. I know very little about the CIA, but I remember how my dad used to talk about Watergate and what happened in the seventies when the CIA was involved with domestic spying during President Nixon's administration."

Jeff nodded. "The White House was wired to eavesdrop on aides and reporters. President Nixon used former CIA agents as spies. These agents were called 'Plumbers.' They were caught burglarizing the Democratic National Committee offices in the Watergate Hotel. Led to Nixon's resignation."

"That was a crazy time, wasn't it, Jeff? Dad kept a scrapbook of articles about it. I've read through them, but they didn't provide any useful knowledge about the CIA."

I withdrew my tape recorder from my tote.

Jeff reached over and put his hand over the recorder. "I can't have my voice on that."

I withdrew my Tandy from the tote. If he didn't want me to record our conversation, I wanted to at least type my notes, rather than scribble everything down and have to decipher later.

Jeff pulled into the circular drive to the house I'd inherited from my parents and parked behind the black Caddy Mom used to own. I rarely kept the Cadillac in the garage. The heavy garage door moved from side to side, rather than up and down. Almost impossible to open and close without pulling a muscle. Sometimes the garage door accidentally shut on its own. Whenever that happened, Mom would blame ghosts and say, *"What house built in eighteen hundred doesn't have ghosts?"* At one time, our garage was part of a carriage house and stables.

Yellow buds had sprouted from the bushes I'd planted recently. Their vines were climbing a white pillar, cleansed from last night's rain.

The light from the chandelier shone through a window in the foyer. I was certain I'd turned the chandelier off when I left. Turning it off was a habit Dad had drilled into me.

Rather than mention this and interrupt Jeff, I listened to him and typed in what he said. He seemed in no rush to check my security system, or perhaps he wanted to finish his train of thought. Or maybe he felt more comfortable talking about this particular subject inside his bullet-proof van.

"As a result of Watergate, the new CIA director James Schlesinger required employees to reveal prohibited activities, past and present. The information Schlesinger gathered became known as the 'family jewels,' a secret document of illegal activities."

When he paused, I read my notes aloud for verification and waited for Jeff to respond and verify, but he sat stone faced.

"What was in the secret document, Jeff?"

"It linked the CIA to domestic wiretapping, assassination plots, mind control experiments, spying on journalists, and so on."

"What kind of mind control experiments?"

"LSD and other drugs were used on U.S and Canadian citizens without their knowledge."

I took a deep breath to keep from protesting what I considered criminal. "For what purpose, Jeff?"

"To observe the effects."

"Could that have happened to Susan? Could she have been drugged, manipulated or blackmailed to free a CIA agent like Virginia Fischer?" This didn't seem plausible in light of everything Marcus had told me about Susan, a strong, empowered woman, but I thought I'd ask Jeff to get his response.

Jeff scanned the landscape. His eyes moved from side to side, as if processing information. "Marcus said Susan was a college friend of Virginia's. That's all I know." He paused and I waited for him to continue. "As a result of the 'family jewels' document, the U.S. Congress created the Church Committee in the Senate and the Pike Committee in the House, and after Nixon resigned and Vice President Ford became President he pardoned Nixon and created what was called the Rockefeller Commission. A number of restrictions were set up to prevent covert operations like assassinating foreign leaders and other operations, considered immoral."

I held up my hand to stop Jeff until I could finish typing his comments.

His eyes continued to scan the landscape while I read back the notes I'd typed. He sat stiffly, as if on alert, anticipating danger.

When his eyes finally shifted toward me, I said, "Marcus had enlisted in the Air Force and was flying B-52s, during the Vietnam War, and Susan was a war correspondent. The War ended in seventy-five. Nixon was President during that time, as I recall. Could you add anything to that, Jeff?"

He nodded. "During that time, the Director of Central Intelligence tried to regulate and control the CIA." He smirked, as if he disapproved. "Those attempts to make the agency less rogue failed. Not many reforms were implemented during the seventies, due in large part to the preoccupation with the Watergate affair. In my service as an agent, Intelligence was disorganized. I had free reign, although it became increasing difficult to know who to trust. I trusted no one. As to why Susan became involved, you'll have to ask her."

"I just think it's strange, Jeff. Why would she choose to go on a secret mission to rescue a friend in enemy territory and not tell Marcus?"

He shrugged. "As I said, you'll have to ask her. She may have been ordered not to inform anyone. I knew a reporter who became a spy because she loved the story of Mata Hari, but I can't speak for Susan."

"I've read about Mata Hari. She was a Dutch dancer accused of being a German spy. The French executed her in early nineteen hundred, as I recall. But that was so long ago, and I'm trying to understand what would make a war correspondent like Susan get involved with freeing a hostage. War correspondents are supposed to follow a code of ethics and I'm just trying to make sense of all of this. In the last few years our newspaper has covered many international stories about spies. One involved a Marine guard at the U.S. Embassy in Moscow. The guard confessed to giving information to the Soviets. He supposedly allowed the Soviets to enter the new chancery building to bug it. We've also run stories about the Iran Contra affair. Do you have any knowledge on that?"

Jeff shrugged. "Only that President Reagan told Congress the CIA would protect El Salvador. Reagan swore he'd prevent Nicaraguan arms from getting into the hands of Communist rebels. When in fact the CIA was arming and training Nicaraguan Contras in Honduras, hoping they would overthrow the Sandinistas in Nicaragua. Much of the information about that has been destroyed, I understand."

"What about you, Jeff? What covert operations and spying activities have you been involved in? You know so much about electronics and installing security equipment. That must have been one of your jobs with the CIA."

"Nice try, Carrie, but I can't comment on my intelligence work."

I gritted my teeth, as I tried to figure out how to connect with him and get him to open up. "What happened to your friend, the reporter who became a spy?"

"She disappeared. I haven't been able to find her." His face softened and his gray eyes misted.

I touched his leather-clad arm. "I'm sorry, Jeff. Perhaps you will see her again one day. Where do you think your friend might have gone?"

He bowed his head. "She was in the Middle East. I have no contacts there anymore. My best contact was Hassan Salameh, a CIA source. He was assassinated in seventy-nine."

"Name sounds familiar. How do you spell it?"

Jeff spelled Salameh's name for me.

"Who was he exactly?"

"His code name was Abu Hassan." He spelled the name. "Stands for *Black September*, an organization responsible for the Munich massacre and other terror attacks."

I grumbled. "How could you trust information from a terrorist?"

"Our government receives information from terrorists all the time. Salameh was Chief of Intelligence of the Palestine Liberation Organization, and we struck a bargain with him."

"What kind of bargain?"

"He provided information on Muslim extremism and promised Americans would be safe in exchange for money and information on our mutual enemies."

"Sounds crazy and risky, to say the least, but getting back to Susan, do you think she could have crossed over and become a spy?"

He squinted. "I think there's a little bit of spy in most reporters, don't you?"

I thought about his question before responding. "If you mean that journalists have pretended to be someone else when they thought it was the only way to uncover the truth, I suppose you're right, Jeff. Even back in the late eighteen-hundreds, Nellie Bly went undercover in a woman's insane asylum. She acted insane to get committed to expose the abusive conditions in there. Before then, she spent six months in Mexico as a foreign correspondent."

As I told Jeff about Bly, I began to understand Susan. She wanted to free her friend, and in the process, uncover a bigger story.

When Jeff didn't respond, I told him I thought it was strange that the chandelier in the hallway was on. "I'm certain I turned it off."

Jeff swung open his van door. "That is strange, Carrie. I drove by here last night on the way to Freemont's. Your house was dark then. That was before the storm hit. Wait here. I'll check it out."

I watched as Jeff turned the knob to the front door and walked inside, as if he didn't need to use my key. I was sure I'd locked up everything and set the alarm when Marcus and I left.

The security system should have gone off if someone had broken in unless the storm disabled it. What was going on? I waited for Jeff to return and tell me, but patience wasn't one of my virtues, as Freemont often said, and I grew tired of twiddling my thumbs while Jeff took his dear, sweet time.

After waiting five minutes, my impatience won. I jumped out of Jeff's van and ran inside the house. It smelled musty. The grandfather clock chime eight times. "Jeff," I called out. I listened. No answer.

If Dad hadn't given his snub nose pistol to Marcus, I would have grabbed it from the hunt board, where he stored the gun until Mom made him give it away.

Jeff wasn't in the master bedroom, the bathroom, the laundry room or in the kitchen. On the kitchen counter, I spotted a wilted yellow rose, which puzzled me. I didn't put it there, though it looked like one of the roses I'd planted next to the veranda. A piece of paper was wrapped around the stem.

I unfolded the note and read the nasty message. I dropped it when I heard growling. I followed the sound to the screened porch.

Jeff—with a broom in his hands—faced off with a little possum. The possum hissed and snarled as Jeff tried to sweep it out the door.

"Come on little guy," he said. "I'm not going to hurt you."

Jeff turned toward me. "Your screen door was wide open. So was your back door. And your front door was unlocked."

"I locked the door and set the security system before I left on Saturday. Someone must have broken in and left a threatening note in the kitchen."

Jeff frowned and set the broom down. "What'd the note say?"

"Told me I'd better watch out and called me a bitch. I'll show you. Why don't you leave the screen door open? And

I'll close the porch off from the rest of the house. That little guy will leave eventually. I'm surprised he didn't play dead. They usually do when threatened."

Jeff followed me to the kitchen and read the note. "A warning rose," he called it. "You're lucky you weren't here. The wires to your alarm system have been cut. Whoever broke in knew what they were doing. I need to finish the walk through. Wait here."

As I waited for Jeff, I stared out the window at the Magnolia tree. I tried to focus on its lush, green beauty, but my anger wouldn't allow me to appreciate anything. I'd been violated. My house had been broken into and burglarized.

I heard footfalls behind me, and jumped as Jeff said, "Appears to be all clear, Carrie. I'll add additional locks on both front and back doors. I can do that today. Also, I can install a video system on the inside and outside of your home. I still need to check for listening devices. And you need to file a police report."

I shook my head. "I'm not popular with the sheriff's office right now. Filing a report wouldn't help."

"I disagree, Carrie. You covered a controversial trial, but not everyone on the force is biased. Regardless, you need to report this. Get it on record. I'll do my best to investigate if you like. Is there anything I need to know in following up?"

I told him about the first note I'd found, though I worried he'd tell Marcus before I had a chance to. Marcus and I had promised not to keep secrets, but I'd kept a huge secret from him. He had a tendency to obsess about my safety and I wanted to avoid that drama. "Two months ago, someone stuck a note in my door. I suspected Neely Nelson, the local Chamber exec."

"I know who she is."

"She has a crush on Marcus. That's obvious, even though Dora Lee recently told me Neeley is having an affair with Detective Nev Powers."

Jeff frowned. "What makes you think Nelson left that note?"

"Marcus and I had gone out to dinner that night, and Neeley showed up at the restaurant soon after we arrived. Not a coincidence, I'm sure, and when I got back home I found the note stuck in my door."

"But you don't have any evidence she left it, do you?" Jeff squinted at me as if he thought I was nuts."

"No, it was just a hunch."

"I'd like to examine both notes, Carrie. Did you save the other one?"

"Yes, of course I saved it."

What about your ex-husband? Exes are notorious for this sort of thing."

"I don't suspect Kyle. He had an alibi. He was directing a play at the theatre. Plus, he seemed contrite when he admitted cheating on me with several women. He firmly denied leaving the note, and I'm certain he wouldn't come near me now. I still have a restraining order against him."

Jeff waited in the kitchen as I retrieved the first note from the hunt board. He placed both notes side by side on the dining room table Mom found at a garage sale, "an antique from England," she'd said.

When my parents were alive, we used to eat supper on this table most nights. Mom and Dad took turns cooking. Mom was "the casserole and crockpot queen." Dad was "grill master." After I turned 16, I was assigned cooking duty. I picked Mondays, but I used to protest like a spoiled brat and sing, "Rainy days and Mondays always get me down." I should have been thankful, not spiteful.

Jeff asked me if he could borrow the notes. I said okay. Marcus trusted him. They'd worked together for many years, but I didn't know how they became acquainted and I'd never thought to ask. Would Jeff tell Marcus about the first note? The question worried me as I watched Jeff wrap the notes in a plastic bag and stuff them inside his leather jacket. He then proceeded to disassemble the kitchen phone. A moment later, he held up a tiny metal "listening device," he called it.

I followed him from room to room, as he searched for other bugs. In the master bedroom, he removed another similar object from that phone. "Now that we're clear, I need to make a few, private calls. I'll use the kitchen phone, if you don't object?"

"I don't mind. That's fine."

He made a circle with his right hand. "Why don't you walk through and around the house and see if anything's missing, Carrie."

My underwear drawer in the master bedroom looked cockeyed. When I opened the drawer, it was almost empty. Someone had taken my good underwear; yet, left the Andy Warhol of Marilyn Monroe hanging above the chest of drawers. Made no sense.

As Jeff instructed, I jotted down the missing items in my reporter's pad before I climbed the stairwell to the second floor. Mom had hung many lovely paintings of local artists, modern and impressionists on the stairwell walls. They all seemed to be in place.

The lump in my stomach hardened, as I walked through each and every room. Mom had furnished them in antebellum style. Nothing seemed to be disturbed.

In the library, Dad's favorite room, I sat in the tufted red-leather sofa and scanned the bookshelves. They reached from ceiling to floor and across three walls. Dad loved to read and write in here.

Similar to many libraries, this spacious room smelled of old books. Some of Dad's favorites were William Shakespeare, John Steinbeck, J.D. Salinger, Mark Twain. He owned every James Bond Novel by Ian Fleming. I spotted his copy of *To Kill a Mockingbird,* signed by Harper Lee.

Dad had collected more than a thousand books, making it damn near impossible to determine if any were missing. But if someone were going to steal books, wouldn't they take the most valuable ones?

From the library, I climbed the stairwell to the attic. In the early 1800s, Annie Justice hung herself in this attic, according to my grandmother's journal. "Annie suffered from mental illness or depression," Granny Justice wrote.

As children, Freemont and I would sneak up here, scared out of our minds, thinking Annie would come after us. We never encountered Annie, but we did find Granny's journal inside an antique chest.

I flicked on the light bulb that hung from the ceiling, but most of the room remained in the dark, despite the angled light, shining through the attic window. Dust particles covered everything. If someone had come up here recently, I should have seen prints and smudges in the dust, but I saw none.

I heard creaking noises. Freemont used to say the creaking came from "Annie's ghost pacing the floor."

I walked into a cobweb, screamed and ran out of the room. Spiders, poisonous or not, scare me more than Annie's ghost.

In the kitchen, Jeff had the radio turned up loud. Otherwise he would have heard me screaming upstairs. But how could he talk on the phone with all that racket?

The news was on and I heard a broadcaster—a woman—say, "Despite efforts to secure his release, Terry Waite, special envoy of the archbishop of Canterbury is still in captivity. Waite was kidnapped in Beirut last month. He arrived in Beirut with the intention of negotiating for the release of hostages held by the Islamic Jihad organization."

"In other news, an autopsy report listed the cause of Liberace's death as AIDS. Liberace was the second major celebrity to die from AIDS. Actor Rock Hudson died of that disease two years ago." No mention of Susan, but perhaps I'd missed that part.

"Atlanta has seen an increase in its crime rate," she reported. "Homicides rose thirty percent over last year. Atlanta officials are baffled at the rise in slayings involving teenagers."

I thought of Preston Campbell, the College Station teen who'd been shot and killed last year. Tatum Brookins was indicted even though he wasn't at the crime scene. Thanks to his lawyer and Freemont's testimony, a jury found Tatum not guilty. Fortunately, the U.S. Supreme Court had prohibited racial bias in the jury selection. Our newspaper published the police interviews verbatim, thanks to Dora Lee sharing the transcripts with me.

Jeff turned off the radio and handed me the phone. "Marcus wants to talk to you."

With my heart thrashing and my knees shaking, I untangled the black cord to sit on the kitchen floor to talk to him. "How are you, Marcus?"

"Hi, Carrie," his deep voice vibrated, but he didn't answer my question.

"Jeff told me about the break-in and phone bugs and those god-awful messages you've received. Under no circumstances are you to stay in that house alone. Go to my house. Lock up. Set the alarm. Stay there until I get back. I've asked Jeff to keep a look out."

My body stiffened as I listened to him. Why didn't he ask me how I was doing, rather than order me around?

"Carrie, I can't believe you didn't tell me about the threat you received in December."

My face burned with anger. "I feel like shit, Marcus, so don't tell me what to do. I feel violated. I had a security system that didn't work. And some pervert stole my underpants."

"Wait," he stammered. "What?"

"You heard me. The pervert, the one who broke into my home, whoever that pervert is, stole my underpants and bugged my phones. And now I don't feel safe anywhere, even at your house, so don't tell me to lock myself up there, where I won't be welcomed if you decide to stay with your wife. I'd rather you tell me you love me. Tell me you miss me. Tell me you want to hold me. And don't order me around."

Marcus blew into the phone, as if he needed to let off steam. God knows I did.

"Carrie, please don't..."

"Please don't what, Marcus? Don't speak the truth. While we're on the subject of truth, why didn't you tell me your jeep is bullet proof? Why do you need a bullet proof car? What's going on?"

Rather than wait for his answer, I slammed the phone down, ran out of my house, jumped in the Cadillac and sped away.

I drove aimlessly with the radio on. As Michael Jackson started singing *Smile*, I turned into a bawling mess and could barely see the road.

I drove by the office, but didn't stop. With so many raw emotions running through me, I didn't need a pity party with my colleagues. I needed to hide somewhere, anywhere. I needed a safe place, but in my mind, at that time, no safe place existed.

On the interstate, I pushed the accelerator to the floorboard, until I reached Peachtree Street. The traffic on Peachtree forced me to slow down.

At Courtland Street, I saw the Hilton and pulled into the hotel parking lot. By then, fatigue was pushing on my eyelids, and I was near collapse. I considered taking a nap in the back seat. I'd fallen asleep many times in this car after a late-night council or commission meeting, but on this day, my paranoia warned me against it. My house had been burgled and bugged by a pervert that may have followed me, for all I knew.

Thinking I'd be safe in the Hilton, I walked inside like I owned it.

A dark-haired man at the reservation desk greeted me with, "May I help you?"

"Yes, I'd like a non-smoking, double or king, three or four floors below the restaurant."

Mom and Dad used to eat at Nikolai's Roof and would sometimes take me. "I'll be staying tonight and possibly tomorrow night."

He looked at his roster. "We have an executive double available. Would that be satisfactory?"

I fished in my billfold and handed him my credit card. "Yes."

As he ran my card, he asked, "Do you need help with your luggage?"

"No thanks." I held up my tote. "I travel light."

He asked for my driver's license, glanced at it and flashed me a sly smile. He may have wondered why I needed a hotel room in the middle of the day. Or perhaps he assumed I was a call girl or a young woman having an affair. But frankly, I didn't give a damn what he thought.

He handed me the room key and directed me toward the elevators. As I walked away, he said something about a complimentary breakfast in the morning.

I got into the elevator with a tall, dark-haired man in a business suit. He leered at me, up and down, and I thought I'd never get to my floor. The lift took forever. When the doors finally slid open, I rushed out, found my room, and bolted the door.

On the verge of an anxiety attack, I inhaled several deep breaths and stood at the window, looking out. A group of people on the street below were walking into the World Congress Center. They laughed as if they didn't have a care in the world.

I continued to breathe in and out, wishing I could absorb their happy energy. But my dark mind wouldn't let me. It preferred to recall a Skeeter Davis song, *The End of the World*.

When my heart stopped racing, I backed away from the window and drew the curtains, shrouding in darkness before I pulled off my boots and plopped down on the bed.

I couldn't keep my eyes open. But sleep eluded me as my brain focused on negative things. I replayed the death of my parents, Kyle's cheating, my divorce and my shattered engagement to Marcus.

I focused on my breathing, as I'd learned to do, but I kept seeing Marcus' face. What if he reported me missing? What if he called his friends at the Atlanta Police Department? I'd disappeared after my house had been burglarized. Would they assume I'd been abducted?

Those questions haunted me until I called Freemont to find out what was going on. He answered on the first ring.

"Hi Free. It's me."

"Where are you, Carrie Sue?" This was his nervous voice, higher pitched than usual, like the time I'd hidden in the woods beneath the kudzu. We were kids playing hide and seek. Night had fallen, but he kept searching for me and calling my name.

"Marcus has called here several times, Carrie Sue, and Jeff came by, looking for you. He said you disappeared out of the blue. We've been in an uproar. Are you okay?"

"I needed to leave. I didn't feel safe. Someone broke in and cut the wires to my security system and left another awful note."

"Why don't you come over here, Carrie Sue? Where are you? You don't sound well. If you've been harmed, say 'yes, yes' two times."

He was using the code words we'd created as children to signal danger. "Yes, yes," meant extreme danger, as did, "Crazy Carrie" or "Crazy Free." If everything were okay, we'd use the code, "clear day." Under normal circumstances, I may have laughed at him, but my depression wouldn't allow laughter. "It's a clear day, but foggy in my heart. I'm at the Hilton in Atlanta on Courtland. Don't tell anybody, okay? Why don't you park at the Marta station and take the train here? I need to talk to you."

He cleared his throat. "Marcus wants you to call him."

"You call him, Free. Tell him you've talked to me, and I'm fine."

"What room are you in?"

I gave him the number. "Don't tell Marcus where I am. Tell him you're meeting me for dinner at Nikolai's Roof, and tell him I'm sorry for hanging up on him."

Freemont huffed, as if out a breath. "I'll call him, but I'd rather you would. If you'd told Jeff you were leaving, you could have avoided all this drama."

"I was too upset, Free. Don't you understand? But if it's not convenient for you to meet me here, that's okay. You've got more to do than you can say grace over."

"I'll get there."

"First call Marcus, but please don't tell him where I am."

"Okay, okay, but after I talk to him, I need to leave Dora Lee a note in case I don't get back in time."

"Thank you, Free. Make sure no one follows you."

Chapter Six

I was having a nightmare about Marcus riding away on a white horse with Susan riding behind him, when I heard a tapping noise.

I shot up in bed. The bedside clock told me it was "5:13."

The tapping grew louder and louder. I finally came to my sense and realized someone was knocking at the door. I peered through the peep hole but saw no one. "Who's there?"

"Clear day," I heard Freemont say.

"Clear day," I answered. Why had Freemont been reluctant to show his face? I invited him to come here. Perhaps he'd become paranoid, too.

I unbolted the door and he rushed in, carrying a duffle in his right hand. He'd worn a black suit, white shirt and black tie, which matched the sling on his left arm.

He plopped his duffle on the luggage carrier and groaned. "I'm glad you're okay, Carrie Sue. You scared the hell out of us. Do we need reservations for Nik's?"

"I'm not sure."

He picked up the phone and asked to be connected to the restaurant where he made "reservations for two at six tonight. Name's Freemont."

After he hung up, he sat in the lounger near the window. His long legs overshot the foot rest.

I sat across from him in a wing-back chair. "Were you able to talk to Marcus?"

"Yes, and he thanked me."

"What did you tell him?"

"I assured him you were okay, but upset. Anybody would be in your situation. He wants you to call him as soon as possible. He thought you were going to his house. I said we were getting together for supper tonight, which is true. When you call him, no reason not to tell him you're staying at the Hilton. You can say you weren't feeling safe, and you knew you'd be safe here, which is also true."

As I glanced at my friend, gratitude welled up in me. No matter what happened in my life, I could always count on our friendship. I trusted him and his wise counsel more than anyone. "I don't feel comfortable calling him at his Mom's. They're supposed to pick up Susan today."

"He said to call him there." Freemont shook his head, obviously frustrated with me. "Carrie Sue, you know how Marcus is. Let him know you're okay, so he won't freak out. Jeff's installing a video camera on the inside and outside of your house. He said you approved it. Doesn't Marcus have a good security system? If you decide to stay at his house, you'll be closer to work, and you'll be safe. 'Course you're always welcome to stay at my house."

"Thank you for calling Marcus and for coming here on such short notice. I feel better now that you're here. But I haven't decided where I'll be staying long term. All I know is

I'm staying here tonight. I still can't believe that asshole who broke into my house stole my underwear?"

Freemont shook his head and grunted. "Ump, do you think it was Kyle? I've always thought he was a pervert and an asshole even before you divorced him."

"Why would Kyle take my underwear? He never seemed that interested in my underwear. Passion went out the window soon after we got married. I wore a see-through, black teddy on my wedding night. Kyle got drunk and passed out. He didn't even notice me or what I was wearing. I'm pretty sure he's not an underwear thief. A freeloader? Yes; a cheater? Yes; underwear thief? No. And he should be happy now. I gave him money to end the marriage."

My face burned at the thought of appeasing a man who'd cheated on me from day one.

Freemont blew out a breath. "Could be the Klan's messing with you."

"Could be. Could also be Neeley Nelson. She's been stalking Marcus. I've always suspected she left that first note."

Freemont stood, pulled open the curtains and looked out. "Why would she take your underwear? Her butt looks a lot bigger than yours."

"I don't know. Stranger things have happened. Remember what Dora Lee said about Neeley Nelson and Nev Powers? They've teamed up."

"Yeah, and don't you know his dad was lying when he claimed his truck was stolen at the Klan rally." Freemont ran a hand over his short black hair. "We may never know the truth." He glanced at his watch. "If we want to make it to

Nik's in time, we need to leave soon. Why don't you call Marcus and we'll skedaddle? I'm hungry."

I hesitated, or as Freemont called it, "dilly-dallied." I washed my face and dabbed on powder and lipstick. "What if his mom answers? And what if he's occupied with Susan and can't talk?"

"Oh, come on, Carrie Sue. Marcus is an intelligent guy. He can figure out a way to talk in private."

I fished Carol Handley's phone number out of my billfold and asked the operator to connect us. The phone rang several times, then the answering machine picked up with a recorded message, female voice, sounded like his Mom. She and I had talked on the phone the day Marcus told her about our engagement: "Sorry we can't come to the phone at the moment. Please leave your name and number and a brief message. We'll call you back as soon as possible."

After the beep, I said, "This is Carrie Sue Justice. Please let Marcus know everything is okay here. If he needs to call, I'm at..." I recited the number of the Hilton and my room number.

As I hung up, Freemont unzipped his duffle and withdrew a Glock.

I froze at the sight of it. "Mama J would turn over in her grave if she knew you were packing. Put that gun away."

He pulled open his suitcoat and stuffed the pistol inside the silk-lined pocket. "I am putting it away."

I fussed at him about carrying the gun as we walked to the elevator. He listened to my objections, then said, "You sound just like Mama. Why don't we talk about something else?" He pressed the button for the restaurant. "Do you remember Johnny Ray Dean?

"His name sounds familiar. Should I remember him?"

"You should, Carrie Sue. He remembers you. Johnny Ray is a detective with the Atlanta Police Department. He's agreed to investigate your burglary. He went to Justice Academy. He used to come over to the house all the time."

"When did he graduate from Justice?"

"He didn't graduate from Justice. His folks moved to Charlotte, North Carolina when he was twelve. He moved back to Atlanta in eighty-five when the department hired him. He said the last time he saw you was in Superior Court. He said you did a great job covering Tatum's trial. Johnny Ray never believed Tatum was guilty. Johnny Ray is certain Detective Nev Powers convinced prosecutor's office to go for an indictment. Powers thought four black boys would look more like a gang than three black boys, so they railroaded Tatum. Tatum never should have been arrested, much less, indicted and tried for shooting that poor white boy. I talked with Johnny Ray for a long time today. That was when I was trying to find out where you were. Johnny Ray said he'd be glad to help investigate your burglary. He's convinced my case and yours are related."

We stepped out of the elevator and walked to restaurant. As we entered, a tall, tuxedoed man greeted us with a broad smile. He led us to a table with a stunning view of Atlanta's skyline. The chandeliers reflected in the giant windows. I remembered when Mom, Dad and I came here. They ordered the Osetra caviar as a starter. I hated it at first, but in time, I began to like it.

The headwaiter handed us menus and said our server would take our orders shortly. Freemont frowned as he opened his menu. "Holy moly, this place is pricy."

"Don't worry about it, I'll pay. You came all the way out here, Free. The least I can do is treat you."

His eyebrows shot up. "No, no. Call me old fashioned, but I was raised a gentleman. I'm paying, and don't give me an argument. I was just making a point and just sayin,' I don't usually eat this highfalutin."

I smirked. He smirked back. He would fight me tooth and nail if I tried to pick up the tab. The last time Freemont and I ate in a nice restaurant, he gave me the same spiel about paying and being raised a gentleman. After his spiel, I excused myself, and secretly paid the bill. Then I instructed the waiter to tell Freemont our meals were on the house, because they loved his mama, which baffled Freemont.

"As far as I know, Mama never ate in this place," he'd said. "She was too fond of saying, 'a fool and his money are soon parted.' She'd never eat in a ritzy restaurant."

A tall man—with black hair, black suit and vest—walked up to our table. "I am Borees," he said with a slight Russian accent. Then he bowed. "I will serve you. What would you like to drink? If you like pinot, I highly recommend the Joseph Swan River Valley?"

I took his suggestion and ordered a carafe.

Freemont ordered water and sweet tea.

After Borees left to get our drinks, I studied the menu. "I think I'll have the Osetra caviar to start. We can share, if you'd like."

"No way will I eat fish eggs." His upper lip curled up, as if the mere thought of caviar offended him.

When the waiter returned with our drinks, I ordered the Osetra and Freemont ordered the scallops. "Cook them plenty done and serve them hot, please."

"Absolutely," the waiter replied, then he recited the specials.

Borees recommended the duck and I ordered it.

When Freemont wrinkled his nose, as if he could smell a skunk, I frowned at his rudeness. "What's wrong with you?"

He told me we'd discuss it later and then chose the beef tenderloin. "Well done, no pink."

After Borees left, I said, "Why did you make such a face in front of our waiter?"

He leaned in and whispered, "I hate the thought of anyone eating a duck."

I took a sip of my wine. "Let me get this straight. You have no problem eating cow, but the thought of eating a duck makes you ill. That's silly, Free."

"Not really. Charlie Rowland used to have a pet duck. Charlie raised it from an egg." Freemont made the shape of an egg with his right hand.

"I don't remember Charlie Rowland. Are you sure you're not making this up?"

He shook his head. "I sometimes forget how white you are. Charlie and his folks used to belong to AME Christian. His Dad, Reverend Mackie, preached there several times. They lived a couple of miles behind the church, near the river."

"He doesn't live there now, does he?"

"No, Charlie's Mom and family moved to Birmingham in the seventies. But when he lived here, we were pretty close. He never came over to my house, and maybe you didn't get to meet him, but I'm sure I talked about Charlie. I'm surprised you don't remember. After church, Charlie would often ask me to go to his house. He was schooled at home and an only child. We were kids when we found that duck egg beside the river. That was the summer it overflowed. Charlie placed the egg on a heating pad. Lo and behold, it hatched. Charlie named the pet duck Do. His Mama hated Do, for obvious reasons. Do made a mess. But Charlie and I didn't care. We loved Do. He followed us everywhere. He grew big and fat. He was a beautiful duck." Freemont shook his head and sighed. "I still can't believe what his mama did to Do."

"What did she do to Do?" I couldn't help but laugh at my silly question.

"Wrung his neck. Plucked his feathers off, and served him for supper."

I gasped. "That's awful, Free."

"You're darn tooting it's awful. And Charlie made me swear I'd never eat duck as long as I lived. Every time I see duck on a menu or in the grocery store, I think of Do."

I jumped up from the table, found Borees and changed my order from duck to tile fish. After I returned to the table, I issued Freemont a warning. "If you have or had a friend who owned a pet fish, I don't want to hear about it."

He laughed. "Come to think of it, I did..."

I put my hands over my ears, and said, "Lalalalala," to drown out his story.

He pulled my hands from my ears, and nodded toward the elderly couple in a nearby booth. "They think you've lost your mind, Carrie Sue, and I'm inclined to agree."

A few minutes later, Borees brought out the scallops and caviar. Freemont ordered a green salad in addition to the scallops and asked the waiter to bring the salad out with his steak.

A few moments after Borees scurried away, he reappeared with a loaf of warm bread.

Freemont smiled widely, showing his gap. "I feel like I'm in hog heaven."

"What did you say, sir?" Borees frowned as if confused.

"Hog heaven is an old expression meaning wonderful, happy state of mind," I explained.

Borees smiled, bowed his head and backed away from our table.

Before we finished the bread, Borees brought Freemont his salad and our main courses. I had already gobbled up the caviar. I hadn't eaten anything that day due to my trauma, but my appetite had obviously returned with a vengeance after relaxing with my friend.

Freemont said his steak was "delish."

For dessert, Freemont chose the chocolate soufflé, and I picked the crème brulee, which we devoured. Then Borees brought us vodka samples: cinnamon, peach and lemon. We drank the samples and ordered more while reliving childhood memories.

Drinking and laughing with Freemont was exactly what I needed. Better than a tranquilizer, which I'd been prescribed after my parents died.

"You're a bad influence, Carrie Sue."

"That's not a very nice thing to say, Free."

"Maybe not, but I wouldn't have drunk all that vodka, if you hadn't encouraged it. Now I'm tipsy." He massaged his forehead.

"I wasn't thinking, Free. I forgot you took the Marta from the Park and Ride. You're in no condition to drive home. If you don't want to take a cab, you're welcome to sleep on one of the double beds in my room, and I can drive you home in the morning."

"If I stay, I'll have to leave here at five a.m. Will that be a problem?"

"No problem at all. It's not late and we'll get to bed at a reasonable time."

Freemont agreed to stay and we got back to my room around nine. The red light on the phone was flashing.

A hotel operator said Marcus had called and wanted me to call him at his Mom's. Then she dialed the number. My heart hammered in anticipation as my mind buzzed from the booze.

Marcus answered with a stern "Yes."

"I like the 'yes.' Does that mean you'll agree to anything I have in mind?" The alcohol had loosened my tongue. Freemont was in the shower and couldn't hear us. Why not enjoy a little phone sex?

"Probably," he said hoarsely.

I plopped on the bed and stuck a pillow under my head. "What are you wearing?"

"A towel."

"Mmmm, I can picture you." I heard a woman's voice in the background, calling his name, and my heart sank. "You're not alone, are you?"

"No," he snapped.

The woman continued to talk. Her voice muffled, and I couldn't hear what she was saying.

"Thanks, Mom. If I need anything, I'll get it." After a short pause, he returned to the phone. "Sorry, Carrie."

I heard the shower turn off, meaning Freemont might hear us. "How are you doing, Marcus?"

"More importantly, how are you doing?"

Typical of Marcus, he never wanted to talk about himself, but I chose not to mention that. "I'm feeling better. Freemont and I had dinner at Nikolai's. We ate like pigs and drank too much. I had wine and we both sampled the flavored vodkas."

"Wish I could have joined you."

"I do, too. Did you pick up Susan today?"

"Yes, and we checked her into the hospital."

"How sick is she?"

He groaned. "She's malnourished, and there are other complications. Docs in Manila gave her antibiotics for bronchial pneumonia and dysentery. Mom is nurse for the hospital where Susan is now. She suspects intestinal parasites, among other problems. They've been running tests and feeding Susan intravenously with nutrients and antibiotics."

My arms itched to comfort him. "I'm sorry. Marcus. Forgive me for hanging up on you this morning."

He sighed. "You were upset, and I reacted badly."

"Have you been hounded by the media yet?"

"We were able to get away at the airport, but we've been harassed with phone calls. News crews are stationed outside. I'm having a press conference at noon tomorrow, three your time. I invited Virginia Fischer's parents, but they declined. They're still convinced their daughter is alive."

My stomach knotted. Would Marcus bring up the details of the helicopter crash and his perceived responsibility for it? He was convinced his carpet bombs had caused the crash, but he had no way of knowing who was in the vicinity of his bombs.

"How much will you share at the press conference?"

"I haven't prepared a statement yet. I'll explain the obvious. Susan didn't die in the crash. She was taken prisoner. Then I'll attempt to answer questions as best I can. I've been conferring with a lawyer here. He's advising me." Marcus cleared his throat. "Thomas will be working on the story for our paper. If you have a problem with that, let me know. In light of everything you've been through, I didn't think you'd want to work on it. If Susan recovers well enough, she might want to provide more details, but she doesn't want to talk about the CIA involvement or Virginia's role in this. Whenever I prod her, she becomes agitated and says she doesn't remember."

As I listened, my heart swelled with sympathy for him. I blinked away tears. Marcus needed to feel in control. Yet he had no control over this situation. "I'm sure she was happy to see you."

He cleared his throat again. "She was in pain."

I wiped my eyes. "Marcus, I'm so sorry. I wish I could say or do something to ease your pain."

He groaned. "Knowing you're safe makes me feel better. Tomorrow or whenever you wish, you can go to my house. You'll be safe there."

I thought about this. What if he returned to Atlanta with Susan? Where would I go then? After my break-in, I trembled at the thought of returning to my house. "Maybe I should stay at the office apartment."

"Mmm, okay. If you think you'll feel safer there."

At that moment, I doubted I'd feel safe ever again. But why tell Marcus that? He had enough on his mind already. He had to prepare for a press conference which could place him in a tricky situation. What would he say? What would he do? Would he incriminate himself?

Chapter Seven

Wednesday Feb. 18

I got up at 4:30 a.m.—after sleeping fitfully—and jumped in the shower. The hot pulsating spray helped me to regain my sanity.

With no clean clothes to change into, I wore the same thing I had on yesterday—Mama J's red velour outfit. I spritzed the clothing with Chanel perfume, Mom's favorite, to cover up the sweaty-fear odor. After Mom died, I started wearing her chosen perfume and kept a little dispenser of it in my tote. It made me feel closer to her. That morning I yearned for her reassuring presence more than ever.

She'd be pleased to know I always carried clean underwear in my tote, a habit Mom had reinforced. "Always wear clean underwear," she used to say, and as I remembered this, my mind segued to my stolen undies.

"What sick pervert would steal my underpants?" I asked Freemont as I drove him back to the Marta Station Park-and-Ride where he'd left Marcus' Jeep.

Freemont shook his head and shrugged, as if he wanted me to drop the subject. He was tired of hearing about it.

From the station, I followed Freemont to his house. I didn't want to be alone, and Freemont said he understood why. He knew me better than anyone.

Soon after we arrived at his house, I called Thomas. It bothered me that Marcus had asked him to write the story about Susan's return, and I could almost hear Dad saying, *"Be aggressive, Carrie Sue. Take charge. You can do anything as long as you have the desire to do it."* I would be defying Dad's legacy if I ignored my duties. He started the Southern Journal before I was born and it eventually became my lifeline after I lost my parents.

"Anderson's residence," Lisa answered. Sleepiness edged her voice. Had I awakened her? I thought not. She often said she awoke with the chickens.

"Hi, Lisa, it's Carrie Sue. Sorry to bother you at home, but I need to talk to Thomas."

"Hi Carrie Sue. I'm so glad you called. We've been worried to death. I'm so sorry about everything. Thomas told me Marcus' wife came back from the dead. Good God, what a mess. How are you doing, dear?" She sounded like Mom.

I inhaled a deep breath to keep from crying. "I'm still trying to cope with the shock." Did she know about the break-in at my house? If not, I didn't plan to tell her.

Lisa sighed. "We're all shocked. Where are you? I don't like the idea of you being alone right now."

I snatched one of Freemont's tissues and wiped my eyes. "I'm with Freemont, at his house. Did Marcus tell Thomas about the press conference?"

"Yes, but how do you feel about that?"

"I'm not sure. Marcus thought it was necessary. Susan is very sick and unable to do interviews, he said."

Lisa sniffled. "Yes, Thomas told me. Marcus gave Thomas the task of writing an article about her return. It's to appear in Saturday's paper. Marcus said Susan never took his last name. She preferred to use her maiden name, Silverman, which I found interesting."

"That's right. According to Marcus, Susan didn't believe women should arbitrarily take the last names of their husbands. I'd like to help Thomas with the story. I'm sure he must be swamped and could use some help right now."

"Sure, Carrie Sue. Let me get him. Before y'all talk, I want you to know we're concerned about you and want you to stay with us. We don't want you to be alone right now."

"Thank you, Lisa. I appreciate your offer. I'm not sure what I'll do yet. I'll keep you informed. Don't worry."

As I waited for Thomas to pick up, I imagined myself at the press conference. What would I ask? I'd want to know every detail. Why did he assume she was dead? How was she captured? Why didn't he receive word she was still alive and in captivity? How was she able to escape? Until two days ago, Marcus firmly believed his bombs killed Susan and a helicopter pilot. Now he thinks his bombs killed Virginia Fischer as well as the pilot. The reporters at the press conference won't be privy to all of those details unless he tells them. Would he? How could anything good come out of this press conference?

Freemont recommended we watch it at my house. Jeff would be there, updating my security system, he said. We arrived at my house an hour before the scheduled time for the press conference and turned on the television in my den. I paced the floor until Freemont said, "Stop walking around and fidgeting, Carrie Sue. You're making me nervous. I remember when your mom and dad bought this TV."

By then, Jeff had finished updating my security system and walked in to join us. Freemont told him that Mom hired a carpenter to build an entertainment center around the TV. "We loved hanging out in here," Freemont said, as a way to lighten the mood.

We all fell silent when Bethany Coffman, a popular anchor, announced: "Susan Silverman, the war correspondent who was reported dead in nineteen-seventy-four, has been found alive. Her husband will be holding a press conference shortly. Stay tuned."

A photo appeared, showing Susan as a blonde child, standing between two adults, likely her parents. Another photo showed a pony-tailed Susan as a cheerleader, holding pompoms and jumping high. This seemed out of character. Marcus said Susan was a staunch feminist, someone who would rather play sports, than cheer for them. My heart sank when I saw the wedding photo of Susan and Marcus. She was dressed in a lacy white gown. He wore a black tux, handsome. They smiled lovingly at each other.

Another photo showed Susan with her hair pulled back. She wore a camouflage shirt and a camera around her neck. She held a reporter's pad in one hand and a cigarette in the other. I once caught Marcus puffing on a cigarette and I'd reprimanded him. He quickly stomped it out and said he'd quit. I responded with, "Apparently not." Since then, I've never seen him smoke another cigarette.

But who am I to judge? During my teens, I used to sneak around and smoke. I carried a long, black holder back then, and thought I was Miss Fancy Pants until my lighted cigarette lodged in the bouffant hairdo of Mary Alice Lee. I didn't even realize her hair was on fire until I smelled it burning. I quit smoking soon after.

"Show time," Freemont said. "There's Marcus."

Marcus filled most of the screen as he walked down the steps of what appeared to be a sprawling ranch house. He wore a tan suit, white shirt, open at the neck, no tie, his handsome face, serious and sad. He stopped in front of an array of microphones and passed a stack of papers to a tan man—perhaps Hispanic—in a white T-shirt.

"I'd like to make a statement before I attempt to answer your questions." Marcus spoke in a confident, rich baritone. "My wife, Susan Silverman, was reported dead December twentieth, nineteen-seventy-four, but we now know Susan is alive. She didn't die in a helicopter crash, near the Mekong River in North Vietnam, as reported. The charred remains of the helicopter pilot, Joseph Henderson and his passenger, that we believed to be Susan, were recovered. All reports indicated Susan and Henderson died in the crash. There were no survivors, and no one came forward to report she'd been captured. When I heard the news of the crash, I traveled to the site in hopes of proving she didn't die. Despite the heavy rain, we were able to find two metal ID tags, one was Susan's and the other was Henderson's. After the war ended, I held out hope that Susan might still return with the other prisoners, but she did not, and we received no word of her captivity."

Marcus ran a hand through his dark hair, a nervous gesture. "Ten days ago, a missionary group found Susan locked up in an abandoned house in a wooded area near Saigon. Her wrists and legs had been restrained with ropes. Samuel Ackerman, a spokesman for the Church of Christ group, said missionaries from his church heard Susan's cries for help and were able to free her. Ackerman regrets he could not attend the press conference today due to a prior commitment. I will provide his contact information." He motioned to the man he'd given the papers to. "Carlos Lopez has that information, and other details, which he will give you. I've also included background on Susan. Her captivity took a tremendous toll on her. She has memory lapses and health problems. She was held prisoner for many years and shuffled from one horrendous place to another. She recalls living in caves and eating mostly rice and drinking unsanitary water. Her doctors believe she suffered amnesia due to the punishment she endured. She is unable to speak to the press at this time, and I'm asking you to respect her privacy as she struggles to recover."

His lips formed a tight smile, as if to rein in his emotions. "I will try to answer your questions as best I can. But it is my hope you will focus on Susan as a dedicated and fearless war correspondent. Many journalists died while covering the Vietnam War. Their numbers have been estimated to be more than sixty. Unfortunately, media workers were not typically accounted for, and some may still be alive. Any questions?"

"Mr. Handley, you've named the pilot, who perished in the crash, but not the other person in the crash. Now that you know it wasn't your wife, are you able to identity that person?" asked a gray-haired man, standing in the horde of other reporters.

Marcus shook his head. "As of yet, we don't have a positive I.D., just conjecture, and I'd rather not speculate. On the contact sheet, you'll find sources who may wish to voice their opinion on that person's identity. As to questions regarding Susan's health, you may contact her physicians, listed on the information sheet."

The camera switched to a tall brunette, with sleek chin-length hair. She wore full makeup, most likely a television reporter. "Has anyone been arrested in connection with your wife's captivity? And can you name her captor?"

Marcus nodded. "The man who owned the house where Susan was held captive has been arrested. For more information, you can call the contact person listed in the press release we've given you."

The tall brunette raised her hand to indicate she had another question. "After so many years of assuming your wife was dead, did you remarry or become involved with someone else? And my last question is: How will your wife's reappearance change your life?"

I gritted my teeth as I watched Marcus close his eyes, as if to hide. He cleared his throat before answering. "After I became convinced Susan died in the crash, I never fully recovered, but as to my personal life, that's personal and not for public consumption. But to answer your first question, as to whether I've remarried yet, the answer is no."

My heart pounded in my throat. Was our engagement over?

Freemont walked over and placed his arm around me. "Carrie Sue, don't freak out. He can't tell them about you yet. He's trying to protect you and Susan. He doesn't want those reporters questioning you and you don't either. That doesn't mean he doesn't love you. You know he loves you, right?"

I started to state the obvious. Marcus is still married, but I hesitated when I heard the next question. "Do we know what caused the helicopter crash, Mr. Handley?" A young blonde woman asked. "Was it a mechanical malfunction, pilot error or was the copter shot down by the enemy?"

"Napalm hit it."

"From the enemy?"

"No, from our widespread carpet bombing. That's what we believe. No communication existed between the copter pilot and our scheduled bombing raids, which resulted in a tragic and deplorable accident."

My heart sank. I couldn't bear another hurtful question or upsetting answer, and in my need to escape, I ran to my bedroom and climbed under the white comforter.

As a child, I used to climb in this four-poster bed with Mom and Dad. Their presence and the mahogany columns comforted and guarded me from storms and imagined monsters. On Sunday mornings, my parents would sometimes linger in bed and read the New York Times together. I often invaded their privacy and pestered them with all kinds of questions, but they didn't seem to mind. They saw those times as an opportunity to educate me, Dad used to say, and on occasion we discussed the Vietnam War.

I was 13 when that war ended. It was the first war to be televised, which meant Americans actually viewed the atrocities. Dad said the war started in the '50s, during the Eisenhower administration. That's when Vietnam split in two. North Vietnam became communist and our government feared that South Vietnam and all of Southeast Asia would fall if we didn't stop the invasion.

President Kennedy inherited the conflict and continued it, I was told. Both President Kennedy and the President of South Vietnam, President Diem, were Catholics, although most of the people in South Vietnam were Buddhist and rebelled against Diem's tyrannical leadership. Our government supported the assassination of Diem, Dad said, as he revealed a very tragic and strange coincidence. Both Diem and President Kennedy were assassinated in November of 1963. Lee Harvey Oswald, a communist, was arrested for shooting and killing President Kennedy, but Oswald never stood trial, because he was shot by Jack Ruby.

Many young men wanted to avoid the draft, which continued through the administrations of Presidents Johnson and Nixon, but the draft ended in 1973. Marcus could have avoided the draft, too, but he joined the Air Force to serve his country, and I knew he must be going through a roller-coaster of emotions.

The phone on my bed-side table kept jingling. Rather than answer it, I sank deeper under the comforter and plopped a pillow over my head to mute the racket.

At the hard knocking on my bedroom door, I tossed the pillow aside and yelled, "I'll be out in a minute."

"Carrie Sue, are you okay?" Freemont called out.

I wiped my teary eyes and sat up. "I'm trying to rest."

"If you're decent, I'm coming in."

"I'm not decent," I said, as he eased the door open. He held up a piece of paper that looked like it had been torn from one of my reporter pads. "I've been answering your phone and taking messages. Maybe you should hire me as your assistant." He flashed a devilish smile.

"In case you haven't noticed, Freemont, I have a machine to do that."

He walked over and sat next to me. "Do you want the whole world to be taken over by machines?"

I studied the paper in his hand. He'd neatly written names and phone numbers. "Call Marcus. Call Lisa. Mary McCarthy will call back. She wants to thank you."

The phone jingled again. Freemont walked over and answered "Justice Residence."

I shook my head to mean, *No, I don't want to talk.*

He placed his hand over the mouthpiece. "It's Mary McCarthy."

She was the lady who called the Southern Journal two Christmases ago, I remembered. What could she want?

Freemont pushed the phone toward me. I took a deep breath and braced myself for the unknown. "Hello."

"Carrie Sue?"

"Yes?"

"I hope you remember me. I'm Mary McCarthy. You helped when no one else would. You wrote an article about my family and how my husband was fired for no good reason from that Atlanta trucking company. Remember? We were relocating from Detroit and our car broke down in Lexington, Kentucky. We used all of our savings to have it fixed."

"I remember."

Mary continued as if she didn't believe me. "We thought we'd be okay after John started working with the trucking company. In the meantime, we had to stay at the cheapest hotel we could find. The people in the room next to us were busted for drugs."

"Yes, Mary, I know. Your husband didn't feel right about leaving you and your children in the motel alone while he traveled on the road, so he took y'all with him in his truck."

"That's right. You do remember. That stupid trucking company said it was against the rules and they fired him."

As I listened, I recalled in vivid detail how her children were looking forward to Santa, but she had no money for gifts and barely enough for food and shelter. They were a sweet family, and their story touched me. I'd driven out to the motel to meet Mary, her husband Joe and their two children, Jeannie, six and Barry, eight. I took a photo of them, and Marcus ran it with the article I wrote.

Soon after the story appeared, I received a call from a man named Enfinger, who said, "I read your article about the McCarthy family. I have a furnished apartment that's vacant. I can let these folks stay there for free until they can get on their feet, if you think they're trustworthy." I vouched for them, but never heard back.

"How are you, Mary. How's your family?"

"We're great. I've been meaning to call and thank you. This year we've been so busy. But I wanted you to know we had a wonderful Christmas, and we're getting ready to move into our new home."

"I'm so happy for you, Mary."

We talked for a while and cried. I was a sobbing mess by the time we said our goodbyes.

After I hung up from Mary, Freemont handed me his handkerchief. "That call should've made you happy, Carrie Sue."

I wiped my eyes and blew my nose. "It does, but my emotions are all mixed up. I have too many tears inside."

He patted my arm. "Well then, you better get those tears out before you drown."

He pointed to the next name on his list. "You remember Louise Samson, don't you?"

"Isn't she the librarian at College Station?"

"Yep, sure is."

"Does she need me to call her?"

"You can call her if you want, but it's not necessary. She just wanted to give an update on Damon Cardoza. He's that homeless man you wrote about."

I frowned, concerned. "Is Damon okay?" I remembered how the Southside libraries were being closed due to computerization. Louise was worried about Damon. He had a habit of walking to the libraries when he couldn't get work. Damon loved to read books about the west, and with the libraries closing she worried he might not have a warm place to go.

Freemont's brown eyes glistened. "Ms. Samson said he's doing great. Wasn't he from some place in Wyoming?"

"Yes. His mom sold the family ranch after his dad died. Damon begged his mom not to sell, but she sold it anyway. He eventually found another ranch to work on. But he fell from a horse, broke his leg and hurt his back. He decided to try another line of work while he recovered and saw a newspaper ad for carpenters. He'd learned to do all kinds of carpentry on the ranch, he said, so he made the decision to follow up on the ad. He took a Greyhound to Atlanta and worked on some of the most luxurious townhouses in the city. But soon the carpentry work ran out, and he started walking to the libraries. He liked the libraries because they're quiet, like his home."

Freemont ran a hand over his short black hair. "Yeah, I seemed to remember reading what you wrote about him. I'm not exactly sure where all the libraries in South Atlanta are located, but I can't imagine walking to them and still having time to read. But he doesn't have to do that much walking anymore, if he doesn't want to."

"Really? Why? What did Louise Samson say?"

Freemont smiled with his whole face. "According to Ms. Samson, a rich lady came into the library after she read your article. She was determined to meet Damon. Long story short, she hired Damon as her handyman. He looks like a different person now, Ms. Samson said."

As I listened to Freemont, I pictured Damon. "He said he wanted to have enough money to return to Wyoming. I hope he's happy."

The phone rang again. I grabbed the receiver and answered.

When I heard Marcus whisper, "Hi," my heart hammered, and I couldn't speak right away.

"Are you okay, Carrie?"

"I'm hanging in. How about you?"

I heard what sounded like a low growl, but he didn't answer. I took deep breaths to slow my heartbeat. "I watched the press conference. You did a good job under difficult circumstances." The question about his personal life had left me feeling a little discarded, but I saw no reason to add to his guilt by revealing that.

"I wanted to stop the media harassment, but I failed. A reporter, posing as a doctor, slipped into Susan's room and took her picture."

"Oh, no, Marcus, that's terrible."

"Susan doesn't feel safe here now. She wants to leave the hospital and return to Atlanta with me." His voice cracked. "An Air Force buddy has offered to fly us in his Lear Jet. Mom said she'll come along, too. She's a nurse, and a PA."

My stomached knotted. Call me selfish, but I didn't want to share Marcus, even though I had no choice. Susan was his wife and had every right to return with him. "How is Susan doing health wise?"

"She has breast cancer. Doctors are recommending surgery. Her mother died from the same disease."

I tried to recall what he'd said about that. Susan's mom had died and his dad had remarried a woman with no intentions of becoming a mother. Marcus' mom had been more of a mother to Susan than the step mom. "I'm sorry, Marcus. But is Susan strong enough to fly here and go through that kind of surgery?"

"The antibiotics seemed to be working on her intestinal problems. She says she's feeling better and wants to have the surgery in Atlanta."

"Have you told her about us, yet?"

He sighed loudly and I wasn't sure if it was a sigh of frustration, fatigue, impatience or all three. "No, Carrie, I haven't. She's not strong enough to hear that. I'm sorry. She's just too fragile right now. I hope you understand."

Chapter Eight

Friday, February 20

For the next couple of days, I walked around in a brain fog, vaguely aware the weather had turned warmer. Plenty of sunshine, not a drop of rain, though it was raining in my heart, like that *Raining in my Heart* song from Buddy Holly. I wrote a column on depression. Easy to write. The article flowed, as if I'd cut a vein and let it bleed.

"Are you sure you want to publish this?" Thomas asked. "It's personal and maybe too private for public consumption."

"Yes, I'm sure." Thomas, Lisa, Lindsey and Jackie had smothered me with their pitiful stares for days, and by Friday, my spirits had dipped, lower than low, bluer than blue.

As usual, I buried my sorrows in work. I wrote a follow-up about Damon Cardoza, but I didn't include a photo. Julie Lasca, the lady who'd hired Damon as her live-in handyman, said she didn't want me to use his picture this time, although the librarian Louise Samson had said he looked like a new man, with shorter hair, clean-shaven face and sporty clothes. "Damon wants his privacy now," Lasca said, when I reached her via phone.

Her husband and son died in a car crash in 1967, twenty years ago. Damon was the same age as her son.

"Damon and I have been searching for land in Montana and Wyoming," she said, "I love the west and look forward to going there."

When she put Damon on the phone, I asked him how he felt about his new situation, and he answered, "I miss home."

Before Lasca said goodbye, she said, "Everything happens for a reason. Don't you think?"

I didn't know how to answer. She'd lost her son and husband in a tragic accident, and I couldn't think of a justifiable reason for that, or why I'd lost my parents in a plane crash, and discovered my fiancé, the love of my life, was still married to a woman he thought was dead. Rather than dispute her, I wished Lasca and Damon luck and asked her to keep in touch. She promised she would.

After I finished the Damon story and others, I ran upstairs to rest. I'd spent the last two nights sleeping in the apartment on the third floor, above the offices. This apartment had become my sanctuary. I could work in peace and avoid the pitiful stares of my co-workers.

I barely had the energy to use the bathroom and pull off my boots before crawling onto the four-poster bed where Marcus and I first made love. I tugged the maroon comforter over me and curled up in a fetal position. This room smelled of old furniture. It reminded me of Mom and how she used to drag me along as she bargained for antiques. This bed was a century old. Marcus had kept the furniture she'd selected, but had remodeled the kitchen and replaced the mattresses on both beds.

I heard the kitchen phone ring several times, but I couldn't force my leaden body up to answer it. Instead I embraced my black hole of despair. When I finally fell asleep, I dreamed of getting lost in a sea of abstract shapes.

My growling stomach awakened me. I'd eaten only half a doughnut that day.

I slipped out of the purple dress I'd fallen asleep in and put on the Atlanta Braves tee, then searched the fridge. It contained yogurt, orange juice, packages of sliced turkey and ham, mayonnaise, mustard, rye bread—Marcus kept the bread in the fridge—salad fixings, and beer. I pulled out the smoked turkey, the jar of mayonnaise, and mustard then made a sandwich with rye and washed it down with a Heineken.

As I ate, I remembered the cassette tape of Lionel Ritchie Marcus had played a few times. It was still in the boom box.

I carried the music to the bathroom, where Lionel serenaded me with *Hello, Endless Love, Lady, Truly, Still, Stuck on You, Three Times a Lady, All Night Long.* Enjoying the music, I stayed in the shower longer than necessary, shampooing and conditioning my hair, shaving my legs and scrubbing my body. Lionel had finished his serenade by the time I'd dried off and stepped out of the bathroom with a towel wrapped around me.

The sound of a slamming door startled me. I glanced through the pointed window in the archives room, which gave a clear view of the front steps of this building and the street below.

Mom's Cadillac was the only car in the parking lot. The guys who ran the presses parked in back, but they would have finished their work by now. Had they forgotten to lock up? Fear rose up my spine. No one should be in here this time of night.

Lisa sometimes retrieved old newspapers from this third-floor archives room, but rarely, and during working hours. Most of the past issues were stored in the larger archives on the first and second floors.

I heard footfalls on the stairs. Someone was coming up here. I ran to the bedroom where I'd been sleeping and locked the door. As I listened for the intruder, I grabbed the pistol Marcus kept inside the nightstand. I knew nothing about firing a gun. Marcus had offered to teach me, but I said no. I preferred Mama J's nonviolent approach.

But as I watched the doorknob giggle, I pointed the gun and positioned my finger on the trigger. Would I be able to shoot someone? If my life depended on it, *yes.*

"Carrie?" Marcus called out.

I exhaled a relieved sigh, then put the pistol back in the nightstand, swung the door open and grabbed him. "You didn't tell me you were coming in today." As I kissed him, I could feel his day's-growth of beard. He smelled and tasted like the whisky he'd been drinking.

"I called here, but you didn't answer." His eyes roamed over me. I realized then I'd dropped my towel.

He grabbed my head and planted another rough kiss. I tugged at the tail of his V-neck blue sweater. He helped me pull it over his head.

As my eyes feasted on his powerful chest and the ribbon of hair trailing from his navel, I unzipped his jeans. He was as hard as a tree limb. I kneeled to kiss him there, but he pulled me up and carried me to the bed. "You first, baby."

"I'm surprised you aren't exhausted."

"Never too tired for you, baby." His warm tongue encircled my breasts and moved downward, lavishing me with his mouth. "God, you taste good."

I could feel our hot bodies humming as we came together. He buried himself deep inside me, pounding hard and swift. I wrapped my legs around him and met him, thrust for thrust.

After I found my pleasure, he allowed himself to come. He cried out like a wildebeest as his body convulsed.

As his breathing slowed, he moved to his side, keeping us attached. "I didn't hurt you, did I, Carrie?"

I gave him what I hoped was a seductive smile. "Do I look like a woman in pain?"

Marcus asked me this same question the first time we made love. Back then, I wondered if he'd hurt another woman and had a slit personality like Dr. Jekyll and Mr. Hyde.

But then he explained he'd injured Susan the first time they'd made love. They were only eighteen. She was a petite, five feet. He was six, five, with a sizable penis. When he entered her, she tore, which caused her great pain. He had to rush her to the emergency room for treatment.

I gave him a reassuring hump. "You're turning me into a sex maniac, and if that's your idea of hurting me, then you've caused irreparable damage."

He sighed, "I feel the same."

I fondled his muscular chest and eased my body back and forth over him then rolled on top. I loved the feeling of being in control of this powerful man. And despite his fatigue and the booze, he got hard again and we were able to make love more gently this time.

As I rolled off, he groaned, "I love you, Carrie," then quickly fell asleep. His beautiful mouth emitted puffs of air in a soft snore.

"I love you, too, Marcus, always and forever," I whispered to his sleeping face.

Chapter Nine

Saturday, February 21

The ringing phone snapped me awake. Marcus shot out of bed to answer it.

The radio clock on the bed stand registered 8:03 a.m. but I didn't have anywhere I had to be and no desire to leave our love nest. I expected Marcus to return to bed and snuggle, but my hopes were dashed when I saw the somber apologetic look on his face as he stood nude in the bedroom doorway.

"Who was on the phone, Marcus?"

He rubbed his eyes. "Mom. She called to let me know Susan is scheduled for surgery this morning. I need to get over there right away, sorry."

As I listened to him, I could feel his emotional wall, distancing me. To conquer the separation and regain intimacy, I jumped out of bed and wrapped my arms around him. "Is there anything I can do?"

He drew me near. "Your being here, being patient, loving me, that's more than I deserve." His guilt had resurfaced, a casualty of the war.

I searched for a way to reassure him. "For me, there's no one better in the whole world than you, Marcus."

He frowned and squinted, as if he doubted my words. "I hate to leave you, Carrie. I hope you know that. I wish I could stay. But I have to jump in the shower and get to the hospital. I want you to relax and enjoy your Saturday, do whatever you need to do to feel good."

I sighed. "You make me feel good."

He kissed my forehead. "Ditto, baby."

"There are so many questions I need to ask you, but I got distracted last night and didn't think to ask them."

His navy eyes glistened. "I can think of no better distraction. I'll have to use that technique the next time you try to badger me with questions and force me to bare my soul."

This had been a running joke between us. When we first got together, I'd ask him personal questions and he'd say he wasn't one of my interviews. I'd agree and say he was my personal life. He often accused me of badgering him and forcing him to bare his soul.

I nodded and poked him in the stomach. "You're overdue for a good badgering. We can talk while I drive you to the hospital."

Freemont still had Marcus' jeep. That meant Marcus had no transportation and would have to take a taxi if I didn't drive him.

He kissed my lips softly. "I want you to take it easy. Don't worry about me. I'll call a cab. Your badgering will have to wait."

I pouted. "If you don't want me to drive you, why don't I call Freemont? He can bring your Jeep over?"

"No, I don't want to put you or Freemont out. I'm taking a cab and that's final."

He'd been drinking last night and made a good choice in taking a taxi. But would he continue to drink as a way of dealing with his problems, now that his life had spiraled out of control?

The question hounded me, but I chose not to broach that sensitive subject with Marcus, and after he left, I walked around in a daze, pondering our relationship and reliving our lovemaking. He claimed he didn't want to leave me. Yet, he rejected my offer to drive him to the hospital, and he failed to say when he'd return or call.

I paced and brooded, searching for answers. My stomach developed a big knot.

I withdrew my Tandy from my tote, turned it on and sat for several moments staring at the blank screen. *"Be patient,"* I could almost hear Dad say.

I waited for inspiration. My fingers were perched on the keyboard ready to respond, but no meaningful words or thoughts came to me. My mind flew from one erratic thought to another.

I eventually gave up and called Freemont. If he couldn't inspire me, no one could.

My hopes were dashed when his voice mail answered. I hung up without leaving a message. I'd monopolized too much of his time already. He needed to focus on his laundry business, his college assignments and his health.

Then I remembered Lindsey had invited me to go with her to see her psychic, Kasandra Rubin. Lindsey had written a column about Rubin, piquing my interest. I'd complimented Lindsey on the column, and she invited me to come with her today for a reading with Rubin, if I could find the time.

I called Lindsey and told her I was free. Rubin lived in Dunwoody and worked out of her home, Lindsey said. "Not far from me, but a little bit of a drive for you."

"That's okay, Lindsey. I'll meet you there."

She recited the address. "I'll call her and make you an appointment, Carrie Sue. She charges a dollar a minute and it's check or cash."

"Are you sure she's worth it?"

Lindsey laughed. "She's been right about me so far. Best psychic I've ever been to. Bring a cassette tape if you want her to record your session. I'm so glad you've agreed to do this. We can do lunch afterwards and have a girl's day. Stan is at a convention in New York. He won't be flying back till late this afternoon."

Her husband Stan was a successful lawyer, though she often referred to him as, "the ambulance chasing barrister I married."

Lindsey had a reputation as the newspaper's answer to Barbara Walters, with a talent for drawing out secrets. She and everyone at the Southern Journal knew about my divorce from Kyle and the return of Marcus' wife, but she didn't know I'd seen Marcus last night or that Susan would be having surgery, which meant I needed to be careful and not share too much. Marcus guarded his personal life like a mama gator defends her young. "Watch your tongue," I could almost hear Mom say.

I put on a pair of old jeans, a yellow turtle neck sweater and my Pumas. Forty minutes later, I'd arrived at Binghamton Road and easily found Rubin's house from Lindsey's description, "white with black shutters." I pulled up onto the hilly drive and killed the engine. Not long after, Lindsey's red Thunderbird pulled up behind me.

She jumped out, waving, as if we hadn't seen each other yesterday. She wore red capris, a jean jacket over a red and white shirt and white tennis shoes. Her large sunglasses hid her brown eyes.

"You look like Jackie O," I said, when I got out of the Caddy.

She waved off the compliment. "I need to tell Stan that. He absolutely loves Jackie O." She gave me a tight hug. "You look great, Carrie Sue, but you always do. Have you talked to Marcus?"

I paused, weighing my words. Sooner or later she'd know Marcus had returned, if Lisa and Thomas hadn't already told her. "He flew back last night."

Lindsey stuck her sunglasses on her head and raised her eyebrows in surprise. "He tried to get in touch with you yesterday. He called the newsroom. I spoke to him, and he talked to Thomas a couple of times. Did y'all finally get together?" She winked.

I nodded. "I'm hoping your psychic can tell me what it all means."

She led me toward the white front door. "I bet she will."

No doorbell, only a black-enamel door knocker in the shape of an angel. Lindsey banged the angel three times and the door swung open. A stunning woman with white hair, in a giant bun on top of her head, faced us. Her black eyebrows and lashes were in stark contrast with the white hair. She could have been anyone's mother or grandmother, but I wouldn't have placed her as a psychic.

She hugged Lindsey. "Come in, come in."

After Lindsey introduced us, Rubin hugged me. She smelled like peppermint. "I prefer to do my readings in the sunroom, as Lindsey knows. Lindsey asked me to do your reading first. May I call you Carrie Sue?"

"Yes of course."

"I'll wait for y'all in the living room," Lindsey said. "I brought along a novel to read, so I'm cool."

I followed Rubin to the sunroom. It was a lovely glassed-in area overlooking a backyard shaded in magnolia trees.

Rubin motioned for me to sit on a fern-green sofa.

"Make yourself comfortable, dear," she said.

As I sat on the squishy couch, a black Persian cat jumped in my lap. The kitty wore a rhinestone-studded collar.

Rubin stroked the cat's head. "This is Witchy. She likes to help me read."

Witchy purred as I petted her. "She's beautiful."

Rubin sat opposite me in a green chair that matched the sofa. "I usually record these sessions. Many of my clients have told me they get more out of their sessions when they're able to listen to them again. If you didn't bring a tape, I can provide one."

I withdrew a cassette tape from my tote and handed it to Rubin. "Lindsey asked me to bring one."

Rubin inserted the tape in a Sony recorder, which looked similar to the one I use when taping meetings. The recorder sat on top of the glass and mahogany table positioned between us.

Rubin inhaled several loud breaths before she clicked record. "When I read, I view events as if I'm watching them on a television or movie screen. Ask me questions, and I'll see if I can envision the answers." Rubin closed her eyes. "But I can see already that you're confused. I see danger and sadness. Do you have a question you'd like answered?"

I winced at her negativity. Lindsey said Rubin was positive. "Yes, will the man I love choose me?"

With her eyes closed, she inhaled and exhaled as if in a trance. "The man you love, his name begins with M. He has chosen you, but he is not free. Is that right?"

"Yes, but I want you to tell me about our future."

"I see you together. You have made a commitment." She shook her head. "Be very careful. Oh, no. You are being watched. You have received threats. Pay attention to them."

I sighed, recalling the last few days, but I didn't want to dwell on the nasty notes and the break-in at my house. As I thought about this, Rubin's hazel eyes popped open. Her stare pierced mine. "These are the same people who hurt your friend."

I gasped. "Do you know who they are and how we can stop them?"

Rubin closed her eyes. "You already know who they are. Believe in your judgement. But be very careful."

"Is my friend Freemont in danger?"

She inhales and exhales. "I see Freemont. He has a beautiful heart. There is an angel around him, his mother. Did his mother die?"

I fought back my tears, but they leaked out anyway. "Yes. Will he be okay?"

Rubin nodded. "And you have angels, too, your mother and your father."

I often bared my soul in my columns. It was possible Rubin had read them. And the deaths of my parents had been widely publicized. Did Rubin know about me already? As to Freemont, she could have read what happened to him as well, but when she described Mom and Dad as angels, I wept. "What about my love, the M you mentioned, what can you tell me about him?"

Rubin took several rapid breaths. If I were to breathe like that I would hyperventilate. "Wow, he's a hunk," Rubin said. "And believe me, even at my age, I know what a hunk is. He's the whole package. But, but, he has anger inside. Life has not been fair to M. You love him dearly and he loves you. Did you know he loved you in another lifetime?"

"No, how could I know that?"

"In this life, he fought his feelings for you, is that right?"

"I don't know if that's right or not."

"This man knows how to love, my, oh, my, he's hot, but he's loyal, the opposite of that other guy you hooked up with. Unfortunately, M has bottled up anger. He was dealt bad juju. He tries to do the right thing and control himself. He feels very guilty. Guilt bottled up leads to anger. Did you know that?"

"It makes sense."

"I see this man as having to fulfill an obligation." She frowned. "Is he married?"

"Yes, he thought his wife was dead for many years, but she came back."

"Ohhhh, I see that. Oh, no, I prefer not to put tragedy out in the universe but in this case, I see something dark and ...." She stopped talking to glare at me.

Rubin's words and stare made me shiver. I cradled the purring Witchy in my arms for comfort. "You're scaring me. Please don't scare me like that."

She gave a quick nod. "You are very talented. The world needs your talent. You are an old soul. You have lived many lifetimes. You and M were together in one of those lifetimes," she said. "You bore his children and died in childbirth."

In my shock, I blurted out, "When was that?"

"Early eighteen-hundreds, I'm unsure of the exact dates. In this lifetime, M moved here, to this area, because his soul sensed you were here," she said. "Did you know that?"

"If he came here to find me, why did he marry his childhood sweetheart? Why didn't he wait?"

She breathed in and out several times, before she spoke again. "He entered this lifetime ahead of you and geographically away from you. Aren't you much younger than M?"

"He's only ten years older." A true psychic would know this, I thought.

Rubin closed her eyes. "A big age difference when one is very young. Not so much now. M is passionate, wow." She fanned her face with her hand. "He chose prematurely in this lifetime. He picked someone he knew well. Someone he thought he could trust. But she is not as passionate as he. Very few are as passionate as he. But you are. You have the passion to match his. You are a true soul match. The other woman is not. Am I right?"

"I don't know the other woman. Only what he's told me."

"She betrayed him. Yet, he cannot bring himself to tell her about you. He wants to tell her, but he feels guilty. He is plagued with guilt. As I look at this situation, this is a very dark area. I cannot see what's going on here."

I wanted to explore why Rubin thought Susan had betrayed Marcus. Susan had failed to inform Marcus of her plans to rescue her friend. Maybe Rubin considered that a betrayal, but I didn't want to waste my minutes with Rubin exploring this. "Why does M think he needs a bullet proof car?"

Rubin took several quick breaths. "M has had threats on his life, due to his job." She sucked in another breath. "And he suspects danger. He has psychic abilities, too."

"Is M in danger?"

She opened her eyes. "He is a smart man and he has taken precautions, but life has been unfair to him. I am hoping this dark cloud will blow away."

"Do you believe the dark cloud surrounding M will blow away, Ms. Rubin?"

"Call me Kasandra, please." She closed her eyes. "I cannot see through the dark now. I'm sorry. This happens to me when the screen I'm looking at is dark. As I said when we first began, I glance at a screen, like a television screen in my head. Parts of the screen for you and M are dark."

I sighed and wanted to leave. I worried about Marcus. What would happen to him? Did I really want to know? Should I be concerned about his drinking? How could I ask her about this without describing the problem?

As I hesitated, Kasandra asked, "You are worried about M, and he is worried about you. Your love is vital for him. He is at a crossroads, and as I see the dark screen, he sees the dark, too. You are his light. Keep your light alive for your sake and for M's. He is a strong man, mentally and physically. Do not worry about him. Look after yourself and your light. This is what he wants you to do, too. I believe you can change a dangerous situation by being careful. Remember, you need to be extremely careful. You have free will, and you can reverse a bad situation if you are aware of the dangers."

Kasandra stood, removed the cassette tape and gave it me. Then she handed me a small package of tissues. As I wiped my teary eyes, she sat beside me and stroked my head. I noticed her wristwatch—with the green cat eyes inside. If the time was right, an hour had passed since I sat down.

Kasandra charged a dollar a minute, Lindsey said, so I wrote her a check, which included a generous tip, and handed it to her. She thanked me, and I followed her to the white-carpeted living room where Lindsey sat on a white sofa with green pillows.

When Lindsey saw us, she closed the paperback she was reading and gave me a sad stare, as if she sensed my distress. She stood and touched my face, without speaking.

I asked Kasandra if I could make a local call. She led me to the kitchen and pointed to a vintage 1930s gold phone, on top of a white granite countertop. The shelf above it held an Atlanta phone book.

I found the number for Emory Hospital, dialed and when the operator answered, I said, "I need to speak to Marcus Handley. Please page him. He's not a doctor or a patient, but he's visiting someone at the hospital." I didn't mention Susan's name. Marcus wouldn't want the news media tracking her there or anywhere.

"What is your name?" the operator asked.

I told her, and she said, "Hold, please."

I waited for several minutes and started to hang up, when I heard Marcus whisper, "Hello."

Rather than say hello back, I surprised myself by singing *Endless Love*. This was not something I'd planned to do. It was spontaneous.

He listened silently until I finished my serenade. "Lovely, thank you. You could easily perform a duet with Lionel Richie."

I laughed, delighted by the compliment. "I was listening to his tape last night before you came in."

"Mm, we should have listened to it together."

"Maybe tonight, Marcus."

When he hesitated and didn't respond, I said, "I hope you don't mind me calling you at the hospital."

"I'd already informed the operator you might be calling. I called you earlier and left a message for you to call me here."

I sighed. "I didn't get your message. I'm sorry. I've been gone most of the day. How are you doing. How did the surgery go?"

"Susan is out of recovery. She's sleeping now. The cancer has metastasized, her surgeon said." I heard fatigue in his whisper.

"Are you saying her cancer has spread?"

"Yes, but we can talk about that later. A team of doctors, oncologists are looking into the best way to proceed. Where are you now?"

"I'm with Lindsey at her psychic's house. She's having her reading done now. I just finished mine."

"Are you kidding? Is that the same psychic Lindsey wrote about in her column?"

"Yes, Kasandra Rubin; I talked to her for an hour. She taped it, but I don't think you'd want to hear it."

"Why wouldn't I want to hear it?"

"You'd probably consider it silly and a waste of time."

"Whatever involves you, I don't consider a waste of time, Carrie. Hold on a sec, will you?"

As I waited for Marcus, I heard a woman's faint voice and became aware of a beeping noise.

"I need to go. I'll call you later. Enjoy your time with Lindsey. Stay safe."

"Will you be coming back tonight?"

"I'll call you."

My stomach knotted at his abruptness. "Okay, I love you."

He hung up the phone without saying he loved me back. I figured he didn't want Susan overhearing.

I tried to bolster my confidence by remembering what Kasandra said. He was my soul mate. We'd been together in a past life. I hoped to tell him this later, though I would exclude the part about the dark screen and the bad juju.

To stop my mind from sliding to the dark side, I closed my eyes and pillowed my head in my arms on the granite countertop. I began to meditate but soon fell asleep despite my uncomfortable perch on the kitchen stool. When Lindsey tapped me on the shoulder, I jumped up, startled by her beaming smile and brown eyes sparkling. She looked ecstatic. No darkness in her reading.

"I can't wait to tell you about my reading and hear about yours," Lindsey said. "Why don't we go to Virginia Highlands for lunch?"

I nodded in agreement. We both liked the eclectic vibe of Virginia Highlands—at the intersection of Virginia and North Highland—not far from the Southern Journal.

I suggested Ethiopian food and we stopped for lunch at the Green Nile. Mom and Dad used to love the Green Nile. Marcus enjoyed the food, too. The first time I ate there, I was about 14 or 15, a picky teenager, who hated exotic, spicy foods. Since then, my pallet has become more educated.

As I wrapped the flatbread (injera) around bits of beef, chicken, lamb and veggies, Lindsey gushed about her reading. "Kasandra said Stan and I would definitely have a baby but she was unclear on the date."

I gasped. "Do you think you might be pregnant?"

She took a sip of the mango smoothie she'd ordered. "Not yet, but we're trying. I've stopped taking the pill. I can't wait much longer. I'll be thirty soon. But don't breathe a word to Marcus, *please*."

"That's your private information, Lindsey, not mine to tell. I won't breathe a word, I promise, and I hope whatever I share with you will remain private as well."

If Lindsey and I could establish a mutual agreement not to blab our secrets, I'd feel free to vent and relax, I thought.

Lindsey touched her index finger to mine, reminiscent of the science fiction character E.T. in the movie by the same name. "Absolutely, Carrie Sue."

"You're still young, Lindsey. Thirty is certainly not old, by any measure. You still have plenty of time to start a family."

She waved me off. "Easy for you to say. You're five years younger."

"Age is only a number. I don't look younger than you, but getting back to what Kasandra predicted, if you and Stan are eager to have children right away, I hope she's right." As I said this, I remembered I needed to schedule an appointment with my gynecologist. "Speaking of which, I have to call Doctor Bush to have my birth control pills reissued. He won't fill my prescription until I see him."

Lindsey squished up her face and snickered. "You have a GYN named Dr. Bush? I would never let a Bush examine my bush."

I laughed. "Who's your doctor?"

"I go to a woman. I like her. Doctor Dooditty."

"You go to a doctor Dooditty?" I snickered.

Lindsey slammed her hand on the table and laughed until the mango smoothie ran out of her nose. Her laughing made me laugh, and we both blamed our drinks, thinking they were spiked. The laughing made my sides hurt, but I couldn't seem to help myself. It had been a long time since I've laughed this hard.

When we finally gained our senses and stopped our giggling, Lindsey asked me about my session with Kasandra. "You looked like you'd been crying when you came out, Carrie Sue."

I told Lindsey about the dark screen.

"Wow, Carrie Sue. Kasandra once told me the same thing. It was a while ago, though. Stan had hired this intern named Bunny. Bunny took it upon herself to call me every day and inform me of Stan's schedule. She wanted to work fulltime in his office as a paralegal, and I didn't have a problem with that. But then, she started telling me how much she enjoyed her lunches with Stan. And God, how she bragged about him. She'd go on and on. She thought Stan was a genius, as if I didn't know him. She said she'd learned so much from him. Mind you, this was over the phone. I'd never met Bunny in person, but I soon decided I needed to meet her face to face." Lindsey leaned across the table and lowered her voice. "And guess what I discovered?"

"What?"

"Bunny looked a lot like me, a much younger me, and I began to wonder if Stan was getting ready to trade me in for this younger version."

"Oh, no, what a terrible thought."

"It was. Stan's secretary, Julie, didn't like Bunny at all, and I found that kind of strange. Julie usually likes everybody. I eventually asked Julie why she disliked Bunny, and she told me Bunny was a goof off and gushed over Stan too much. That's when I decided to get some guidance from Kasandra."

"What did Kasandra say?"

"Same thing she told you about the dark screen. Kasandra told me I needed to light up our home fires. Our bedroom looked very dark, Kasandra said."

"So how did you light up the home fires?"

"I brought out the heavy artillery in the form of see-through lingerie, showcasing my tits and twat."

I laughed. "Apparently your artillery worked."

"Yep, and it didn't take long for Stan to wake up and fire Bunny. She was making too many mistakes, he said. Funny how he'd overlooked those mistakes until I started relieving his horniness. Men are such simple creatures."

As I listened to Lindsey, I couldn't imagine Stan cheating on her. When I first met him, he reminded me of Jerry Lewis, in that old nutty professor movie. I couldn't figure out what she saw in him. Lindsey still looked like the fashion model she used to be. Also, she's clever, a talented reporter and writer.

"I don't think Marcus is a simple creature. He's very complex."

Lindsey shrugged. "You're right. Marcus is an exception, but he still has a penis, and the penis has the power to control the mind."

I thought back to when Marcus and I first made love. He couldn't control himself, because I behaved like a shameless hussy. "I hope Marcus doesn't regret getting involved with me."

Lindsey stood, walked around to my side of the table and hugged me. "Are you kidding? Marcus is nuts about you. He's a different person now that he has you. At first, I wasn't exactly sure what brought about the change in him. But I knew something drastic had happened. I told Stan I thought the heavens must have opened up and replaced the old Marcus with a new, happier version. Stan was the first to think he'd fallen in love. But I just didn't know he'd fallen for you. Then I started noticing the way he looked at you. His face lit up. He would actually blush when he saw you. Very sweet. I never noticed Marcus blushing before you two got involved." She returned to her seat. "Don't worry. He'll do the right thing and tell his wife he loves you."

"I wish I could be sure of that, Lindsey. He flew back with her last night, and his mom came with them. His Mom is a nurse, and when Susan was growing up, his mom was like a mother to her. Marcus said Susan has metastasized breast cancer. Susan's mother died young from that disease." I paused to question whether I should have shared this with Lindsey. "Promise you won't tell anyone about this, not even Stan."

Lindsey's eyes widened. "I promise, Carrie Sue. I won't tell a soul, but I do wonder what kind of treatment she's getting. Is there any hope for her?"

"I don't know. She had surgery today. It's very sad. I can only imagine how much she's already suffered and now this. How can Marcus tell her about me when she's fighting for her life? If he told her, it might destroy her."

The waiter brought one check, and Lindsey grabbed it. "I'm getting this."

I nodded. "Next time, it's my treat."

Lindsey placed her hands on her hips, defiantly. "Hush, Carrie Sue. You've treated me countless times. I just wish I had the magic words to make you feel better. When I'm down in the dumps, I try to be grateful, but sometimes when I'm in a funk, it's almost impossible. From where I sit, I see a young, intelligent, talented, healthy and beautiful young woman. You are loved, baby cakes. Your friends and coworkers love and admire you. And the man you love, loves you. I have no doubt about that."

"But I'm not sure of our future, Lindsey. What if it doesn't work out?"

"You can't give up hope. You have to believe."

I wiped my wet eyes and blew my nose on my napkin. "There's no way Marcus will desert his wife now. He wouldn't do anything to destroy her will to live. Marcus already suffers from guilt as a result of the war. For years he thought his bombs were responsible for killing his wife."

Lindsey placed her hands over mine. "Why does he think that?"

I explained about the carpet bombing and how he didn't know Susan or any American was in the path of his napalm. "And I'm positive Marcus would never do anything to jeopardize her recovery."

Lindsey threw down enough cash on the table to cover our meals, plus the tip. "We need to stop this depressing talk. Let's go shopping. You need a mood lift."

I agreed to the retail therapy, and after we left the restaurant, we walked to a vintage clothing store Lindsey liked. She bought a flapper hat and a corset. I bought a 1950's nightgown made of thin lace and chiffon.

As we walked out of the store, I told Lindsey I needed to buy new underwear, but I didn't mention the break in at my house. She suggested a boutique close by, and we shopped for another hour. I bought several pairs of lacy underpants and matching bras. Then Lindsey held up a V-neck sea-blue top with lace trim and bell sleeves. "This is the exact color of your eyes, Carrie Sue. It's darling. Looks like you. Why don't you get it?"

I bought the top she suggested, and after we left the boutique, Lindsey spotted a spa across the street, where we indulged ourselves in facials, massages and pedicures. I chose fire engine red. She chose purple.

Lindsey's eyes looked sleepy when we walked out of the spa. "I'm going home and pour myself into bed. Stan's supposed to fly back tonight. I hope to God he's eaten before he gets home, because there's no way in hell I'm preparing supper." She huffed a sigh. "If necessary, we'll get take out."

I thanked Lindsey for inviting me on such a lovely excursion. "We need to do this again soon," I said and she agreed.

Driving back to the Southern Journal, my mood shifted to high alert when I spotted a white Ford LTD tailing me. I slowed, hoping it would pass. Night had fallen with fog, and I couldn't make out the driver in the glare of the headlights.

When I parked in my usual spot in front of the office building, the car turned around and drove off. My spine buzzed with uneasiness as I got out of the Caddy and hauled my packages up to the main entrance.

As soon as I unlocked the door, I turned on all the lights then relocked the door before I checked my phone messages. I had two personal calls, one from Marcus—he'd left that message earlier. I'd talked to him since then. The other message was from Freemont.

He invited me to have supper with him and Tatum Brookins at the College Station Diner, two blocks away from the office. It was already 6:30, and he'd said 6, but I figured he and Tatum would still be there.

The streetlamps illuminated my path as I walked to the diner. The lights made me feel a little safer, though my nerves were still prickly from being followed. I studied each passing car and everyone I met on the sidewalk. A couple of men greeted me with, "hello." I said "hello" back, even though I didn't recognize them. "It never hurts to be kind. Kindness can diffuse ill will and anger," I could almost hear Dad saying, and he would often add, "But keep your guard up, too, and carry a healthy dose of suspicion."

When I reached the diner, I heaved a relieved sigh. As usual, the diner was crowded. The yummy aroma made me salivate, though I'd eaten a big lunch. The diner's buffet offered a salad and soup bar, turnip greens, mac and cheese, mashed potatoes and gravy, peas and butterbeans. The meats varied. On Saturday and Sunday, it had Chicken fried steak and fried chicken. On Monday, it was meatloaf, Tuesday—spaghetti, Wednesday—Turkey and dressing. Friday—fried catfish.

Owner Lucy Sumner greeted me and led me to the burgundy booth where Freemont and Tatum were sitting. They smiled and stood as I approached—true gentlemen. Freemont wore gray trousers with a crisp white shirt. Tatum had on jeans with a brown shirt, a shade lighter than his skin, and a tan jacket.

I hugged Freemont before I hugged Tatum. I still couldn't believe such a sweet and gentle soul had been arrested, indicted and forced to stand trial for a murder he didn't even witness. Thankfully, he was acquitted after the evidence proved his innocence.

Lucy asked me if I wanted the buffet or a menu. I chose the buffet and told Lucy I'd have water with lemon to drink.

The aroma from the buffet had piqued my appetite. I chose chicken fried steak and a sampling of the veggies.

As I returned to the booth, I realized Freemont and Tatum had already cleaned their plates and were eating dessert: pecan pie for Tatum, coconut cake for Freemont.

I sat next to Freemont. His wide smile couldn't conceal his fatigue and half-closed eyes. "Tatum has been studying quite a bit. He's maintained a B average."

I smiled. "That's great, Tatum. Congratulations. You've worked hard."

Whenever Tatum reached certain goals, Freemont rewarded him with an item on his wish list, and one of those items had been phone service for his family.

Tatum looked up from his pecan pie and smiled, showing his white teeth, which made me recall what his mom, Latrice, had said, "I try to teach my kids good manners and good morals, but I have to thank God for their good teeth and good looks."

Freemont had assigned Tatum three books to read. "After I get through them, Mr. Freemont is taking me to a Braves game," Tatum said.

Tatum lived in public housing with his Mom and his two older brothers. His dad died nine years ago, and Latrice, as a single mom, struggled to feed her family and provide the necessities. She cleaned houses during the day, but made every effort to be there when her three sons returned from school.

Tatum withdrew a sheet of paper from his shirt pocket and handed it to me. "This is what he wants me to read. He's goin' to test me after I read them. I don't know how long it'll take me."

I looked at the list: "*The Adventures of Huckleberry Finn, To Kill a Mockingbird, The Catcher in the Rye.*"

I returned the paper to Tatum. "Wow, these are great books."

Freemont nodded. "We checked them out of the library today. He's already started on *Huckleberry Finn*, one of my favorites."

I cut off a piece of fried steak. "Mine, too."

Freemont gave me a sly, side glance, as the waitress refilled our water glasses. "Tatum said somebody's been sending his mama cash in the mail with no return address. And she doesn't know who to thank. I told him it wasn't me."

I feigned a puzzled expression. I didn't want anyone to know I was the one who'd been mailing cash to Latrice. I hadn't even told Freemont, but from his sly stare, he'd guessed my secret.

Tatum squinted at Freemont. "Mama doesn't believe you, Mr. Freemont. She says you been sending the money."

Freemont cleared his throat. "That's not the way I operate, Tatum. I want you to earn what you get. I had to earn everything I got." Freemont smiled, reminding me of Mama Jackson's smile. "My Mama always said, 'Nothing comes from nothing. You got to work for everything in this life. But you got to never give up. I had to work a whole year before Mama would buy me cowboy boots. But as to who's sending your mama money for no reason, I'm thinking that benefactor wants you to pay it forward."

Tatum frowned, as if confused. "What do you mean?"

"I mean you should try to find another family who needs help and help them. I'm not talking about now. I'm talking about when you become successful. That's what I mean by paying it forward. You don't repay the person who gave you the money, because you don't know who that person is. So, you need to choose another person or family who needs your help."

Tatum nodded and smiled. "I get it now, okay."

As I listened to the exchange between Freemont and Tatum, I spotted Nev Powers and Neeley Nelson as they walked in. Nev had on a blue warmup suit, not his usual Rea-ganesque detective garb. His chest looked a little thick and I thought he might be packing. He had the same boyish face as he did in high school. His short brown hair stuck up like a well-used brush. Neeley had on pink sweats that showed off her big boobs and camel-toe crotch. She'd captured her long carrot-red hair in a ponytail. Men gaped as she walked in.

I didn't know if Freemont had noticed, so I tapped his uninjured, right arm. "Don't look now but Nev Powers and Neeley Nelson just walked in."

Freemont's brown eyes darkened. We were both convinced Nev and his dad were guilty of shooting Freemont and burning a cross in his yard.

Lucy led Nev and Neeley to a table, near the front and away from us, thank God. Neeley hugged everybody she recognized and worked her way in our direction. I turned toward Freemont, hoping to avoid her.

"Hi Carrie Sue, how are y'all doing tonight?" Before I could respond, she pursed her pink lips and stared at

Freemont. "We haven't been officially introduced, but I know who you are. You're Freemont Jackson."

Freemont nodded. "Ever since birth."

Neeley feigned a sad face. "I was so sorry to hear about your injury. How're you doing?"

Freemont took a sip of his sweet tea before answering. "Better and better."

She smiled widely. "That's great."

Neeley narrowed her eyes at me. "I heard about Marcus' wife being rescued. You must be devastated." My stomach knotted. The nerve of her. She chased after Marcus from the moment she came to town. She blatantly flirted with him, batting her lashes and wiggling her hips, as if to say, *come and get it, baby.* She brought him cakes, pies and cookies like some Penthouse Betty Crocker.

When her green eyes caught mine, I remembered the nasty note left in my door, and judging from her cruel gleam, I could see she thought her words had struck a blow, but I was determined not to show my distress. "I want what's best for Marcus. Maybe that's something you can't comprehend, Neeley."

She smirked. "Oh, I comprehend all right. Now if you'll excuse me. I have to scoot to the Ladies room." She waved her pink and white manicured nails. "Nice chatting with you."

Freemont patted my hand. "Don't let her get to you. She's just jealous."

I grabbed the check. "I think it's time to scoot."

Freemont reached for check. "I invited you, remember?"

I jumped away to keep it out of his reach. "No, let me get it. Please don't make a scene."

Tatum fidgeted in his seat and turned toward the front of the restaurant. His eyes widened, sensing trouble, no doubt. Nev Power had been nothing but trouble ever sense I'd known him. I dated him once and only once in high school. That was before I knew he had anger issues. He lashed out at my friend Jimmy Johnson for no reason and should have been arrested for calling Jimmy a "coon" and punching him in the face. Nev later said he thought Jimmy looked like the drunk driver who caused the automobile accident that paralyzed his Mom and killed his twin brother Nathan. His accusations made no sense. Jimmy was a young teen, not old enough to drive at the time of that accident.

I leaned over and whispered to Freemont. "Where're you parked?"

"Out front, I'm driving Marcus' jeep."

I whispered, "Marcus flew home last night."

Freemont stood and motioned for Tatum to do likewise. "Why are you whispering, Carrie Sue? We're not in a library."

I rolled my eyes. "I'll explain later." I caught Nev staring at us, even as Neeley returned to his table. "You and Tatum go on outside, Free. I'll pay the bill and meet you. I can drive y'all back home and then bring the jeep back here for Marcus. If that's okay with you."

Freemont stood. "That's just plain crazy, Carrie Sue. But if you insist, and you're not too tuckered, you can ride with me. I'll drive Tatum home 'cause I know the way."

"Okay scoot," I whispered. "I don't want trouble."

Freemont raised his eyebrows along with his voice. "Carrie Sue, I'm not afraid of anybody, especially not a Klan jerk who hides behind a costume and pretends to be law enforcement."

I shushed him and shook my head in despair, then hurried to pay Lucy at the cash register.

Nev grabbed my arm on the way. "Are you too stuck up to speak, Carrie Sue?"

"I'm in a hurry, Nev. That's all."

Freemont inserted his giant frame, all 6 feet, 6 inches of him, between us. I stiffened, expecting all hell to break loose.

Lucy Sumner rushed over. She had a knack for breaking up fights. Prior to buying this diner, she worked as a bartender in an Atlanta strip club.

Nev pouted his bottom lip like a child then released my arm and turned away. I rushed toward the cash register and was in the process of paying Lucy when I heard Neeley Nelson say—loud enough for everyone in the restaurant to hear: "Why do you bother with her, Nev? She acts all high and mighty, but believe me, she's no angel. She's as down and dirty as the next one."

Freemont scowled and mouthed, "Bitch," referring to Neeley. Mama Jackson would have scolded him up and down if she'd heard him. To avoid a fight, I pulled Freemont toward the front door. "They're not worth your trouble, Free."

"Sorry you had to witness that, Tatum," Freemont said.

When Freemont refused to let me drive, I got in the back seat and sat quietly. Freemont needed to focus on the road, not conversation. The foggy night required slow, careful maneuvering, and Freemont was at a disadvantage with his left arm incapacitated in a sling.

Tatum stared out the window as if mesmerized by the ghostly vapor. "Thank you for supper, Miss Carrie Sue, and thank you, Mister Freemont, for taking me to the library.

Freemont nodded. "You don't have to keep thanking me, Tatum. I enjoyed it, too."

As we approached the public housing project where Tatum lived with his mother and two older brothers, Tatum turned his head around toward me. "I don't know if I should tell this, but ..."

When he hesitated, I said, "You can tell us anything, Tatum."

"I don't know if Mama wants me to. She might get mad."

Freemont parked in front of the *College Station Housing* sign and turned toward Tatum. "If she asked you not to repeat something, you shouldn't."

Tatum shook his head. "She didn't say not to."

I touched Tatum's shoulder to reassure him. "Is it something we can help you with, Tatum? Something we need to know?"

"Yeah, I'd like to help my cousin, Jolene. Detective Powers did an awful thing to her."

"Oh, god." Sensing the worst, I grabbed a reporter's pad and pen from my tote. "What did he do?"

"Jolene said he raped her, but cops don't believe it. They say she waited too long to report it. She was scared is the reason. When Jolene told Mama what was done to her, Mama took her to the police station to report it, but Jolene waited too late, they said."

I swallowed the bile in my mouth as Freemont said. "Tatum, I don't want you getting involved with this. Carrie Sue and I will follow up. You got it?"

Tatum nodded.

I jotted down what Tatum said. "How old is Jolene?"

"Sixteen."

Freemont slapped the steering wheel. "How did Jolene's parents respond? Did they support her?"

"She lives with Gramma, my daddy's mama. Gramma's in a wheelchair. She has a muscle disease. Jolene's mama is my Aunt Clarisse. Aunt Clarisse lives in Alabama. Mama says Aunt Clarisse can't look after Jolene."

"What about Jolene's dad?" I asked.

"Aunt Clarisse never told Jolene who her daddy is."

"Jolene is a minor," I said. "And if we can prove Powers raped her, we can have him locked up. From what you've said, your Aunt Clarisse is your deceased daddy's sister. Is that right?"

"Yeah."

I continued to take notes, but my stomach sickened at this tragic news. I had to keep swallowing the bile in my mouth to keep from throwing up. I was already in a tentative emotional state, but I was determined to get the facts right. "I want to make sure I heard you correctly, Tatum. Jolene is your Mama's niece and your cousin. What is Jolene's last name?"

"Brookins, same as me. They don't live with us. They live next door."

After I wrote this down, I put my hand on Tatum's shoulder to reassure him. "Freemont's right, Tatum, you need to stay out of this. But I'm glad you told us. That was the right thing to do. Freemont and I will take it from here. We don't want you having a problem with Detective Powers or the police. You need to focus on school and your own life."

"But didn't y'all say I should pay it forward and help someone?"

As I heard his innocent question, my eyes teared, and with the fog, the red-brick buildings where Tatum lived appeared ghastly. I squinted to see the group of teenagers, a few feet away, hanging out on the sidewalk. They were bigger than Tatum. He'd have to walk past them. Would they harass him? I remembered what Atlanta's Police Chief once told me. He called these projects "crime infested," and said, "I'm even afraid to walk through them at night."

Freemont smiled at Tatum. "Yes, I did say that, but I was talking about helping someone when you're in a position to do so. Not now, but down the road. Right now, you need to concentrate on your school work and stay out of trouble. Okay?"

Tatum opened the car door. "Okay."

Freemont turned to me. "Hop in front. I'm walking with Tatum. I'll be back in a minute. Keep the doors locked. Don't talk to anyone."

I did as he instructed, but as I waited for him to return, fatigue washed over me. I closed my eyes and despite my troubled mind, I fell asleep.

A tap on the window, awakened me. My head shot up to see a thin, dark man in a black leather jacket and skull cap.

It's okay, I told myself. *The doors are locked, and I'm in a bullet-proof Jeep.*

He pointed at a cigarette, dangling from his mouth, indicating he wanted a light. I shook my head no.

He made a motion for me to roll the window down. I shook my head no.

This back and forth continued for a few moments. Then I spotted Freemont jogging toward the Jeep. The mere size of him would frighten anyone, but with his left arm in a sling, I worried he might appear vulnerable.

"You're not harassing my lady friend, are you?" Freemont used a gruff voice, uncharacteristic of him.

The stranger shook his head. "Naw."

I unlocked the driver's door, thinking Freemont would hop in, so we could get the hell out of there. Instead, he walked around the jeep toward the stranger.

My heart pounded in my throat. *No, Free,* I wanted to yell. *What if this man has a knife or a gun?*

Freemont scowled like Mike Tyson, getting ready to punch out Trevor Berbick for the heavyweight title. "Find another place to be, man."

The stranger stared at Freemont, as if refusing to back away. I rolled down my window and smiled. "You don't mean any harm, I'm sure, and I don't want anyone to get hurt, so it might be best if you'd leave and find a safe place for the night."

The man held his hands up in a gesture of surrender. "I'm cool, okay. I was just wanting a light." Then he took off running and disappeared behind one of the buildings.

Freemont hopped behind the wheel of the Jeep, without mentioning the incident, then handed me a slip of paper. "I got this from Latrice, Tatum's mom."

I stared at the paper with Jolene's name, phone number and address written neatly.

I wrote Jolene's information in my reporter's pad and tried to figure out a way to help her. I was unfamiliar with the legal statutes regarding rape, but as a crime reporter, I'd covered rape trials and observed the way rape victims had been mistreated when they brought charges and testified against their attackers. Some defense attorneys tried to expose a victim's sexual history, in an effort to convince the jury the victim had been complicit in the rape.

During one of those trials, a victim actually cried out, "I was a virgin when he raped me."

The defense attorney, who'd been cross-examining her, said, "Your word against his."

"I'll discuss this with Marcus," I told Freemont. "He has vast legal knowledge. Also, maybe Karl Silkman can provide some advice." Silkman had defended Tatum and helped to exonerate him.

Freemont nodded. "I'll talk to Silkman. When do think you'll get a chance to talk to Marcus?"

"I'm not sure. Susan flew back with him. She's in the hospital now. She had surgery today. She has breast cancer."

"How are you handling all of that?"

I twisted my engagement ring. I'd been twisting it a lot lately, irritating my finger. "I'm sad. I saw him last night, but this morning he had to leave and go to the hospital because she was having surgery."

Freemont grimaced. “Has he told her about you yet?”

“She’s struggling to live. It would be cruel to tell her now.”

Freemont scowled his disapproval, but said nothing as he drove to his house.

When we arrived, he invited me to stay, but I told him I needed to get back to the office apartment, in case Marcus called or showed up there. I soon regretted my decision. With the fog bearing down, I could barely see two feet in front of me and was forced to drive at a snail’s pace.

By the time I parked in front of the Southern Journal building, my body ached from stress and fatigue. I sat in the Jeep for a few minutes to gather my strength and think about what Tatum shared. In the thick fog, the old Victorian house looked eerie, like a haunted house in *Poltergeist*. I had a strange premonition: Someone was following me.

After I got inside and relocked the front door, I turned on all the lights and called out, “Anybody here?”

No answer.

I checked the phone messages. Marcus had called again. He spoke softer and slower than usual. “I was hoping we could talk. I have to stay at the hospital tonight. Mom needs a break. She’s taking a cab to my house.” His voice cracked. “Sorry I can’t be with you.” After a pause, he said, “Mom would like to meet you, Carrie. She’ll call you when she gets up tomorrow. You can call her, too, of course. I hope you’re okay with that. If possible, I’d like for you to drive her back to the hospital tomorrow. She may tell you to drop her off, but I’d rather you come inside. I want to see you ... and maybe you can meet Susan. Sleep well, baby. Lock up and stay safe. I love you."

I replayed his message. The thought of meeting his mom and Susan scared the hell out of me.

I kicked off my shoes and climbed into bed with my clothes on. I thought I'd fall asleep right away, but my mind buzzed with negative thoughts. "Damn, Nev Powers, he'd raped Jolene." I had no doubt he'd violated her in the worst way.

When sleep refused to claim me, I got up, grabbed my pad and pen to make a "to do" list:

1. Meet Marcus' mom at his house
2. Ask Marcus how we can help Jolene Brookins.
3. Meet Jolene, get details.
4. Find out who Jolene reported her rape to.
5. Talk to witnesses, if any.
6. Talk to Tatum's Mom, Latrice.

After I finished the list, I drank a beer, brushed my teeth, washed my face, slipped into my Atlanta Braves shirt then listened to Lionel Ritchie.

Chapter Ten

Sunday, February 22

The ringing phone woke me up. I glanced at the clock on the bed stand: "9:44."

As soon as the ringing stopped, it started again. But at that moment, I didn't have the energy to get out of bed and walk to the kitchen to grab it. An invading sun peeked through the bedroom blinds. I watched the light beams until I remembered Marcus' mom was supposed to call me. When the phone rang again, I jumped up to get it.

"Southern Journal, Carrie Sue speaking."

"Hi, Carrie Sue, this is Carol Handley. Did I wake you?"

"Hi Carol. Did you just try to call? I heard the phone ring, but I couldn't get to it in time."

She laughed. "That was probably Marcus. When you didn't answer, he called me and got me out of bed."

I rubbed at my eyes, grimy from sleep. "Do I need to call him back?"

"You can, dear, but I wouldn't bother. He's at the hospital. He said you'd be picking me up. Is that the plan?" She sounded relaxed and happy. No one would have guessed she'd been caring for a loved one with a grave illness.

"Right, yes, I need to take a shower and get dressed. I should be there by 10: 30. Is that okay?"

"Of course, it's okay. I'm looking forward to meeting you. I'm planning to wear grey sweats and tennis shoes. So please dress casually. Do you think we can go for breakfast or brunch? I don't feel like cooking. I have a craving for pancakes. Is there an IHOP nearby?"

"IHOP sounds good. There's one on Clairmont, not that far. I'll probably wear jeans." I thought of the V-neck blue blouse with the white lace cutwork I bought yesterday. It should go well with my jeans, black leather jacket and boots. "I can't wait to meet ... you." I almost said my future mother-in-law. That would have been a mistake. She would never be my mother-in-law, as long as Marcus and Susan were still married.

After we hung up, I ran to the bathroom, showered, brushed my teeth and groaned at my reflection in the mirror. My long, curly hair stuck out in every direction. I pulled the tangled mess into a bun and thanked God for bobby pins.

I powdered my face and dabbed *Cherries of the Snow* lipstick on my mouth. It was 10: 45 by the time I jumped in Marcus' Jeep and headed for his house. My stomach was a total knot.

Carol Handley waved as I drove up and rose from the lounge chair on the front porch. Sunlight framed her lovely face. She had salt and pepper hair, captured in a ponytail. True to her word, she was dressed casually in grey sweats. She reminded me of the actress Anjelica Huston.

We hugged as soon as I jumped out of the Jeep. She smelled like vanilla. Her navy eyes were a replica of her son's.

They both shared high cheekbones, full lips and dark coloring.

Carol cradled my head. "You're exquisite. You look like one of my porcelain angels. I collect them."

I smiled, delighted with her compliment. "Wow, thank you!"

She grabbed my left hand and studied my engagement ring. "Beautiful, we have so much to talk about."

She and I hopped in the Jeep and headed to IHOP. "I look forward to learning more about Marcus and you and your family. He hasn't told me much about his childhood."

Carol laughed. "He's like Benjamin, his father. God rest his soul. I miss him so much, but it was like pulling teeth getting him to talk."

I smiled, hoping she'd say more. "I'd love to hear about Marcus as a child."

"He was a dream baby, always laughing, playing, happy, rambunctious. His teen years were a challenge. He loved motorcycles, and to my horror, Benjamin encouraged him to ride. After Marcus saw Evel Knievel perform, he was hooked. Do you remember Evel Knievel?"

"Only by reputation. Isn't he that dare-devil stunt rider who broke nearly every bone in his body?"

Carol threw her head back and laughed. "Yes. Marcus was about eleven or twelve the first time he saw Evel Knievel jump over cars. To my horror, Benjamin took Marcus to see him, and when Marcus turned sixteen, Benjamin bought him a Yamaha bike. I couldn't stand to watch Marcus risk his life. He'd do those wheelies, or whatever they call them, and stand up on the seat without holding on. Crazy."

"Wow, do you have films of him doing that?"

She shook her head. "Oh, heavens no, I could never film him endangering his life. And Benjamin was never one to take photos or use a movie camera. He was always too busy. Aliza, his sister, begged to go riding with Marcus, but I said absolutely not. Thank God, Benjamin backed me up on that."

I smiled, imagining Marcus in his teens. "He's never mentioned riding a motorcycle, but he did say he took piano lessons. He plays beautifully."

She smiled and nodded. "I thought he might become a concert pianist. Mr. Stephens, his piano teacher, said Marcus had natural talent, but there are just so many hours in the day, and Marcus had many things he loved to do. He loved to ride his cycle. He loved to play football, and he loved to run track. The piano took a back seat for a while. Thank God, he gave up the motorcycle and continued his piano playing."

"Why did he give up the motorcycle?"

She grimaced. "A friend of Marcus,' Trever Taylor, was killed on a motorbike. And after Trever died, Marcus lost his enthusiasm for riding."

I gave Carol a sad glance. Why didn't Marcus tell me about the death of his friend? "Did Marcus always want to be a journalist?"

She smiled showing her white, even teeth. "He caught that bug from Benjamin."

"Marcus told me your family owned a number of newspapers but sold them after his dad died. I've often wondered why he moved from California to Atlanta and bought our newspaper business rather than continue with your business." I remembered what Kasandra the psychic had said. Marcus was drawn here. He and I had shared a past life. Was that true?

Carol looked down at her hands and massaged her fingers, as if they ached. Her fingers were long and graceful, with delicate lines, testifying to an active and compassionate life. "It was difficult for Marcus to return to the same place where Benjamin died. Benjamin had a fatal heart attack as he and Marcus were working side by side. Marcus blamed himself. He thought he should have been able to save his father. But there was nothing anyone could have done. Ninety percent of Benjamin's coronary arteries were blocked, according to the autopsy. He refused to have regular checkups. I begged him, but he refused. He wouldn't even let me take his blood pressure. I wanted him to have a stress test. He said no. He wouldn't stop smoking. He had a horrible diet. I tried to get him to eat more vegetables and salads. He preferred meat and potatoes and pizza. Benjamin was a wonderful man, a loving husband and father. Irreplaceable."

I pulled into the IHOP and turned off the motor. Carol's eyes had teared. I reached across the center console and squeezed her hand to offer comfort.

She withdrew a tissue from her purse. "I didn't want Marcus to leave, but I was unable to stop him. The offer from the syndicate came in, and Marcus wanted to sell the business and go."

"I sort of understand why he did that, Carol. I was depressed after I lost my parents. It must have been excruciating for Marcus, losing his dad, especially after all that had happened during the war. I know he felt responsible for what happened to Susan, too."

She dabbed at her eyes with the tissue. "When Marcus returned from the war, I didn't recognize him. He had changed. He was deeply depressed. Thank God, he was willing to seek counseling. When Benjamin died, Marcus wanted to leave and start over. I told him no matter where he went, he wouldn't be able to run away from himself, but regardless of what I said or did, I couldn't make Marcus stay in California. Soon after he flew to Atlanta and met your father and mother he was bound and determined to be here. He loved your parents. He talked about you, too, Carrie." She smiled. "He said you were quite the pepper pot."

"He called me a pepper pot?"

She nodded. "I think he meant it as a compliment, meaning you are assertive and speak your mind, which he admires. I knew he was attracted to you from the beginning."

I studied Carol as she told me this. Was she serious? When I first started working with Marcus, I thought he considered me a wet-behind-the-ears upstart, someone Dad had hired him to train. "He never acted like he was attracted to me at all, until recently."

She reached over and squeezed my shoulder. "Marcus takes his responsibilities seriously, but I knew by the way he talked about you. Take my word for it. A mother knows these things."

I smiled, delighted. "He gave me no indication. At work, he pushed me to achieve above and beyond what I felt capable of doing. I often wanted to strangle him."

She laughed, although her tears leaked out. "That's because he saw your potential and he cared for you. Marcus said your parents were wonderful, generous people. He learned a great deal from your father. Your father was completely devoted to you and your mother, Marcus said. He also told me your mother owned a decorating business and was resourceful and creative."

I tried to bite back my tears, but they leaked out. "Yes, Mom and Dad were amazing. Mom went everywhere looking for deals, and she'd often drag me with her." I groaned, as I remembered. "Sometimes I'd make up an excuse not to go. Then she'd drag Dad. Dad didn't seem to mind. He enjoyed being with her. They both loved to travel. After Marcus took over as managing editor, they traveled more and more." I cringed, remembering how they'd died in a plane crash.

Carol sighed. "I wish I could have known your parents. They must have enjoyed life to the fullest. Your dad enjoyed working, I'm sure, but it doesn't sound like he was a workaholic like Benjamin. I wish Benjamin could have relaxed and traveled more." Carol shook her head and closed her eyes. "My husband always needed a challenge. What I considered stressful, he loved. Right after we were married he bought a struggling newspaper. Destined to fail, I thought, but he didn't see it that way. He loved news and loved to write, and he proved me wrong. Eventually, he was able to turn that failing newspaper into a thriving conglomerate. Then he started looking around for another business to transform and decided to buy a winery of all things. He knew nothing about running a winery, but he bought one anyway. I thought he'd lost his mind when he said he'd purchased five hundred acres of vineyards and a winery. We all had to pitch in. He had to hire an experienced manager and a slew of workers and wine makers. Now the winery is doing quite well."

My stomach growled, demanding food. "I've sampled some of your wine. It's delicious."

She touched my arm. "Why don't we go in and continue this."

I hopped out and hoped we'd get around to talking about Susan. But Carol hadn't mentioned her so far, which seemed strange.

After we ordered —a waffle, scrambled eggs, bacon and grits for me, and a fruit bowl and blue berry pancakes for Carol — I summoned the nerve to ask, "How's Susan doing? Marcus said she had a double mastectomy yesterday."

Carol sighed. Her navy eyes revealed deep sadness. "I was hoping she'd be able to have a lumpectomy, but she wasn't given that option. The cancer has spread. Her doctors have prescribed a drug to counteract the cancer. They mentioned performing a hysterectomy, but they're thinking another surgery could be too much for her body to recover from at this point." Carol sucked in a breath, squinted and squeezed out tears.

I grabbed a napkin from the table and handed it to her. "I'm so sorry. Marcus said you were like a mother to Susan, and I know this is very painful for you."

Carol wiped her eyes. "When she called to say she was alive I was shocked but ecstatic. Of course, we had no idea then how sick she was. She's shared a few things about her captivity, but not much. I don't know if it's because she'd rather forget those horrors or if her mind can't recall everything." Her voice cracked. "I know this has been a shock for you, too, Carrie."

As I listened to Carol talk about Susan, I could feel a black cloud of pain and heartache moving in. I almost wished I could stop this conversation, but I knew I couldn't live in denial and ignore the elephant in the room. "Do her doctors think she'll recover?"

"I don't think anyone knows, Carrie. Susan needs invasive therapy to kill the cancer, but she's very sick and her doctors are weighing the risks. She needs a miracle, and she may get one. I'm a nurse, and I've witnessed miracles before. Medical science doesn't have all the answers."

The IHOP waitress brought our food and refilled our coffee. Carol excused herself. "You go ahead and eat. I'll be back in a moment." I watched her walk to the Ladies Room, as if she carried the weight of Susan's illness on her shoulders.

By the time she'd returned to the table, I had eaten most of my eggs, bacon, grits and waffle.

She sat and pointed to the few morsels left on my plate. "My, Carrie, you were hungry."

"I did sort of inhale my food, didn't I?"

She laughed and poured blueberry syrup on her pancakes.

I finished off my waffle and considered the best way to ask about Susan's relationship with Marcus. "Marcus mentioned that he and Susan had been childhood sweethearts."

Carol narrowed her eyes. "Carrie, Marcus told me you have a gift for getting people to talk. No wonder you're such a good reporter."

I thanked Carol, although I didn't think of my nosiness as a gift, but as a way of appeasing my curiosity. I preferred to focus on others, dissect their lives, rather than peel away the layers of my pain. "I hope I'm not being too nosy. Marcus has accused me of badgering him with personal questions he wishes to avoid. But I love him, and I'm naturally curious about him and his past. Do you think I'm being nosy?"

She stared at her food, as if her hotcakes beaconed. "No, not at all, but I thought you might feel uncomfortable hearing certain things." She took a bite of the pancakes and chewed thoughtfully.

"It's part of Marcus's life and I'm interested, but I don't want to intrude on your memories."

Her navy eyes widened. Had my probing astonished her? If Marcus were here, he would have accused me of tormenting his mom.

She thanked the waitress for refilling our coffees and glanced around the busy restaurant. "Let me start by giving you a little history. Susan's mother, Rachel, and I were close friends, 'two peas in a pod,' was how Rachel described it. We met at the Y. We took tennis lessons together. We were both newlyweds. She'd recently married Ted, and I'd just married Benjamin. We became pregnant about the same time." She paused for a moment. Ordinarily, I would have jumped in with another question, but I kept my mouth shut to keep from interrupting her train of thought.

"A few months after Susan was born, Rachel found out she was pregnant again. But I'm sad to say, she had a miscarriage. About a year later, I found out I was pregnant, and Rachel insisted on giving me a baby shower, even though she'd been diagnosed with breast cancer. I told Rachel if I had a girl, I'd planned to name her Aliza, which was Rachel's middle name." Carol's hands trembled, as if shaken by the memory. "Oh, how she doted on Aliza after she was born. Susan was only three, and she was always wanting to hold her. Susan was such a precious child. She was not quite four when Rachel passed. I promised Rachel I'd always be there for her sweet girl. Ted remarried soon after Rachel died. He dearly loved Rachel, but he was lonely and sad. The woman he married, Elizabeth, was a successful attorney, and she was involved in her career. She didn't have time for children and wasn't nurturing to Susan. Susan began to resent Elizabeth. Their disagreements drove a wedge between Susan and her father. Every time I tried to talk to Ted about this, he asked me not to interfere. But he allowed Susan to spend more and more time at our house. She became a part of our family. Marcus and Susan were more like brother and sister then. But things changed when puberty kicked in." Her eyes searched my face, and she paused for a moment. "Are you sure you want to hear this?"

I nodded. "Yes, if I didn't, I wouldn't have asked."

She chewed on her bottom lip. "If I say anything that troubles you, please stop me, okay?" She paused for a moment, probably filtering her words before she spoke them. "When Marcus and Susan were around fourteen or fifteen, I caught them kissing in the den."

Carol placed her hands over mine. "They said they were playing a game. Susan confided later she had practiced kissing with a couple of her girlfriends, but she wanted to practice with a boy. She adored Marcus, and Marcus was the only boy she wanted to kiss, Susan said." Carol shrugged. "I had a talk with Susan and asked Benjamin to talk to Marcus. Benjamin didn't seem worried. He said Marcus understood. Marcus was mature for his age. He was taller than the other boys. At fifteen he was almost as tall as he is now."

"He's very handsome, Carol. I'm sure he must have been very popular with girls." As I said this, my insecurity surfaced. Why did Marcus want to be with me when he could have his pick of any woman? Would he have picked me if I hadn't forced myself on him? I didn't know.

"Yes, lord, he had girls calling him, mostly older girls. One seventeen-year-old girl took him on movie dates. By then, Benjamin had given Marcus an ultimatum. If he had sex with a girl and she became pregnant, he'd have to marry her, support her and the baby. Marcus said he had no intention of ruining his life like that."

I pictured Marcus receiving this harsh talk. "Was Susan jealous of the other girls?"

She shook her head. "She didn't seem to be. She had a slew of friends and a busy social life. Her father bought her a car when she turned sixteen. She said he bought the car to get her out of the house and stop the friction between Susan and Elizabeth. Marcus didn't seem to want a car back then. He preferred motorcycles. Susan would hop on his bike and ride with him."

As I listened to Carol, I began to get a better understanding of the relationship between Marcus and Susan. "Sounds like Susan and Marcus were very close."

She squinted. "They were, but they had their disagreements."

I pushed the envelope with my next question. "What did they argue about?"

She rolled her eyes. "Oh, I'm not completely sure. She might accuse him of putting other things ahead of her. Marcus worked at the newspaper, ran track, and played football. She might want him to go to a movie and he might want to do something else. They didn't like the same movies, but they were so young. If she wanted to see *The Valley of the Dolls,* he'd want to see *The Dirty Dozen.* It was that sort of thing, just little spats. Or he'd want to go running and she'd want him to do something else." Carol narrowed her eyes. "They had only one major disagreement that I recall."

I leaned in close to hear and observe Carol's body language. "What was that major disagreement about?"

"Getting married, she wanted to and Marcus wanted to wait. They broke up for a few months over it. Marcus had graduated high school early and went on to Whittier College. She graduated a year behind him, although they were the same age. He had taken accelerated classes and attended summer school. After Susan graduated, she followed him to Whittier."

She sighed. "Marcus was a lot like his father, a workaholic. He'd earned a bachelor's and master's degrees in less than four years. Then he joined the Air Force, something I objected to, but his father had served in the Air Force, and Marcus wanted to learn to fly."

As I listened to Carol, I became confused. Up until then, I thought Marcus had become a workaholic to escape his guilt, but according to Carol, he'd always been a workhorse, even before the war. "When did they finally see eye to eye and get married?"

Carol paused before she answered. "They went to a Celebrant or Justice of the Peace after Susan found out she was pregnant. She later miscarried."

Would Marcus have married Susan if she hadn't been pregnant? I wanted to ask Carol. But how could Carol know the answer to such a hypothetical question? According to Marcus, Susan had been a feminist. She'd kept her maiden name after they married. But as I listened to Carol, I saw Susan in a different light. If she had been an activist, why didn't Carol mention that? Instead, she shares how Susan followed Marcus and wanted to marry him.

"Susan miscarried in her first trimester, not uncommon for first pregnancies. Half of all first pregnancies end in miscarriage."

Marcus had never mentioned this miscarriage to me, but he'd said he and Susan had difficulty having sex in the beginning. He was large and she was small. He'd torn her, he'd said, and the injury had been serious enough to require emergency medical treatment. I wondered if he would have shared this information with me had I not badgered him about his personal life. He often balked when I asked him about his past, and after talking to Carol, I realized how little he'd shared. Carol said Marcus and Susan were both 19 when they married. At 19, I was still a virgin. When I was 18, Dad hired Marcus as managing editor. Would I have given up my virginity for him back then? In a heartbeat.

"Were Marcus and Susan happy in their marriage?"

Carol glanced at the ceiling, as if it held the answer. "They were so young, and as many young couples do, they struggled. They both worked hard at school and took odd jobs. Marcus earned money writing. He wrote articles about college life for our newspaper. He worked in the school cafeteria, too, and he was a dorm monitor. Susan typed papers for other students and occasionally wrote an article for our paper. She was a stringer for *The National News* and was later hired as a war correspondent. She worked full time for them after Marcus joined the Air Force. When he went overseas, he lived in the barracks in Da Nang, Vietnam. Susan wasn't allowed to stay there with him. Marcus' supervising officer said if the Air Force had wanted him to keep a wife, they would have assigned him one."

I tried to imagine how painful that must have been for Marcus and Susan as I listened to Carol share her memories. I was grateful she'd opened up. She seemed to enjoy revisiting the past. Talking to her made me feel less of an outsider and more a part of their family.

By the time we'd left the restaurant and headed toward Emory Hospital, I could understand why Susan thought of Carol as a mom. Carol reminded me of my own mom. She was warm and loving. She was a professional woman, who loved working, but she'd never sacrifice her family for her job. Family came first.

At the hospital, I rode around searching for a parking spot. When I finally located one, a driver in a red truck with oversized wheels stole it. "Rude sob," I blurted out.

"Look, Carrie Sue, there's a better spot over there, near the entrance." She pointed.

I pulled into the spot she'd found, and as I killed the motor, my mind whirled. I longed to see Marcus, but my conscience told me I had no right to be here.

In the hospital, Carol guided me through a maze of halls, smelling of disinfectant. Rather than take the elevator, we trudged up several flights of stairs. Carol said she needed the exercise.

We were out of breath by the time we'd reached the floor where Susan was. Carol led me to a small waiting area with plastic chairs. "I'll get Marcus. Let him know you're here." We hugged before she left, and she thanked me for taking her to IHOP and sharing conversation. "You have exceeded all my expectations, Carrie."

I smiled at her kind words, but my stomach filled with butterflies as I anticipated seeing Marcus. I sat next to a woman holding a wiggly little boy. He looked about two. He wore blue overalls and a red shirt. He soon squirmed out of her lap.

The woman watched with sad brown eyes as the toddler ran back and forth, climbing up and down chairs. His antics increased my nervousness. I eventually stood and started pacing.

When Marcus walked in, I gasped at the sight of him. He wore a crisp white shirt and blue jeans. His dark hair was neatly combed back. His handsome face looked clean shaven. He smiled when he saw me, and I rushed to hug him. He smelled like soap and spicy aftershave and his own unique, manly odor.

"Let's go somewhere more private, Carrie," he said and ushered me out of the waiting room.

"I brought your Jeep. I can show you where its parked, if you want to go out there."

Rather than comment, he led me down the hall to a door marked, "Chapel."

It was a dimly-lit room with a piano and several rows of straight-back chairs. A lectern stood in the back of the room. A golden cross hung on the wall behind the lectern.

"I can picture you coming in here and playing the piano, Marcus."

He smiled and nodded, as we sat side by side in two of the upright chairs. I could feel the heat radiating from his body.

"I've missed you, Marcus." I flashed him a seductive smile.

His eyes gleamed. "I've missed you, too." He stroked my face with the backs of his fingers. "How do you feel about meeting Susan?" He drove a hand through his hair, a sign of nervousness.

I chewed on my lips, not knowing how to respond. My heart raced from being close to Marcus, but my stomach knotted at the prospect of meeting his wife. What if she sensed my feelings for him? I've never been able to hide my emotions very well, and Marcus knew this.

He wrapped an arm around me. "Relax, it's going to be okay." He stared into my eyes as if he could read my soul. "Mom said you could've been a psychotherapist; which I translate to mean she spilled her guts to you."

I grunted a laugh. "Your Mom is such a lovely woman. I really like her."

"What did you two discuss?"

"You as a child and you growing up. Your family."

He shook his head, as if exasperated. "You badgered Mom, didn't you? I should have properly prepared her."

I smirked. "Your Mom has no secrets to hide. Can her son say the same?" I could almost see fire brightening his navy eyes. They looked cobalt at that moment.

"Her son is similar to you."

"What is that supposed to mean, Marcus?"

He reached over and played with a stray strand of my hair. "You're uncomfortable talking about the past, and I am, too." His eyes misted over. "As to Susan, I wish I could tell her about you. But I can't, not yet."

"I understand, Marcus. You're trying to do what's best for her. She's sick." My heart fluttered and I could feel the tears burning my eyes.

"I haven't been available to you. I've been unfair to you, and I'm sorry."

"You haven't been available to yourself, Marcus. You need to take time to nurture yourself and not worry about being available to me. I know you're doing your best. You're in an impossible situation. You never expected Susan to return after all those years. You were convinced she was dead. You're in shock."

His eyes studied mine. "I suppose I am. Being with you is just about the only time I feel alive. But I don't want to take advantage of you, Carrie. I want to be fair. I don't want to leave you hanging." He closed his eyes. "But I damn sure don't want to lose you." He ran a hand over his face. "Why don't we talk about something else? Tell me about your visit to the psychic."

Typical of Marcus, he wanted me to talk. This allowed him to escape his pain, and I understood his need to escape. I shared the same need. "It was interesting. Kasandra said you and I were soulmates. We knew each other in another life."

He flashed an amused smile. "What lifetime was that?"

"We were married sometime during the eighteen hundreds. She couldn't pinpoint the exact date. But sadly, I died giving birth."

Marcus winced. "That is sad."

I searched for something positive to say. I couldn't dare mention the dark screen. He'd been through enough darkness already. "She said I was your light, and I needed to keep my light alive for you."

His eyes gleamed. "Now that I can believe. You're definitely my light." He placed a finger over my mouth. "But don't say that's sweet." This sweetness thing had become a running joke between us. When I first started calling him sweet, he didn't know how to take it. He thought the word sweet didn't apply to him. Grumpy? Yes. perfectionist? Yes. Sweet? No.

I nibbled at his finger. "Sweet, very sweet."

He cradled my face and moved his mouth toward mine. We were an inch away from kissing when we heard a door slam. We both jumped at the noise.

A young man, about my age, walked in. He had on a blue shirt with beige trousers. There was something about him, his smile and rich brown skin maybe, that reminded me of Tatum and the need to tell Marcus about Jolene Brookins.

"My wife just had a baby boy," he announced. "And I wanted to come in and properly thank God."

"Congratulations," Marcus and I said at the same time.

"We named him Jeremiah, from the Bible, Jerry for short. He's healthy and almost as beautiful as my wife."

He kneeled before the cross, bowed his head and folded his hands in prayer. We reverently watched him until he rose from his kneeling position. "Have a great day," he said, as he walked out.

"You, too," Marcus and I said. We laughed at our synchronicity.

Marcus blew out a heated breath. His sad eyes offered an apology. "I'd better get back. Or I won't be able to leave. Are you ready to meet Susan now?"

I searched for a way to postpone the inevitable. "Can we wait a sec. I need to discuss something with you first."

He squinted. "What is it?"

"Last night I had supper with Freemont and Tatum. We ate at the College Station Diner. While we were there, we ran into Neeley Nelson and Nev Powers. They came in together, and we had a few tense moments."

Marcus frowned. "Did Powers threaten you or Freemont?"

"No, but after we left the diner, Tatum told us something shocking."

"What did he say?"

"Nev Powers raped Tatum's cousin, Jolene. She reported the rape to police, but not right away, and Tatum said the cop she reported the rape to, said she should have come in sooner and not waited. By waiting, she had reported the rape too late, he said. Jolene lives with her handicapped grandmother, which is next door to Tatum and his mom and brothers. Jolene's grandmother is also Tatum's grandmother. Tatum's mom, Latrice, is Jolene's Aunt. Jolene is only sixteen, Tatum said. I need to talk to Jolene. I haven't had a chance to do that yet."

Marcus rubbed his eyes. They looked fatigued. "Christ, that must mean she didn't get a medical evidentiary examination."

"I don't know, Marcus. All I know is what Tatum told us. It's my understanding she was afraid to report the rape. But Latrice must have convinced Jolene she needed to report it. I don't know the time period in all of this, but from what Tatum said, Jolene waited too long to officially report what happened to her."

Marcus grimaced, as if in pain. "Rape victims need to be examined within seventy-two hours. Unfortunately, these victims are traumatized and don't seek help or report the assault within the legal time frame. But talk to her, if she'll talk to you. Powers could have warned her not to tell anyone and threatened her if she did. And she may not be his only victim. If she's affiliated with a church and feels comfortable talking to her minister, encourage her to do that. The minister and congregation might stand with her on this and perhaps help to identify other victims, if there are other victims. We need to find out where and when the rape occurred. Were there witnesses? What were the circumstances? If she reported it, who did she report it to?" He paused and blew out a breath. "Here's another thing, if she's pregnant as a result of this rape, genetic testing can determine paternity. And you said Tatum and his mom live in the projects, and Jolene is their neighbor, right?"

I nodded.

He blew out another breath. "Whatever you do, don't go out to the projects alone to talk to anyone." His eyes studied mine, as if he could read my thoughts. "We already suspect Nev and his dad in Freemont's shooting, and if we can prove Nev Powers raped Jolene, we can stop him from hurting anyone else."

I nodded.

"Is there anything else you need to tell me, Carrie?"

I shook my head no.

He smiled but his eyes looked sad. "Are you ready to interview Susan?"

A groan slipped from my lips. "I'm wondering why she wants to see me."

He stroked my hair. "I've talked to her about our work and what we do. I've given her a little history on the Southern Journal, your parents, you and the staff. And she said she'd like to meet you and would be amenable to an interview."

My stomached tightened. What if Susan suspected Marcus and I were lovers? That question worried me as we walked.

When we reached the door of Susan's room, he held up his hand. "Wait out here. I need to make sure she's awake and okay."

As he opened the door to the room, I heard Beethoven's *Moonlight Sonata* playing from inside. Marcus had provided that music, no doubt.

My heart drilled against my chest as I waited for him. Deep breathing did little to calm me.

When Marcus returned, he whispered, "Susan is awake and eager to talk to you." He glanced at his aviator's watch. "I'll be back in thirty minutes."

I shot him a questioning glance. Why would he leave me alone with her? Wasn't he afraid I'd blurt out something inappropriate? "Aren't you going in with me? I want you there."

"You'll be fine." He hiked up the left side of his top lip in a conciliatory smile. "Go interview her. She's waiting. If Susan grows too fatigued and can't continue, Mom will alert you. Don't worry. Mom's in there." He touched my lips with his then turned away and strolled down the hallway.

Old fears resurfaced, similar to the first day of school. Mom had left me with strangers, when she had always cautioned me not to talk to strangers.

I inhaled another deep breath and pushed open the door. The sun shone through the partially closed blinds. Susan was propped up to a sitting position in the hospital bed. Her short blonde hair was feathered around her narrow face. Her large eyes reminded me of the big-eyed waif paintings by the artist Margaret Keane. Mom loved those paintings.

I smiled to greet her. "Hi, I'm Carrie Sue."

Carol motioned me in. "Susan's been expecting you, Carrie."

Carol positioned a chair near the bed, away from the bag of fluid feeding into a tube attached to Susan's left hand.

Susan returned my smile. "Hello." She looked more like a child than a woman.

I took her extended right hand, careful not to squeeze it and hurt her. "Nice to meet you, Susan. How are you feeling?"

She closed her eyes before she answered. "I'm still alive ... and grateful to be alive and with the people I love." She enunciated well but her voice was soft, not what I expected of a staunch feminist. She had on a baby blue gown, and when Carol switched on the bedside light, I could see her blue eyes, similar to mine.

Carol arranged a small pillow behind Susan's neck and head then motioned for me to sit in the chair near Susan.

As I sat in the chair, I realized I still wore the ruby and diamond ring Marcus had given me. Would Susan ask me about it? "Marcus said you might be agreeable to an interview."

Her eyes roamed over my face. Was she seeking clues, searching me out, wondering about my relationship with her husband?

"Yes, I think I'm ready. I trust you. Marcus refers to you as Carrie, but you introduced yourself as Carrie Sue."

"Most people call me Carrie Sue."

She smiled, without showing her teeth. "Marcus said you're smart, hardworking, honest and talented, but he didn't mention how beautiful you are."

Her compliment surprised me, and I had to pause for a moment to weigh my words before I responded. "Thank you, Susan, but beauty is subjective, in the eyes of the beholder, as they say."

She placed her right hand to her chest and grimaced, as if in pain. "Marcus places intelligence above physical appearance."

"Unlike my ex Kyle who visually undressed every attractive woman he saw." I could feel my face burning as my words slipped out. I shouldn't have given her that much information. Too much upon meeting her for the first time, and I was the one interviewing her, not vice versa.

She stared at me with questioning eyes. "You look so young. How old are you, if you don't mind my asking? And how long were you married?"

As she asked the question, I realized I'd opened the gates to my personal life, and I needed to close them pronto, but I couldn't avoid answering. It would be rude. "I don't mind. I'm twenty-five. Kyle and I were married for only a year. Sorry I brought him up. I guess I'm still venting."

To gain control of the interview, I reached inside my tote and pulled out a pen and reporter's pad. I often record interviews on tape, or type them into my Tandy, rather than resort to speedwriting. But with Susan, my instincts told me that pen and paper would seem less intrusive.

"I'd rather talk about you, Susan."

She shifted in bed and grimaced. "What do you want to know, Carrie Sue?"

I flipped open the reporter's pad. "Can you tell me about the day you were captured? Marcus said you were trying to rescue your friend Virginia Fischer, who worked for the CIA."

"I made a terrible mistake by not telling Marcus my plans. I didn't have to go. But I wanted to go. I felt confident

Virginia would make it out alive. Being young then, I thought I was indestructible, and I thought I'd have a great story at the end of it."

"Why were you given the task of rescuing her?"

"As I said, I didn't have to go, but Virginia and I were close. I loved her, and I loved her mom and dad. And I was fascinated by her work with the CIA. She'd earned double majors in criminal justice and international affairs. She was bilingual and had a gift for languages. I admired her very much. She was fearless and I guess, during that time, I was fearless, too. We were very much alike. We even looked alike. When I heard she'd been captured, I was devastated. Her family was blackmailed. They sent money to her captors, but heard nothing back. It was horrible what her family went through."

"How much money did the family send?"

"I'm sorry I can't tell you that. But when we heard nothing after the ransom had been paid, we were afraid Virginia might be dead. Our government enlisted the help of a South Vietnamese sympathizer that had gotten assigned to a prison where Virginia was being held in North Vietnam. The sympathizer's family had fled to the United States. He was hoping to join them. He verified that Virginia was still alive, but in poor health."

"What was the sympathizer's name?"

"Sorry I can't tell you."

"Who gave you the okay to go in and help with the rescue? Didn't you have to get some kind of official clearance first?"

She sighed. "I'm sorry I can't tell you that either. It's confidential."

I nodded in agreement. "What can you tell me about the day of the attempted rescue?"

Susan glanced at her left hand—with the IV tube attached—as if it helped her think. "We were instructed to land in a specific area, where the sympathizer had agreed to meet us with Virginia. The plan was for him to give drugs and alcohol to his comrades, get them intoxicated and unconscious. He had planned to flee with Virginia in the helicopter. Our pilot glided down into the designated area. It was a dark night, stormy with lightning and thunder. When we landed we were surrounded by trees on three sides and the Mekong River on the other. We were wearing night googles. We waited for almost an hour. I asked Joe, the pilot, if we'd landed in the right spot. He had a map. I studied it, got out and looked around. I saw these figures running. Then I heard gunfire and yelling. The sympathizer, or I think it was the sympathizer, jumped in the river. I have no idea what happened to him. I saw Virginia fall, as if she'd been shot. I ran to help her up and get her in the copter. The next thing I heard was this awful explosion. The copter caught on fire."

"What caused the fire?" Marcus told me his B52 caused it, but I wanted to know what Susan would say.

"Our government had ordered bombing raids, but I didn't know that then. I ran away from the fire. The last thing I remember is feeling a sting." She pointed to her head. "I still carry a bullet there."

"How terrible, why hasn't the bullet been removed?"

She smiled, as if my question amused her. "It's too risky, I was told. I couldn't speak or function for ... oh ... I don't know how long. I lost my memory for a time. I lived in a fog. I couldn't even feed myself. I wanted to die. After they released me from the hospital, if you can call it a hospital, I lived in caves like an animal. I didn't know who I was for a time. My memory came back slowly, mostly in my dreams. I dreamed about Marcus and Carol and Dad. Those dreams fortified me and gave me the will to live."

I bowed my head to hide my tears. "At the press conference in California, Marcus said missionaries heard your cries for help. Can you tell me where you were then?"

"A shack in the woods near Saigon. My captor — I only knew him by Chad—kept me constrained. My feet and wrists were chained together and attached to a concrete block. He had a family, a wife and kids in the city, he said. He'd leave food and water close to me while he was away. I slept on a cot on the floor and used the portable toilet next to the cot. I tried to get free, but I couldn't. I didn't have the strength. I hated myself for not being able to find the strength to escape."

"It amazes me how you had the strength to survive. Did he sexually abuse you?"

"I'm sorry I can't talk about that. I'd rather talk about how my dreams and prayers kept me alive. I prayed constantly for a miracle. The day I was rescued, I heard this beautiful singing, like angels. They were singing *Amazing Grace.* That has become my favorite song. I screamed as loud as I could. By some miracle, they heard me. They said they were in that area to build a church. They had just started breaking ground for it." She cried and swiped her eyes with the heel of her right hand. Carol handed her tissues, then gave me a tissue before wiping her own tears.

"I hope Chad was prosecuted and punished for what he did to you."

She closed her eyes and nodded. "He was arrested but denied abusing me. He said he saved me from death. But believe me, he never saved anyone. He said he paid for me and owned me. He was a monster. I have nightmares about him still. I've seen a psychiatrist, and I've tried to talk about the nightmares and torture. But it's too painful now to continue that therapy. If I survive the cancer, I will try the hypnosis and eye movement therapy, but I'm not able to do that yet."

I shivered as her blue eyes mirrored mine. "When you write your article, Carrie Sue, I'd like for you to tell your readers how important it is to cherish each and every moment. I feel blessed now to be with the people I love. I'll never take my freedom or my loved ones for granted again. I'll never forget to say I love you. I used to get angry about the silliest things. But I know now it's more important to listen and understand and respect the opinions of others. No one is right all of the time. It's senseless to fight and go to war. Don't you agree, Carrie Sue?"

"I do."

She smiled, but her eyes looked tired and sad. "We should try to get along and understand each other. We live in a world of differing cultures and beliefs. Why not celebrate our differences, rather than fight over them? Our country is about freedom, and we should be free to express our opinions without oppression. As for me, I've started counting my blessings, which may seem strange for someone who has cancer. And my cancer has spread. But I thank God, I'm still alive and I'm living now in this wonderful country where I can fight to live and cherish my loved ones for as long as I live. Love, I've learned, is the most important thing in this world. We have nothing if we don't have love. I've lost twelve years of my life, twelve agonizing years, due to the bad decision I made. Nothing can give me those years back. But it's my hope your readers will learn from my mistakes. Don't do as I did. Never, ever make an important decision without weighing the pros and cons. Always consider the consequences. Listen to your instincts. When I left on that mission to rescue Virginia I had a premonition, a warning." Susan ran a hand over her stomach. "But I ignored that warning. And I regret I didn't discuss my plans with Marcus. He had every right to know. He was my husband. I should have informed him. But I was driven by ambition. I wanted glory. I wanted to rescue my friend and write this great story."

She leaned her head back on her pillow and closed her eyes. "I have this lovely memory of going to the beach with Marcus. Marcus and I would ride on his motorbike to Newport Beach. We'd spend the day together." Her voice cracked and faltered. She stared at the IV in her left hand, as if it confused her.

I could feel my face burning with embarrassment and guilt. Sadness flowed through me, and I could almost feel her pain. She had every right to complain about her dire circumstances. Yet she'd offered advice on how to make better choices and avoid mistakes. Despite the torture she'd suffered, and the cancer in her body, she was grateful to be alive.

Love is more important than anything, she'd said. She cherished the good times, like when she and Marcus went to the beach and spent the day.

"Maybe you'll be able to relive that beach experience, Susan. Tybee Island isn't far from Atlanta. It's on the Atlantic Ocean. The Savannah River empties into the Atlantic near Tybee. It's about five hours away. In lieu of a motorcycle, you could fly there. Maybe you and Marcus could go for the day. Another option would be Florida. Panama City Beach is only a five-hour drive from Atlanta. An hour by air."

Susan's smile brightened. "I've never been to those areas. Tell me more."

"The sandy beaches in Panama City are white, like sugar crystals. It's on the Gulf of Mexico. It's called the Emerald Coast. The Gulf there is the color of emeralds. The areas along the Florida Panhandle are like that. Mom and Dad and I used to go to Panama City, mostly in the summer, but also in the fall and winter. One year we spent an unseasonably warm Thanksgiving there."

She rubbed her eyes. "Sounds lovely, but I'm not sure I'll be able to go. I'll talk to Marcus and see what he thinks."

I touched her right hand. "I should go now and let you rest. I'm afraid I've stayed longer than I should have. I really appreciate your time. Thanks for sharing so much with me."

Our eyes connected again. "I trust you, Carrie. I'm glad I've had this opportunity to meet you."

I stuffed my notebook and pen inside my tote and closed my eyes to hide my guilt. "Thank you for your confidence and trust."

The door swung open and Marcus strode in. My face burned at the sight of him.

Susan's blue eyes widened. She smiled and held out her right hand. "Hi Darling, Carrie Sue and I were having a lovely chat. It didn't seem much like an interview."

As I watched him take her hand and stare at her with love and admiration, my heart sunk. After a moment, he shot me a piercing glance, as if he could read my thoughts.

Carol, who had been listening quietly, said, "Susan's had quite a day. I'd like her to rest now."

A man in green surgical scrubs strolled in. A nurse followed him. He glanced through some pages attached to his clipboard then placed a hand on Marcus' shoulder. "We need to examine Susan, Marcus."

"I'll wait outside, Doctor Sanders. Let's talk after you finish your exam." Marcus motioned for me to join him.

I said my goodbyes to Susan and walked out of the room with Marcus and Carol. Carol hugged us both. "I'll be back in a moment," she whispered then disappeared into the Ladies Room.

Marcus stroked my back in a comforting gesture. "How did it go with Susan?"

I inhaled a fortifying breath. "There were some painful things she couldn't share, and other things she wasn't at liberty to share, or so she said."

"Are you referring to confidential details of her rescue mission?"

"A couple of the questions she couldn't answer due to that. She preferred to talk about what she'd learned from her mistakes and how she wanted to pass along that knowledge to others. I took copious notes, and I'd rather you read the article when I've finished it, rather than ask me questions now."

His eyes seemed to darken. "Is there anything I need to know?"

"There was one thing. Susan said she has a fond memory of going to the beach with you. Maybe it's something you'd want to consider. I told her about Tybee Island and Panama City Beach. And she said she'd never been to those places, but she seemed pleased by the idea."

"I'll mention that to Sanders. See what he thinks."

I touched his chest. His heart galloped.

I reached into my tote. "I need to give you the keys to your jeep. Carol knows where it's parked."

He grabbed my hand. "I want to drive you back. I shouldn't be long. Can you wait?"

WHEN WE ARRIVED AT Marcus' Jeep, there was a grey pickup parked next to it. The pickup had its hood up. A young woman seemed to be studying the engine, while cradling the smallest baby I'd ever seen. The baby was barely visible in the blue blanket.

She turned to us. "Can you give me a jump. My car won't start."

Marcus connected the jumper cables and had her engine running in no time. She thanked him.

"What's your baby's name?" I asked.

"Tucker. He's two weeks old. I couldn't get him till today. He was born pre-mature. They kept him in the incubator. When he reached five pounds, the hospital let me take him home." She introduced herself as Taylor, and looked like a teenager. Tucker slept peacefully in Taylor's arms unaware of her distress.

"Are you sure you're going to be okay to drive with him?" Marcus asked.

"My mom and dad are less than a mile down the road. I'm staying with them." She thanked us again, placed her son in an infant seat, waved goodbye and drove away.

"Someone in her family should have come with her," Marcus said. He put in a cassette of classical music then maneuvered his Jeep away from the hospital.

"I learned a great deal about you today, Marcus."

He squinted and paused for a moment before responding. "You mean from your conversation with Mom?"

I nodded. "But I'm still curious about something."

"What's that?"

"Your relationship with Susan—how would you describe it?"

He shook his head, as if he disliked the question and didn't want to answer. "We've been over this before, Carrie. Susan and I grew up together. She was a part of our family. In looking back, I realize I didn't give her the attention and time she deserved."

"Didn't you enjoy spending time with her?"

"I was ambitious and selfish."

"Do you regret marrying her?"

He shot me a stern glance. "That's an unfair question. We did marry, but we were young. I regret we didn't communicate as well as we should have. Mostly my fault, I can be controlling, as you know. If I'd taken the time to listen to her, she may have shared her plans to rescue Virginia, and I would have known about it. Perhaps I could have helped her. But, but I can't change the past. Why dwell on it?"

"Do you regret asking me to marry you?"

He sighed. "Ah, Carrie, when I asked you to marry me, I had no doubt you were the person I wanted to spend the rest of my life with, but now I'm not in a position to make promises. And I don't want to be unfair to you. God knows I wish I could tell Susan about us. But if she knew, she might lose hope. The truth might devastate her." Marcus took his hand from mine to wipe his eyes. "We don't know if her recovery is even possible. Sanders has prescribed drugs to fight the cancer. Susan is weak. It's uncertain how she'll respond to those drugs." Tears leak down his cheeks.

I stroked his right arm. "I want you to know. I'm not going anywhere. I love you, Marcus. You're stuck with me."

He drove the jeep into his drive and killed the engine. His face looked flushed and fevered.

I touched his cheek. "Are you feeling okay, Marcus?"

He turned around in his seat toward me. "I'm frustrated." He began to remove the bobby pins from my bun, placing them in the console between us. After he'd taken the bobby pins out, his fingers started combing through my hair. His smile and tender eyes told me he enjoyed what he was doing, though my hair must have looked a wiry mess. Maybe he thought this was something he could tame and control.

I cradled his head in my hands and planted a firm kiss on his mouth. A tornado of passion flowed through me.

He scooped me up like a baby and carried me, tote and all, inside his house. His ambidexterity amazed me. He juggled me in his arms, unlocked his front door and disarmed his security system without fumbling.

He carried me to his bedroom and began undressing me. I popped off one of his buttons in my urgency to undress him. My blood boiled hot. I didn't even recognize my own voice moaning as he explored me with his tongue. I begged him to enter me.

We pounded away at each other. Our bodies slick with sweat. We were two desperate lovers, seeking satisfaction as if our lives depended on it.

He cried out as my body contracted around his volcanic eruption. I was trembling from head to toe when we finally collapsed together, our hearts hammering in sync. Guilt did not enter our minds then and for several precious minutes we were able to find relief. We held each other, even as he shifted to his side—breathing as if he'd run a marathon.

"Oh, god, Carrie," he huffed. "I have no control when I'm with you. I never thought it was possible to feel like this. You're my lifeline. I can't give you up. Most of my life I've worked with words, and loved words, but there are no words to express how much I love you. You're my fantasy. But you're as real as anyone I've ever known. I love everything about you. Your happiness is my happiness. I love your passion. I even love your badgering, even though I complain about it, and I love the way your eyes turn steel blue when you're angry. I love all your emotions. I can't believe my good luck in finding you. But damn, I'm in an awkward position. I'm being unfair to you and unfair to Susan. And I can't seem to do a damn thing about it. I need to make sure Susan gets the best care she deserves. And I pray that she recovers. I love her like a sister, like a member of my family. But the way I feel for you is more powerful than any love I've ever known."

"I feel the same about you, Marcus. I love you with all my heart and more."

He wrapped me in his arms. We kissed again, deeply and passionately. I could feel his excitement growing. His ability to recover amazed me. Then the phone rang—a loud, shrill sound, dampening our desire.

Marcus pulled away. "Sorry, I'd better get that. Might be Mom." He sprang from the bed and answered, "Marcus Handley."

I rose up on my elbows to get an eyeful of his muscular backside, and after he listened to the caller for a moment, he straightened out the black cord and pulled the phone to the bed. "It's Freemont. He wants to talk to you."

I grabbed the receiver. "What's up, Free?"

"Sorry to call you there, but I've tried everywhere else. I even left a message in the roses." He laughed, indicating he was okay and in good spirits. "I thought you'd want to know Jolene has agreed to talk to you today. Sunday is her only day off. She works at *Papa's Chicken and Burgers* after school and also cleans houses with Latrice. This is the only day she has free."

When I caught Marcus' questioning stare, I relayed what Freemont had said. Marcus didn't want me to visit the projects. He'd already expressed his concern, but I needed him to understand this might be my only opportunity to talk with Jolene.

Marcus said, "Why don't you ask Jolene to come here. Perhaps Freemont can bring her. I need to go back to the hospital for a while. On my way back, I'll pick up some steaks and whatever you wish. We'll grill out. Eat around 6:30."

When I told Freemont about the invite, he said, "Sounds like a plan. See you tonight. I'll bring Dora Lee, too, if that's okay. She needs a break."

By the time I'd hung up the phone, Marcus had already dressed to leave. He thanked me for sharing Susan's dream of going to the beach. "I think I'll rent a house somewhere between Panama City and Destin. I mentioned the idea to Dr. Sanders, and he's in agreement. He thinks Susan's treatment can be coordinated with one of the local hospitals there. I'll arrange around-the-clock care, so Mom can enjoy the beach, too."

"Are you planning to stay in Florida?"

"No more than two or three days a week."

This news shocked me. Susan had mentioned a day trip, but Marcus was actually planning to rent a house and spend considerable time there. Didn't he know how much I'd miss him? I wanted to tell him, but I didn't want to appear selfish. "That's very generous of you, Marcus."

"I have you to thank, Carrie. Susan may never have told me, but she told you."

FREEMONT ARRIVED AN hour early with Jolene and Dora Lee. He abhorred the stereo-type "colored peoples time," and always made a point to disprove what he considered a racist label. If he arrived late, I knew something was wrong, like on the night he didn't show for supper, and we found him on his front porch bleeding from a bullet wound in his chest.

I greeted Dora Lee and Jolene with a hug. Jolene smiled sweetly, but other than saying "Hi, nice to meet you," she spoke only when someone asked her a question. She had on a yellow V-neck top with long sleeves and white pants. She appeared older than 16 and possessed a classic beauty. She reminded me of the pictures I'd seen of a young Lena Horne.

Marcus and I had agreed to stay away from controversial subjects and keep the conversation light. Fortunately, that wasn't difficult. No one asked about our engagement or inquired about Susan.

Freemont wanted a tour of Marcus' house, which Marcus obliged. The rest of us trailed along.

Marcus was justifiably proud of the way everything had turned out after many months of renovation. Freemont seemed most interested in the gym with its Nautilus equipment and free weights.

Freemont has always exercised, and whenever possible he'd go to the Y to work out. After the surgeries to his chest and rotator cuff, he'd undergone quite a bit of physical therapy. Marcus told Freemont he looked fit. I agreed and said he looked spiffy in his black trousers and white turtle-neck sweater.

Marcus had on jeans and a blue V-neck, which outlined his musculature. He usually ran three or four miles daily and lifted weights in his gym.

"I can't wait to get this thing off." Freemont pointed to the sling holding his left arm. "The PT I'm working with wants me to swim. It's not as hard on the joints. I can't run yet."

"You'll be back running like a gazelle before you know it," I said.

I'd baked potatoes and prepared a large salad. Marcus had marinated the steaks with what he called his secret sauce, a combination of soy sauce, minced garlic, honey, olive oil and a splash of Worcestershire before putting them on the grill out back. Everyone, except Freemont, had ordered their steaks medium rare. Freemont wanted his "done, no pink."

We ate at the farmhouse table and listened to a classical music tape. I'd heard Marcus play many of those same songs on his piano.

We continued to converse on the safe subject of exercise as we sat down to eat. Dora Lee said she used to run track in high school. She looked stunning in a gray, form-fitting dress. Her silky dark hair tumbled past her shoulders.

I sat beside Jolene at the table and tried to engage her in conversation. "What about you, Jolene? What do you do for physical exercise? Do you have PE at school?"

She glanced down at her plate. "Yes, and I help Aunt Latrice clean houses. She says that's the hardest work-out there is."

"I agree with your Aunt Latrice," I said. "But it's not the form of working-out I enjoy."

She smiled. "What exercise do you like to do, Miss Carrie Sue?"

I glanced at Marcus. He once said making love was the best exercise you can do in a small space, but I wouldn't dare repeat this to Jolene. "I like to run, but I don't run as much as I used to. In high school, I ran cross-country."

Freemont cut off a piece of his steak and speared it with a fork. "Carrie Sue's being modest. She won first place in the district."

"Wow," Jolene said.

I remembered the look of pride on my parent's faces when I won that blue ribbon. Such a happy day, but as I thought of Mom and Dad, I began to miss them even more. To keep from crying, I changed the subject by asking Marcus to identify the song on the stereo.

"*Pathetique* by Beethoven," he said.

"What does pathetique mean, Marcus?" Freemont asked.

"Passionate. This composition is unique for its time. It has three movements." Marcus' face glowed as he spoke. "The first movement starts off heavy and dark, but becomes fast paced. The second movement is my favorite. It's calm, warm and one of Beethoven's most beautiful melodies. The third movement is happy and fast and seems to bring all of the pieces together."

Everyone at the table listened attentively. Freemont asked about other composers he'd heard, and by the time Marcus finished his lesson on Beethoven, Bach and Mozart, Freemont said he'd gained a new appreciation for the music.

"The music is almost as good as the food," Freemont said. He'd devoured his filet, several helpings of salad and two baked potatoes. "I can't eat another bite."

Marcus started collecting the plates from the table, but I stopped him. "Go relax, Marcus. I'll clean up." He'd spent many hours at the hospital. He'd shopped for the groceries, marinated and cooked the steaks, and set the table.

Dora Lee stood and began collecting the steak knives and silverware. "I'll take care of all of this." She held up her right hand, clutching the knives. "And don't give me any arguments."

Marcus flashed a smile. "I make it a point never to argue with a knife-wielding woman." He turned to Freemont. "I'm thinking the den will be safe. There's a game on if you want to watch it." Marcus slipped his arm around me. "Call me if you need me, Carrie."

Jolene walked over to the sink. "I'll help, Miss Dora Lee."

Dora Lee turned toward her and smiled. "No sweetie. I've got this. You and Carrie Sue go talk."

Jolene's brown eyes questioned me. Had she changed her mind?

I led her to the living room, with its cozy mixture of vintage and contemporary furniture in blue, red, white, grey, brown and black. This room represented Marcus well—earthy and passionate.

Jolene ran a hand over the top of the ebony grand piano. "Can you play this?"

I smiled and shook my head. "No, I can't. but Marcus plays beautifully."

"He's a smart man, and I can tell he loves you a lot."

I nodded and smiled. "He was my mentor before he became my love. But before I got to know him, I wanted to strangle him."

She frowned. "You did?"

I laughed, even though what I said about Marcus was true. "He didn't like anything I wrote in the beginning. He always found something to criticize. I once told him he'd criticize Hemingway."

She smiled. "Really? But I bet he likes what you write now."

"I hope so. My folks taught me to keep trying, never give up, and that was great advice. They used to say as long as I was trying I wasn't failing. Failure is when you stop trying, they'd say. And now I have to admit I've become a much better reporter and writer as a result of Marcus pushing me to be better. But that's enough talk about me. I want to talk about you."

I led her over to the black leather sofa, shaped like a horseshoe around a stone fireplace. We sat side by side on the sofa. She stared into the crackling fire. Marcus had placed a tape machine on the blue slate end table.

"Do you mind if I record what we talk about, Jolene? No one else will hear what you have to say. I promise. It's only for my information, not for publication."

She knotted her hands together. "Okay. Sergeant Peters at the sheriff's office in College Station has already recorded my statement, but he said I waited too long."

When I pressed record, she looked down at her hands, clasped tightly in her lap. "I felt scared and guilty. I shouldn't have accepted a ride from that man. He's a detective and I thought he'd be safe." Tears trickled down her cheeks.

I looked around for tissues, but didn't see any. "This was not your fault, Jolene. You have no reason to feel guilty."

"He said I'd be sorry if I told." She hugged herself.

"I'm sure that's why you were afraid to come forward right away. I know this is difficult for you. But can you describe what happened the night Nev Powers hurt you?"

She stared into the fire. "I was working at *PCB* that night. It was ..." She counted on her fingers. "Five Fridays from last Friday. I work Mondays, Wednesdays and Fridays after school. On Saturdays, I work on the morning shift. I thought Detective Powers was nice at first. He'd come in and talk to me and ask me about school. You know ... things like that. I noticed he started coming in more and more. I didn't think much about it, but I did feel a little uncomfortable when he told me I looked pretty." She paused and glanced at me, as if to check my response.

I nodded to reassure her.

"I usually get off around seven and if Aunt Latrice can't pick me up, I catch the bus home. That Friday it was raining. There was thunder and lightning. He said he didn't want me walking in the storm to the bus stop. Aunt Latrice would have picked me up, but she was working late that night, cooking for a family. I wanted to wait for her. But he said he just happened to be going near where I lived."

"How did he know where you lived? Did you tell him?"

"No. And it made me feel funny that he knew. So, I kept saying I needed to wait for my aunt to come. I thought he'd leave. But he waited around for an hour or more. He kept saying, 'Looks like your aunt got busy and forgot about you. I didn't want to be rude. He was a sheriff's detective. So, I agreed to let him take me home. When I got in his car, I had a weird feeling. He had handcuffs hanging over the front mirror. And then he patted me on the knee. I scooted away from him and said I needed to hurry up and get home. I had homework to do. He said okay, but he needed to make a quick stop first. I should have known better and gotten out of the car, but I didn't. He rode down this dirt road. It was dark, lots of trees. No houses anywhere. At the end of the road, he stopped and said he'd been thinking about me. He said he thought I was beautiful, and he really liked me. The next thing I knew he grabbed me and kissed me real hard. I begged him to stop and to take me home. When I tried to fight him off, he slapped me. He held me down and handcuffed my wrists. He kept saying it was my fault. I was driving him crazy. I told him my aunt would be worried, and she'd call the cops. He just laughed. He said he was the cops." Jolene broke down in sobs. "I tried to scare him. I told him my boss and some other people at the restaurant saw me leave with him. I just told him that. I didn't know for sure."

"That was a smart thing to say, Jolene." I wrapped an arm around her. "I'm so sorry this happened to you. This was not your fault. I hope you know that. He knew you were only sixteen, didn't he?"

She nodded. "Yes, and he knew where I went to school."

"That means he's not only a rapist, but he's a pedophile."

Her body trembled, and I worried she might suffer a breakdown. "You don't have to talk about this anymore, Jolene, if you don't want to. I'm here for you. I want you to know that. I want to help you, not hurt you. Would you like some water?"

She nodded and wiped her eyes. "And some tissues please."

"Okay, I'll be right back." I found a packet of tissues in the master bathroom and when I went into the kitchen to pour a glass of water, I noticed Dora Lee had already cleaned up. I heard the television and her laughter coming from the den.

Back in the living room, I offered Jolene the tissues and glass of water. She wiped her eyes and drank every drop.

As I watched her, I debated whether I should continue. Her chest heaved, her eyes were glazed over, as if in shock.

"It must be unbearable for you to relive this horror again, Jolene. Would you like to continue this another time?"

"No, I came here to tell you, and I need to." She hugged herself and rocked back and forth. "After he handcuffed me, he forced me down. And ... and ... he tried to make me ..." she paused and pointed to her crouch. "Suck him there. He said it was my fault he couldn't get hard. I gagged and couldn't do it. He started playing with himself until ... you know ... he got hard. He told me not to move until he finished. I just wanted it over." She covered her face with her hands.

I stroked her head. "Did he come ... Did he get semen in you?"

She grimaced. "Some of his yuck got on my dress. I shouldn't have waited to tell Aunt Latrice. She took me to report what happened. We brought along the dress. It used to be my favorite dress. It has American Flags on the skirt. Sergeant Peters took it. That's when he said I'd waited too long. I should have told Aunt Latrice right away. But I was scared and ashamed."

I turned off the recorder. "Is there a possibility you may be pregnant, Jolene?"

She heaved a loud sigh. "No, thank God. I got my period a week later. I was worried about that. I don't need a baby. I want to go to nursing school. I've been saving up. I want to be an RN. Nurses make good money, and I can get a nice place of my own, maybe help Aunt Latrice and my cousins get out of the projects. I'd like to help Gramma, too. She has muscular dystrophy." Jolene studied her hands. Her calloused fingers proved she worked hard.

"Are you afraid he might hurt you again?"

She balled up her fists. "I'm afraid and angry. I hate that man. I wish he was dead. I know it's not right to wish people dead. Gramma is always saying if you carry hate, hate poisons you, but I can't help how I feel. He keeps coming in the restaurant, just like nothing's ever happened. And I want to crawl in a hole when I see him. I'm sure he knows I reported him. You'd think he'd stay away, wouldn't you?"

"He's obviously crazy, Jolene, and a megalomaniac. He does what he damn well pleases, no matter who he hurts. Why don't you report him to the restaurant manager? Do you feel comfortable telling the manager?"

"Yes, mam, I had a talk with Mr. Elmore. I told him I didn't want to serve that man again. Mr. Elmore asked me why, and I said I didn't want to talk about it. Mr. Elmore is nice. He told me I was a good worker, and I wouldn't have to serve that man if I didn't want to. Now when he comes in, Mr. Elmore finds something for me to do in the back." She twisted her hands. "Aunt Latrice has been picking me up after work, and I'm with her whenever I can be. I help her clean houses when I'm not in school or working."

I turned her face toward me. "I'm so sorry this happened to you. It's not your fault. I hope you know that. You were a victim. Nev Powers is a criminal and a pedophile and should be punished for what he did to you. I wish I had the power to make that happen. I promise I'll do everything I can to help. In the meantime, do you belong to a church with a minister you'd feel comfortable talking to?"

She shook her head. "I haven't been to church much lately. Sunday is my day off, so I don't really have an excuse for not going. I guess I'm just a little lazy on Sunday. Aunt Latrice and I went to the Easter services at the AME church where Mr. Freemont goes. A couple of times we went to Ebenezer where Dr. King used to preach."

I smiled to reassure her. "Maybe we can all go together next Sunday. I'll ask Freemont. And if you don't object, I'll call Reverend Samuel and arrange for you to meet with him. Freemont claims he's a great listener and counselor. Reverend Samuel is very active in the community. He might be able to help us. It's possible you're not the only girl Nev Powers has raped, and if we can prove that and get others to come forward, this will help your case against him."

Her eyes widened. "Okay, I'll ask Aunt Latrice what she thinks."

As I sat there with Jolene, her fear spread through me. No one would be safe as long as Nev Powers was on the loose.

Chapter Eleven

Monday, February 23

A *shadow chased me. But I couldn't move my legs to escape.*

I jerked awake, thankful to be out of the nightmare. My heart hammered, and I inhaled deep breaths to calm down.

In the darkness, I saw a strange vision, like a white light, at the foot of the bed. The vision looked like Marcus, but it couldn't be. He was asleep beside me.

As I stared at the vision, it vanished. But whatever it was, it made me feel safe enough to fall back asleep.

The next time I awoke, I smelled coffee brewing and saw a rosy light peeping through the blue curtains. The digital clock showed 6:15. Marcus was no longer in the bed beside me.

I threw back the covers, got up, used the bathroom, pulled on my Atlanta Braves shirt then made my way to the kitchen. I expected to find Marcus there, but he wasn't.

I poured a cup of coffee into a mug that said, "Coffee is a hug in a mug," and heard groaning coming from the back of the house. I followed the groans and found Marcus in his boxers, lying on his back, bench pressing.

I studied his toned, muscular body covered in perspiration; his dark underarm hair drenched. "I don't know if that's helping you, Marcus, but it sure is helping me."

He dropped the stack of weights with a bang and sat up. I laughed at his surprised expression.

He grabbed a towel from the end of the bench and wiped away his sweat. "Would you like to join me?"

I walked over and kissed him on the mouth. His boxers winged out in front. I ran a hand over him there.

He grabbed my fondling hand and kissed it. "I love where this is heading, baby, but I'm nasty and sweaty. If you don't want to work out, why don't you join me in the shower?"

"Only if I get to lather you first."

He agreed and I washed him from head to toe. He returned the favor. We lingered in the shower and made quick love. Our bodies were slippery and steamy when we stepped out.

"We have an hour before our staff meeting, Carrie." I was amazed at how quickly he switched to work mode. I wanted to continue cocooning with him.

He tucked a towel around his middle. "How about a breakfast shake."

In the kitchen, I watched him throw frozen strawberries, milk, oatmeal and honey into a blender. A minute later, he was pouring two glasses of this concoction.

He handed me a glass. I took a sip. "Tasty, and I'm assuming it's good for me."

He smiled and winked. "I hope so."

As we drank our shakes, I told him about my conversation with Jolene.

He listened attentively, shaking his head and grimacing at the awful details of her rape. "We should do a series of articles on rape crimes, Carrie. Maybe the first article should give advice and safety tips." He handed me a reporter's pad and pen to write down what he was saying. "Why don't we include the procedures for reporting a rape? Victims are required to seek medical attention from a hospital or medical center. It should be a facility that has rape kits. Not everyone is aware of the proper way to report. We have a duty to inform our readers. Also, we need the latest statistics on reported rapes and let's interview local therapists and psychiatrists. Contact the Department of Family and Children's Services, along with crisis hotlines, and so on. Gather all of the information you can. Find out the ratio of rapes versus prosecuted rapes. A pattern should emerge. As to Jolene's case, we can't mention her by name of course. Unfortunately, she didn't go to the hospital. There was no rape kit evidence. Only the dress she gave to Peters. That dress should contain fibers, hairs, semen, blood, and so on. And we need to make sure Peters and his forensic team follow up on Jolene's case. Talk to Peters. Get his version. Let him know we're aware of what happened."

"I don't want to do anything that will hurt Jolene in any way, Marcus. We absolutely cannot identify her. She's a minor. I promised her anonymity."

"I agree with you, Carrie." He placed our empty glasses side by side in the dishwasher. "An emergency nurse or counselor at one of the hospitals should be able to walk you through the procedure that rape victims are required to go through. Jolene was frightened and in shock. She didn't know what to do, or where to turn. We have the ability and responsibility to provide a service for other victims who may be too afraid to come forward. That's why we should promise anonymity. Not reveal names, but write their stories. We want stories that ring true." He paused again and rubbed his forehead as if it helped him think. "If Nev Powers has attacked other women and girls, we might be able to locate his victims. I like the idea of talking to that pastor at the AME church. He may have counseled rape victims and could offer insight and information." He smiled as our eyes locked. "I'll help all I can with this, Carrie."

"Okay, but I can also ask Jackie Steiner to do research. She enjoys that, as you know."

He nodded. "You might assign her a couple of articles to research and write, give her a chance to do something other than obituaries and the crime report." He puckered his bottom lip. "I've been thinking we might even create a special edition for this and publish it on Wednesday. We have several health-related articles already to go. Our subscribers will appreciate this bonus."

I held up my hand in a stop sign. "Wednesday? That doesn't give us much time. And if you're thinking of publishing the first article about rape that soon, I'll need to talk to Jolene before then and prepare her. I'd like to get her feedback, and assure her we'll keep her identity private. I'll stop by *PCB* sometime today and chat with her about it."

"Okay, sounds good, Carrie. Why don't we include that article you're writing on Susan in our special edition? That is, if you have time to write it. No pressure." He hiked up the left side of his mouth in a lopsided smile.

"When you say, no pressure, I assume that's the new Marcus and not the old Marcus speaking. The old Marcus would have pressured me, but the new Marcus has been known to be a little more lenient, right?"

"We must never assume, Carrie, but when you say 'old Marcus,' it worries me."

"Why does that worry you?"

"Well, for all I know, you could be thinking I'll soon need a cane." He made a pretense of hobbling toward me.

I laughed and hugged him. I wanted to hug him longer, but he worked his way free of my embrace and slapped my bare bottom. "We need to get dressed, baby."

Marcus put on a gray pinstriped suit, blue shirt and red paisley tie for our staff meeting. I slipped into a conservative black dress and bobby-pinned my hair into a French twist. He straightened the sheets then threw the blue comforter over the bed, his way of making it.

He held up one of my pearl and diamond earrings. "I found this in the bed."

Mom called these her *"good luck earrings."* She'd forgotten to wear them the day of the crash. I'd been wearing the earrings ever since.

"Thank you. I can't afford to lose these."

"I know how much they mean to you."

I hugged him. "You look very handsome."

"You're always beautiful, baby."

Despite his compliment, an unexplainable dread washed over me. I struggled to breathe. My chest heaved. I saw a black wash as the blood drained from my head. "I need to sit down a minute, Marcus." I plopped down on the bed.

"What's wrong, Carrie?"

I put a hand over my eyes to hide. I didn't want him to see me this helpless and out of control. Mom and Dad raised me to be independent, not helpless. "I'm a little panicky. I'm not sure why."

"I shouldn't have hurried you. We don't need to rush, Carrie. We have time. I still need to call Binky Bailey. He's a Realtor in Seagrove." He pulled the black phone over to the bed and sat beside me.

After he dialed the number and exchanged pleasantries with Binky, he explained the purpose of his call. "I need a beach house, wheel chair accessible, facing the Gulf." Marcus paused to listen to Binky before he continued. "Sounds good. I'd like to rent it for a month. If I really like it, I may buy it."

I couldn't believe my ears. Was he actually thinking about buying a beach house? Why hadn't he discussed this with me?

I wanted to ask him, but as soon as he hung up from Binky, he called Carol and Susan at the hospital to tell them they should be able to leave for the beach tomorrow.

My head whirled, my stomach knotted, and I could feel a full-blown anxiety attack coming on. I'd had several of these attacks after I lost my parents. The worse one occurred in a shopping mall. I fainted and woke up in a hospital. The attending nurse gave me some wise advice: "The next time you feel an attack coming on, breathe, in and out, in and out," she demonstrated, breathing deeply and slowly. "Rate your anxiety—one through ten. While you're rating it, stay where you are. Keep breathing until you've lowered your number. Your attacks shouldn't last longer than thirty minutes."

After the nurse gave me this advice, she shared her own experiences with panic attacks. She used to be agoraphobic, she said, afraid to leave her house.

As I listened to Marcus, I used the techniques I'd learned and managed to lower my number to five, low enough to survive the staff meeting and immerse myself in work.

At the office, I assigned Jackie the task of gathering statistics and interviewing medical professionals. Jackie's green eyes brightened when I asked her to write a sidebar with her by-line.

"I have the perfect article in mind, Carrie Sue. I've had friends who've said 'no' on dates, but were forced to have sex anyway. I'll write from that angle, okay?"

"I like your idea and your enthusiasm, Jackie."

She flashed a toothy smile. "And I like the fact that Marcus has promised to pay double for overtime. I see a cruise in my future." I couldn't help but laugh, despite the graveness of our special edition.

How in the world would we be able to pull everything together in two days? Rather than worry and obsess about the lack of time, I committed to the deadline and quickly finished the article on Susan.

Lisa asked us what we wanted from the College Station Diner. "Is it noon already?" I couldn't believe it.

Marcus left for the hospital soon after lunch. We barely had time to discuss the data Jackie had collected. He told me to make an executive decision on what to include.

I rolled my eyes. "You say that, Marcus, but I know you'll edit out what you don't like."

As night fell, Lindsey and Jackie left the office. I stayed at my desk, working, until Lisa announced, "Time to call it a day, Carrie Sue. Marcus is on line one for you."

I answered with, "Is this my slave-driving boss?"

"Guilty. Why don't you take a break and allow me to redeem myself?"

"I don't think you can."

"I'm willing to do whatever it takes."

"How willing?"

He sighed. "Very willing and very eager. I'll grovel if necessary."

"What time will the groveling start?"

He sighed a laugh. "I'm at the hospital now. I'll leave soon."

"The traffic is probably a bear, Marcus. Be careful. Oh, and I almost forgot. I need to tell Jolene about our special edition and assure her we won't publish her name or her comments in this series. While I'm at *PCB*, I'll pick up some comfort food. What would you like?"

"I'm up for anything you provide."

Thinking about his playful words excited me as I drove to *PCB*. I parked on the side of the building opposite the drive thru with its long line of cars.

Jolene was standing behind the cash register when I walked in. She had on a yellow shirt with the familiar logo of a chicken holding a burger. Leroy Stacy, owner of the restaurant franchise, had designed the logo, according to the article Lindsey had written about him.

Jolene's brown eyes widened as I greeted her. "Hi Miss Carrie Sue, I didn't expect to see you tonight."

"I had a hankering for barbeque chicken. I also wanted to talk to you privately for a sec, if you can spare the time."

She smiled, but her eyes flashed fear. "I'll see if Martha Jane can cover for me. Let me take your order first."

I glanced at the menu printed on the billboard above her head and ordered eight pieces of barbeque chicken, two orders of coleslaw, green beans and mashed potatoes with gravy. Jolene rang up the order, and after I paid, she asked me to wait at one of the tables while my order was being prepared. "I'll bring it out to you when it's ready."

I sat at a corner table, and watched Jolene take orders from other customers. As soon as the line thinned out, Martha Sue took over the cash register, then Jolene brought me the yellow bag, with my order.

I thanked her and asked her if she could sit a moment.

She sat across from me. "I can't stay long. I'm sorry. We're real busy."

"I'll be quick, Jolene. I wanted you to know the Southern Journal will be publishing a special Wednesday edition concerning rape and violence against women. Marcus thought it would be a good idea. We'll offer advice and hopefully protect other girls from being victimized. Your name won't be mentioned. I promise you that. But I thought I should come by and talk to you personally. I didn't want you to pick up the paper and panic."

Her eyes widened. "I won't panic. I trust you."

Susan had said the same, even though I didn't deserve her trust. "You inspired this special edition, Jolene. I wanted you to know that. And I wanted to assure you, your name and identity will not be mentioned."

She smiled, but said nothing.

"There is another thing. Is it okay for me to talk to Sergeant Peters? I'd like to follow up with him. Make sure he plans to have his forensic folks check out your evidence. You did say you gave him the dress you wore when you were attacked. We need to find out what's going on with that."

Her brown eyes darkened. "He took it, but he said I waited too long. Remember I told you that?"

"Yes, you did, but even if Peters thinks you waited too long, that doesn't mean he shouldn't move forward with your case. I'd like to think he'll do the right thing. I've had a good working relationship with him in the past. But if you don't want me to contact him about your case, I won't."

"I don't object to it, but ..." She looked up. "Oh, no." Her body folded inward. "It's him. He just walked in."

I turned to see Nev Powers facing Martha Sue at the cash register. He had on a brown two-piece suit. His jacket looked bulky from the shoulder holster with gun and ammo pouch detectives wear. When I turned back to Jolene, I saw horror in her eyes. I could almost read her mind. He'd assume she told me about the rape.

I pointed in the direction of my car. "Why don't I drive you home? I'll wait for you to get off work."

She shook her head. "You don't have to. Aunt Latrice is coming to pick me up tonight."

A tall, stout man the color of coffee beans walked up to us. "Is everything okay?" He looked familiar, but I couldn't place him.

Jolene stood. "This is Carrie Sue Justice, Mr. Elmore. She just needed to talk to me for a minute."

He extended his hand. "Hi Carrie Sue, I'm Eugene Elmore. I used to play football with Freemont Jackson. I've been reading your columns. My favorite is the one about him giving you a brown thumb. I've ragged him about it."

I stood and shook his hand. "Thank you, Eugene. Freemont thinks I owe him a public apology for writing that article. But by all means, continue to rag him."

He chuckled. "Oh, I will. Good to see you. Is there anything you need?"

I shook my head. "No, thank you, Jolene has already served me, and we've been chatting. I hope I haven't monopolized too much of her time." I grabbed my yellow sack. "I guess I'd better scoot and let y'all get back to work." I waved goodbye and darted out the side door, away from Nev Powers.

Inside the safety of my locked car, I took deep breaths to calm my racing heart. Powers was still standing stiffly with his hands on his hips. The bright lights and large windows of the restaurant gave me a clear view of him.

He turned in my direction. Had he seen me?

My stomach knotted with fear for Jolene as I watched. I could no longer see Jolene inside. I hoped Eugene had allowed her to work in the back. She said he'd help her avoid Powers.

As I cranked up and drove away, my fear lingered. I turned on the radio to relax. A Supernova was expected to reach Earth that night, according to the news woman.

"The original explosion began approximately one-hundred-seventy-thousand years ago and nearly one-million-trillion miles from Earth," she announced.

I glanced up at the cloudy-night sky and saw nothing resembling a shooting star. As a child, I used to lie on the grass, and gaze up at the stars for hours.

"I saw them through my eyes, and no one could see them the way I saw them," I told Mom. That's when she educated me on Vincent van Gogh's *Starry Night.* She had a copy of that painting hanging in our hallway. I'd never paid much attention to it until then.

"This is how Van Gogh saw the stars," Mom said.

In reliving the memory, I could almost feel her presence in the car, a 1982 Cadillac, a birthday present to Mom from Dad. I wouldn't trade it for any car in the world. Dad placed a giant red bow on its hood the night before her birthday. When she got up the next morning and saw it in the drive, she'd cried tears of happiness and excitement.

I started crying as I pulled behind Marcus' jeep and killed the engine. Memories of Mom and Dad are still too raw.

I was wiping my eyes when Marcus walked out. He opened my car door and greeted me with a kiss then grabbed my tote and the bag of food before ushering me inside. Elvis was singing *And I Love You So,* one of Mom's favorites, on the stereo.

"You left this tape in my jeep, Carrie, and I've been listening to it."

"That's Mom's tape. She adored Elvis. When Elvis came to the Omni in 1973, we went to see him. I was only twelve, but when I saw Elvis, I knew I'd reached pubescence." I forced a laugh.

Marcus flashed his Elvis smile and pulled me into a slow dance. "This song reminds me of us."

I nestled in his arms, inhaling his aftershave, a spicy musk. A lit candelabrum was on the farmhouse table.

I pointed to it. "That's lovely."

"It's a gift from Mom. Traditionally, the Shabbat candles should be lit on Fridays after the sun goes down," he said. "But I decided to make an exception and light them today."

His handsome face glowed in the candlelight as he explained this. He still wore his suit trousers, but he'd taken off his coat and unbuttoned his shirt collar.

I remembered Mom and her Jewish tradition, as I watched him set the table . "My mom used to light the Shabbat candles, too. She'd pray for peace and blessings."

He poured two glasses of chardonnay and said he would be flying Susan and Carol to the beach house the next day. "I have to stay there for a couple of days to get everything set up for them."

I listened, sipped the wine and ate the barbeque chicken with my fingers. My mood had turned somber, and I didn't feel like talking.

His eyes pieced mine. "You seem upset."

"I'm just a little tired that's all."

"Are you pleased with the article on Susan?"

"Yes, she wanted me to focus on the positive, rather than the negative, and wanted others to learn from her mistakes. She gave good advice, and I tried to convey that."

He used his napkin to wipe barbeque sauce from his lips and hands. "Could you give me a summary of what you wrote?"

"I'd rather you read the article, Marcus. It's difficult to summarize. As I said, she hopes others will learn from her trials. She regretted her impulsive decision to rescue her friend. She wished she'd informed you. Instead, she acted without thinking or weighing the pros and cons. Her tragedy taught her to cherish each and every moment. She counts her blessings. She feels blessed to be alive. She cherishes her freedom, even with the cancer. Love is the most important thing in the world, she said."

I paused, collecting my thoughts. "I wrote about her captivity and the events leading up to it, but I honored her wishes to deliver her positive message of survival."

As he listened, he wiped his eyes with the back of his hands. "I look forward to reading it." He sucked in a breath. "How was your meeting with Jolene?"

"We didn't talk long. I assured her we wouldn't use her name in our special edition, but I wanted her to know she had inspired it." I rubbed my stomach, in an attempt to dislodge the sick knot. "Nev Powers walked in while we were talking. I felt terrible. What if he suspects she told me about the rape? I asked her if she wanted me to drive her home. She said no, her aunt Latrice was going to pick her up."

Marcus scowled. "Damn, he's stalking her. Son of a bitch. Don't blame yourself, Carrie. Your intentions were good."

"Nev Powers makes me sick, Marcus. He needs to be stopped. He thinks he's above the law. I'm worried about Jolene. She's working hard to make a better life for herself and her family. She's only sixteen. I wish we could do more to help her. Jolene said she didn't object to me talking to Raymond Peters about her case. Now I'm wondering if that's such a good idea. What if he tells Nev? You know how that good ole boy system works."

Marcus took my hands. "Isn't Peters the audio-visual guy, the one who tapes most of the police interviews for the sheriff's department?"

"Yes, he taped the interviews of Jeremy, Calvin, Leroy, and Tatum. He also testified for the prosecution. Since then, he's been promoted to sergeant. Jolene reported her rape to him. She gave him her clothing from that night."

Marcus nodded. "I'll talk to Jeff tomorrow and ask him if he knows someone who might be able to keep an eye on Jolene. I'm thinking she'll feel safer with a woman guarding her."

Fatigue swept over me then. Marcus must have sensed it. "Why don't you take it easy, Carrie. Go lie down. I'll clear the table and put the food away.

Rather than argue, I gave him a kiss and walked to the master bedroom, where I kicked off my boots and plopped down on his sleigh bed without turning back the comforter.

I had already fallen asleep when he awakened me with, "My turn to treat you." He undressed me in record speed and uncapped a bottle of lavender scented oil.

"Why don't you flip over on your stomach?"

I did as he instructed and he began kneading my neck with his strong fingers. Fatigue soon overpowered me again, and I fell back asleep.

I awakened when he asked me to turn over. As I did, I saw his erection. “My, oh, my, you obviously need relaxing, too, Marcus.” I poured a puddle of the massage oil in my hands.

“Not yet, baby,” he whispered and walked out of the bedroom.

With a confused frown, I waited for him to come back. It must have been at least five minutes before he reentered the bedroom, this time gloriously naked, his erection still prominent. He scooped me up in his arms like a baby, and carried me to the Jacuzzi.

As we sat in the hot pulsating water, we kissed and fondled. I wrapped my legs around him and rode him hard.

After I found my pleasure and he found his, he began to wash my hair, as if we had all the time in the world. I’ve never spent this much time washing my own hair, but I have to admit, this was almost as intimate as our love making.

With my head resting on his knees, he rinsed out the lather and applied conditioner. When he finished, I returned the favor by washing his hair. He hummed his enjoyment and thanked me when I was done.

My legs, like rubber, needed his help getting out of the Jacuzzi, and in less than a minute, I fell into bed. As I drifted off to sleep, he whispered, “Keeps getting better and better, baby. I love you more than anything, never forget that.”

Chapter Twelve

Tuesday, February 24

I awoke with the morning sun seeping through the blue curtains. Marcus was lying on his side, staring at me. "How long have you been awake, Marcus?"

"I don't know. I've lost track while watching you sleep."

I snuggled up to him. "I wish we could stay like this forever. I don't feel like facing the world today."

His fingers combed through my tangled hair. "How often do you get your anxiety attacks?"

His question stunned me. I'd never complained about my anxiety to him. "It depends. I started having them after I lost Mom and Dad."

"I get them, too. Mine are usually accompanied by flashbacks. What about yours?"

"I don't have flashbacks. I just feel panicky. My heart pounds, and I get scared and sick to my stomach. I've learned how to deal with them. I take slow, deep breaths and wait for them to pass. They don't last long."

He seemed to be studying my eyes, reading my mind. "At least you don't hit the booze as I've been known to do. Being with you has certainly helped me, but before I found you, I tried psychotherapy, hypnosis, and eye-movement therapy." He glanced at the ceiling and frowned.

"What exactly is eye-movement therapy?" Susan had mentioned it during our interview.

He sucked in a breath. "It relocates traumatic memories in the brain and prevents those memories from reappearing in the present moment. In my case, the psychiatrist asked me to share certain events from my past, events that might bring on flashbacks. As I shared them, he moved his finger back and forth. It's a form of hypnosis."

Marcus demonstrated by moving his index finger in front of my eyes. "It seems to have the ability to place traumatic memories in a different section of the brain. They're relocated and filed away, not forgotten entirely, but they're not as disruptive. I don't have to relive them in the moment, as if they're happening all over again."

"But you still have nightmares."

He nodded. "True. Nightmares provide a method to deal with trauma. I'm having fewer and fewer of them, as time goes on. Although I still struggle with flashbacks."

"Did you get flashbacks before you were in the war?"

He exhaled a groan. "No."

"Have you ever regretted your decision to join the Air Force?"

He pillowed his head in his hands, exposing his dark underarm hair. "I wish no one had to go to war, Carrie. I hate war. But I did go, and as a B-52 pilot and commander I killed people from the air and told myself I was serving my country, as my Dad served before me." His dark eyes pierced mine. "I have plenty of regrets. I caused death and destruction, but I can't change the past."

I stroked the smooth hairs on his chest. "How did Susan feel about your volunteering for service?"

He grunted, as if he didn't want to answer this question. "She was opposed to the war. She didn't want me to go. I probably would have been drafted if I hadn't joined. We had the draft back then. Susan and I didn't communicate well. We were too young to get married, but I thought it was the right thing to do at the time."

"Your Mom said you balked at getting married until you found out Susan was pregnant."

He shook his head. "Carrie, I swear, you could make a priest confess."

"I guess you'd like to avoid that question."

He raised his eyebrows. "You made a statement. You didn't ask a question."

"You're right. I'll rephrase. Would you have married Susan if she hadn't been pregnant?" My heart thudded in anticipation of his answer.

He cleared his throat. "I probably would have waited, but I couldn't ignore my responsibility to her. I wasn't a good partner back then. I was ambitious, worked most of the time, like my dad, and I don't think I knew the true meaning of love, other than the love I felt for my family." He blew out a breath. "When I heard Susan had died in that crash, I realized I'd failed her. The love I had for her wasn't what it should have been. I loved her as a dear friend, as a part of our family. Those feelings haven't changed. She's suffering, and it hurts to see her suffer. I'm hoping this beach trip will bring the miracle she needs."

His eyes turned darker. "Carrie, I know this has been extremely difficult for you. But I hope you know how much I love you. I've tried to show you how I feel. I love spending time with you, talking to you, working with you, making love, everything. You've brought me the greatest joy I've ever known. I've never experienced this kind of love before. When you're happy, I feel your happiness, and when you're sad, I feel that, too." He cradled my face in his hands. "It's been difficult for me to open up. But I'm trying my best to communicate with you." He wrapped his arms around me. "I'm the luckiest man on earth to have found you."

As I listened to him, I remembered what Kasandra said: Marcus and I were together in a past life, which was the reason he'd been drawn to move here.

The phone rang before I could talk with him about that. He pulled away to get it.

I propped up on my elbows to admire him. Whoever said the human body looked better with clothes on hadn't seen Marcus in the nude.

He answered with a gruff, "Yes," and after a moment, he handed me the receiver. "It's Freemont, Carrie. He needs to talk to you."

My stomach knotted, and I sensed something horrible had happened. "What is it, Free?"

"Jolene is missing."

"Are you sure, Free? I just saw her last night at the barbeque place."

"Latrice's car broke down. She couldn't pick up Jolene from work. By the time Latrice was able to call the restaurant, Jolene had left. Latrice thought she'd caught the bus, but when Latrice got home, Jolene wasn't there. Latrice called the bus station, but no one could tell her anything. She reported Jolene missing but was told she couldn't be considered missing yet."

"That's terrible. We've got to find her."

I turned to Marcus. "Freemont said Jolene is missing. No one knows where she is, not even her aunt."

Marcus took the phone. "Freemont, tell Latrice we'll help every way we can. If Jolene isn't located by the end of the day, we'll post her photo in our special edition. It'll go out tomorrow. And we'll print flyers. Get her photo, bring it by the paper or have Latrice bring one in. A recent school picture should do. And I'll call Jeff and ask him to join us in the search. Most missing persons are found within the first forty-eight hours. Let's hope we find Jolene within that timeframe."

I swallowed the bile in my mouth to keep from throwing up. "Oh, no, I'm sure Nev Powers must have seen me talking to Jolene last night. Oh, God..." I cried out.

Marcus grabbed me. "Take deep breaths, baby." He stroked my back. "If Powers took her, he's left a trail. We can't give up hope. And remember, this is not your fault."

"I told Jolene the same thing, Marcus. We have to find her."

"We need to talk to Sergeant Peters. Insist that he cooperate on this. He doesn't strike me as a bad cop."

"If I can get an appointment with him, I need to meet him somewhere away from the sheriff's department."

"I agree, Carrie. Time is our enemy. We need to hurry, work fast.

I slipped on a black dress while Marcus made coffee and another breakfast shake. "My sick stomach can't drink or eat anything," I told him. He seemed to understand.

We both felt compelled to get to the office right away, and the minute I walked in, I called Latrice to find out everything she knew. I also called the bus line and was able to talk to the driver on Jolene's route. He said he remembered dropping her off at the scheduled stop, a block from where she lived.

Meanwhile, Marcus read and edited my article about Susan. "Great job, Carrie. You focused on the lessons she learned from her tragedy, rather than the tragedy itself." He apologized for having to leave that afternoon.

I asked him to postpone his trip a day or two, until we found Jolene, but he said he couldn't. He'd already scheduled an ambulance to take Susan to the beach house from the airport, and he would be flying Susan and Carol there. In addition, he'd scheduled meetings with specialists that would be coordinating Susan's care. He also needed to lease a car for Carol so she'd have access to transportation while at the beach, he said.

He was explaining all of this as Lisa knocked on his office door to announce Latrice's arrival. We walked out to greet her, a petite woman, about 5-foot 3, with russet skin and short black hair, her brown eyes etched in despair.

She handed Marcus the photo of Jolene. "If it's okay, I'll wait for you to print the fliers."

As she waited, I longed to comfort her. She felt guilty for not picking up Jolene, she said.

"You mustn't beat herself up over this, Latrice. Your car broke down. It wasn't your fault." Even as I tried to convince her she wasn't to blame. I shared her guilt. I should have listened to my gut and insisted on taking Jolene home from the barbeque place.

When Marcus came back with the fliers, Latrice stared at them and cried. They showed Jolene's lovely face, her age, school, phone numbers to call, where she was last seen. Marcus had offered an award for information that led to finding her.

Latrice thanked him, took a stack of fliers then rushed out. Soon after she left, Lindsey pulled me aside.

"I just got off the phone from Kasandra. She can help us locate Jolene."

"What did Kasandra say?"

Lindsey grabbed my hands to gather my attention. "She had a vision of a young woman, long black hair, light brown skin, lying close to a river, near a cabin. She asked me to fax her a picture of Jolene."

I handed Lindsey one of the fliers Marcus had prepared. "Did she say what cabin, what river?"

"Not yet. When I send her this pic of Jolene, she might be able to tell us."

"Tell us what?" Freemont said, walking up behind me. I turned to greet him and Dora Lee. Freemont was dressed "church ready," as Mama Jackson would say, in a pinstriped suit, white shirt and a tie with swirls of blue, his arm still in the sling. Dora Lee wore jeans and a blue turtleneck sweater. "We came by to pick up Jolene's flyers," Freemont said.

After Lindsey said "hi" to them, she said, "Kasandra didn't say specifically where she saw the body. I'm praying Jolene is still alive. But I was hoping Kasandra could help us find her. She seemed positive she visualized a body of a young woman near a cabin that's on the river." Lindsey turned and walked away to fax Jolene's photo to Kasandra.

Freemont frowned, "What's Lindsey talking about? Who's Kasandra?"

"She's a psychic."

Freemont squinted his disapproval. "What she said doesn't make much sense. Does it, Carrie Sue?"

Dora Lee's mouth gaped open. "Oh, my God. Nev Powers owns a cabin near the Chattahoochee. It's in Cleveland, a little north of here. I've never been to it, but he used to talk about that cabin all the time. He even tried to get me to go up there with him. I still have the map he gave me. It wouldn't hurt to check it out. Do you want to drive up there, Carrie Sue? I can leave early tomorrow morning, but not today. I'm delivering laundry this afternoon." She glanced at the stack of flyers. "It breaks my heart to think anyone would hurt this sweet girl."

I swallowed my nausea. "I'm hoping we'll find her today. I'm meeting Sergeant Peters at *PCB* for lunch. I've already spoken to the bus driver. He said he remembers Jolene getting on his bus. He dropped her off at the bus stop a block from where she lives, he said."

"I'd like to go with you to *PCB*," Freemont said. "I talked to that bus driver, too. He told me the same thing." Freemont glanced at his watch. "We'd better get going now, Carrie Sue."

Before we left, I called Eugene at *PCB* to prepare him for our visit. "Will you share with Sergeant Peters what Jolene told you about Nev."

"I'll do anything that will help find Jolene," Eugene said.

"You remember seeing Nev Powers last night, don't you, Eugene?"

"Yes, I saw him."

"And I'm sure the lady who waited on him remembers seeing him."

"Probably, but he didn't stick around. He left with his takeout."

"Do you know what time he left."

"No, we got really busy. I couldn't even hazard a guess."

After talking to Eugene, I walked in Marcus' office. He was on the phone. I didn't have time to wait, but he interrupted his phone conversation long enough to give me a kiss and say he'd call me later.

My heart dropped as Freemont and I walked out of the Southern Journal. I had no idea how long Marcus would be at the beach. I already missed him terribly, but I had to push my sorrow aside to focus on finding Jolene.

Freemont gave me a comforting hug. "You look as sad as I feel, Carrie Sue."

On the drive to *PCB*, Freemont startled me when he said, "If Dora Lee insists on going up to that cabin and breaking in, you tell her no. Her ex used to be a locksmith, and she learned that trade from him. She has a set of picking tools like you wouldn't believe. But you need to stop her from breaking and entering, okay?"

"If we can find Jolene, it'd be worth it."

Freemont's frown deepened, as we pulled up to the restaurant. Sergeant Peters was standing beside his patrol car. Thin, medium height, with brown hair, Peters appeared bookish in his horn-rimmed glasses. If not for his police uniform, no one would have guessed he was a law enforcement officer.

I shook his hand. "Thanks for coming, Sergeant Peters."

He smiled as if he didn't have a care in the world. "Thanks for the invite. I love this place."

We walked inside and found Eugene at the front door; his face pinched. Worry shaded his brown eyes. He saw us drive up and had been waiting for us, he said. He gave Freemont one of those manly, bear-hugs, before he took our orders.

When he delivered our food, Freemont gave him some fliers to post. We had already given Peters a few as we sat down.

"Jolene was walking out to the bus the last time I saw her," Eugene said. "It was dark. But there's a light at the stop. I thought she'd be okay. She'd taken that bus many times. She lives in a rough area though. Everyone here likes Jolene. She's a good worker, very dependable, very kind and friendly with our customers."

"Did Jolene ask you to help her avoid Nev Powers, Eugene?" I asked the question to make that point with Peters. "Was she afraid of him?"

Eugene nodded. "He made her uncomfortable. He could be crude. He had a tendency to flirt and run his mouth. Jolene was nice to everybody. She never complained. If she had a problem with him, she had good reason. She didn't say what it was he did or said. She just wanted to avoid him."

Peters withdrew a notebook from his shirt pocket and scribbled some notes. "Did you ever see her alone with Powers?"

Eugene nodded. "He gave her a ride home once. It was stormy that night. Her aunt was at her work and couldn't pick her up." Eugene rubbed his forehead as if it hurt. "I wish I'd paid more attention. But when we get slammed, it's difficult. One thing's for sure, I could always depend on Jolene to show up on time and work hard. She's the hardest worker I have."

I turned to Peters. "I was here last night. I came to pick up supper. I chatted with Jolene for a couple of minutes. As we were talking, Nev walked in. She froze when she saw him. I could see the fear in her eyes. Eugene came over and we chatted. He said he remembers seeing Nev. Isn't that right, Eugene."

"Yeah, I saw him."

I sighed. "Martha Sue was at the cash register, as I recall. She waited on him. When I saw Nev, I was afraid for Jolene. I talked to the bus driver who picked her up from here last night. He told me he remembers dropping her off a block from where she lives, but that doesn't mean Nev Powers wasn't waiting for her there. He'd warned her not to tell anyone he'd raped her. Yet, she reported her rape to you, Sergeant Peters."

Eugene leaned in and slapped the table. "Detective Powers raped Jolene?"

Peters glared at me as if I'd committed a sin. "She made a report against him, but we couldn't bring charges. She didn't follow proper procedure. She reported it days after the alleged incident. And it was her word against his. No witnesses. He admitted he gave her a ride home. He swore nothing happened. Just between us, Nev can be a jerk, but what she claimed he did is a serious crime and without proof, we couldn't charge him. Forensics has her dress, the one she gave me. They'll look at skin, hair, blood, bodily fluids, etc. But they're backed up. It may take a while."

Eugene glared, his eyes darkening with alarm. "God, have mercy. I had no idea. I wish she'd told me. Jolene stayed after her shift was over last night. She always works late if we get busy. We were short-handed. One of the workers didn't show. Once it calmed down, Jolene left. She was waiting for her aunt. When her aunt didn't show, she took the bus."

Freemont grumbled. "Latrice's car broke down."

Eugene shook his head. "Oh, my, my, my, I feel awful."

"Don't beat yourself up, Eugene," I said. "I wish I'd done more, too." I turned to Peters. "We're doing a series on rape. Our first edition will come out tomorrow. We can't mention Jolene's case of course. She's a minor, but I definitely believe her. If we don't find her before our deadline, we're going to run Jolene's picture and report her missing in our special edition. You said your forensic folks will be examining Jolene's dress. When they do, I'm confident they'll find a link to Nev Powers. But you could bait him and say a link was found. He might then claim the sex was consensual, which it wasn't, of course, but it's like him to say something like that. And in this case, Jolene is a minor. Having sex with a minor is a serious crime."

Peters nodded. "Yes. But he claims he didn't touch her."

Anger flared in Eugene's eyes. "Sergeant Peters, Jolene wouldn't report something that's not true. I've never known her to lie. I had no idea he'd hurt her that way. God Almighty, this is terrible, terrible." Eugene kept shaking his head.

Freemont asked Peters if anyone, other than Jolene, had ever accused Powers of assault or rape.

Peters closed his notebook then placed his pen behind his right ear. "First case I've heard of. He's an observant detective, good at gathering evidence and making a strong case. He's believable in court. But he's not someone I socialize with outside of work. I don't know him very well personally."

I studied Peters. He must have known or heard of other women who have complained about Nev Powers. Was he protecting him? The good ole boy system at work.

Peters finished his burger. "I need to get back to work. Thanks for lunch." He grabbed the fliers Freemont had given him. "I'll be sure to distribute these. We'll see what we can do to help find her."

"We're counting on you, Sergeant Peters," I said.

After lunch, Freemont and I drove all over South Atlanta handing out fliers. We must have talked to more than a hundred people who agreed to join in our search for Jolene.

As night fell, I drove Freemont back to his house. On the way, we talked about the best ways to search for Jolene.

He would be joining forces with Jeff Daniels, Freemont said. "I'm praying she'll be back home before tomorrow."

He invited me to spend the night in his guest room. "Thanks, Free, but I need to get back to the office and pursue leads. If she's not found by tomorrow morning, Dora Lee and I are driving to that cabin in north Georgia. I'll ask Kasandra Rubin to go with us. It wouldn't hurt to take a psychic along. What do you think, Free?"

Rather than answer, Freemont glared at me, as if he thought I'd lost my mind.

Chapter Thirteen

Wednesday, February 25

An orange and pink sunrise bled over rolling hills as we approached Cleveland, Georgia. Dora Lee rode with me in the Cadillac. She'd brought along a search and rescue German Shepherd named King. Kasandra followed us in her silver Thunderbird.

Dora Lee was dressed like a soldier in her camo outfit. She hid her dark hair beneath a brown and green cap. I wore jeans and a blue sweater. I hid my hair under a camo cap that Dora Lee gave me. Kasandra wore a multi-colored peasant dress and red bonnet. So much for camouflage.

As I drove, I remembered what Freemont said, "Don't get arrested for breaking and entering."

Dora Lee and I had not discussed the possibility of prison. We were women on a mission. Damn the consequences.

Dora Lee popped in a Jim Croce tape: *I Got a Name, Operator, Time in a Bottle, Bad, Bad Leroy Brown, You Don't Mess Around with Jim*. Croce was killed in a plane crash in the early '70s.

We sang along with Croce on some of the songs, and we talked quite a bit. Dora Lee explained how she acquired the map to Nev's cabin.

"I was depressed when I first started working with Sheriff Barnum. I'd gone through an awful divorce. I didn't have good sense back then. Nev seemed nice. I thought he was cute. Obviously, I didn't know him. He flirted with me and bragged about the cabin he'd bought. He said he needed to get away from his house for the sake of his sanity. He lives with his mom, who's paralyzed. He helps his dad take care of her, he said. His cabin needed, 'a woman's touch,' or so he claimed. He asked me if I could help him decorate it. I told him I wasn't a decorator by any stretch of the imagination, but I could maybe drive up one Saturday. Take a look. Give him my two cents. He asked me to ride with him, but I said no, I'd rather meet him at the cabin. So ..." She waved the map, a simple drawing on lined paper. "He wanted to make sure I knew the way. My plans changed when Tiffany got real sick. I didn't want to leave her. She'd been with Mama all week. Mama looked a bit puny herself, like she might be coming down with something. Nev had planned to drive up to his cabin the Friday before. I tried to reach him to let him know I couldn't make it and why. But I didn't have a phone number for the cabin. He hadn't given me one. I tried his two-way but couldn't get up with him. I found out later there was no phone in that cabin."

"Was he upset when you didn't show?"

"Yes, very. A reasonable person would have understood, but no, not Nev Powers, he was pissed off, big time."

"Must have been awkward for you, working with him after that."

"You could say that. After he lost his temper, I mostly ignored him. Later, after he cooled off, he kept saying I needed to make it up to him. He pestered the bejesus out of me, trying to get me to drive up the following Saturday. I told him it wasn't convenient. But he kept asking and asking. I kept making excuses. I thought he would get the hint. But no. The more I refused him, the more obsessive he got. Then one day he forced me into a corner and felt me up."

"Oh, no, he should have gotten fired for that."

"I thought so. I told the Sheriff. He just said he'd have a talk with Nev. But Nev denied he did anything wrong. He claimed I came on to him, which was bull crap. But it was my word against his. Barnum told me to keep my distance from Nev, and told Nev the same."

"And did he keep his distance?"

"More or less. He still made rude comments. You know how he is. He tells dirty jokes, thinking they're funny."

"I'm surprised Barnum kept him on. I thought the Sheriff respected you. Y'all seemed to get along pretty well."

"It's a boy's club over there. You know how that goes. But all in all, the sheriff was respectful to me, as long as I didn't try to clean or organize his messy desk."

I smiled, recalling the pile of papers on Barnum's desk. "How does he find anything in all that clutter?"

"Beats me. He's the complete opposite of his wife. She's a perfectionist. She can't stand for anything to be out of order. When I worked with Sheriff Barnum, I used to go to their house for supper once in a while. His wife rules the roost at home. She's in complete control there. I kind of teased him about it. He said, that was okay, she could be in charge at home, but never at his office."

As I listened to Dora Lee, my thoughts turned to Marcus. He liked to be in control and informed, but I'd failed to tell him about the trip to Cleveland. I didn't want him to worry. He was already dealing with so much in his personal life and at the office. When he'd called from Florida last night, I heard the frustration and exhaustion in his voice. The Seagrove house he'd rented needed a larger ramp to accommodate Susan's wheelchair. The arrangements for her medical care would take longer than he'd expected. He had no idea when he'd be able to return to Atlanta.

King's loud bark startled me back to the moment. Dora Lee stroked his brownish-gray head to settle him.

King had worked as a K-9 cop until the Sheriff's department forced him into retirement. His handler and owner, Bobby Lewis, was no longer connected with the sheriff's office, but still worked in law enforcement as a state trooper. "King has an amazing talent for locating missing people," Dora said. "I brought along Jolene's scarf for him to sniff." Dora Lee gave King a bone-shaped treat then studied the hand-drawn map to Nev's cabin. She waved the map and a Cleveland travel brochure in her right hand.

"I'm glad I didn't throw these away. I'm always getting on to myself for not cleaning out my purse. In this case, I'm glad I didn't." She unfolded the brochure and read from it. "This says Cleveland was named after a General Benjamin Cleveland. He served in the war of 1812, and was the grandson and namesake of Revolutionary War Colonel Benjamin

Cleveland. Wow. Did you know Cleveland is the home of two Jewish summer camps? Amazing, isn't it? And get this, Carrie Sue. Xavier Roberts is from Cleveland. Do you know who he is?"

"His name sounds familiar."

"It should, Carrie Sue. Xavier Roberts created the Cabbage Patch Kids. He learned his sewing and quilting skills from his mother, it says here. Isn't that something?"

I nodded in agreement. Dora Lee was trying to lighten the mood. I didn't want to discourage her, though my stomach was queasy and my mood dark. "I love your enthusiasm, Dora Lee. You've always been such a positive person. If anyone can chase away sadness, you can."

"Aw, what a sweet thing to say, Carrie Sue. Call me Pollyanna. But in all seriousness, I haven't forgotten we're on a mission."

"Doesn't hurt to learn about the area and create some positive energy, Dora Lee. I appreciate your efforts to do that."

"Thank you, Carrie Sue." She smiled and pointed to a red-clay road, about fifty feet ahead to our right. "Nev's map has us turning here."

I turned as instructed. The dirt road was filled with pot holes. I drove slowly to avoid damaging the car. We bumped along for a mile or more. Nothing but trees and bushes on both sides of the road.

When we reached a wooden sign with "Clay Hollow" in fading red letters, I turned to Dora Lee. "Is this where we're supposed to turn?

"According to the map."

Two cars couldn't pass safely on this dirt road. Trees and bushes scraped the Cadillac as we drove for at least two miles. The area looked deserted. No house or anything that would indicate someone lived nearby. Eventually, we came to a black mailbox on the right side of what I considered a path, not a road. "Is this it, Dora Lee?"

"No, his box has a confederate flag on it, he said."

We bumped along for another mile and found the box she described. I stopped and glanced down the trail where Dora Lee said we'd find Nev's cabin. "Why don't we park and walk the rest of the way?"

"Good idea. We don't want to be too obvious. And we certainly don't want to run into him."

"Didn't you call the sheriff's department and make sure he was working today, Dora Lee?"

"I did, but that doesn't mean he won't take off and dilly dally. He makes his own schedule."

I drove a half a mile down Clay Hollow and backed up between two giant cedar trees. Kasandra parked beside me.

Dora Lee clicked on King's leash and let him smell of Jolene's hound's-tooth scarf then slipped on her backpack. "This thing weighs a ton. I've got lock-picking tools, two thermoses—coffee and water. I brought along some paper cups for us, too, and food for King. I even have garbage bags for collecting evidence. If we get hungry, I'll open the can of spam I brought. I like mine on crackers, and I brought plenty of saltines."

"Everything but the kitchen sink, right?"

She laughed. "Right. I came prepared."

As we stepped out, King started leading us. Dora Lee reigned him back at the sound of an approaching vehicle. We all hid in the bushes and waited. It turned out to be a black truck, spewing red clay.

The evergreens blocked the morning sun. Only a few freckles of light leaked through.

Dora Lee and I wore sunglasses, in our attempt to disguise ourselves; whereas, Kasandra refused to have her green eyes shielded with shades. This made sense. She was a seer.

I heard gurgling, water sounds, but I couldn't see the river. "I have no idea how long it'll take us to walk to the cabin," Dora Lee said.

"Are you sure this is right, Dora Lee. I haven't seen a cabin anywhere around here. What do you think, Kasandra?"

"I think this gravel road will lead us to it. King knows where he's going."

We dutifully followed King. He tugged at his leash, obviously eager to work.

"I agree," Dora Lee said. "We're headed in the right direction."

Kasandra nodded. "Yes, we need to follow King. He will help us find her."

Dora Lee patted King's head. "I'm glad I brought him. Aren't y'all?"

"He's a good detective and so are you," Kasandra said.

"Nice of you to say, Kasandra. But I could never be a detective. I hate guns."

I nodded. "That makes two of us."

"Firearms have their purpose," Kasandra said. "But gun owners are more likely to shoot a family member and kill themselves than a burglar."

I inhaled the cool air and swallowed my nausea. Unusual for me to have a sick tummy. When I was a teenager, Dad accused me of having a superhuman digestive system after I ate three hotdogs at a Braves game and god only knows how many roasted peanuts. "My mom disliked guns, too. She made Dad give away his prized snub nose. It was the same type of gun Jack Ruby used to kill Lee Harvey Oswald. Marcus has it now. I didn't know Dad had given it to Marcus until Marcus told me. Marcus owns a number of guns. He claims they're for sport and protection."

Kasandra shot me a piercing stare. "Marcus has received threats."

My heart stuttered. "From who?"

"Crazy kooks."

"Who are the crazy kooks?"

"I cannot see them clearly. As I've told you before, darkness surrounds him."

I swallowed my bitter saliva. "Do you think he'll be okay?"

Kasandra touched my arm. "Don't worry. You worry too much."

I started to protest when Dora Lee chimed in. "Do you remember when Larry Simpson and Percy Anderson got shot and killed, Carrie Sue?"

"What a tragedy. They were good cops, too."

Dora Lee took off her sunglasses and rubbed her eyes. "Saddest funerals I ever attended. I apologize for bringing that up, but they popped in my mind when we started talking about guns. I still can't believe they got shot and killed with their own pistols. Larry had been an officer for thirty years. He was getting ready to retire. He was a father and a grandfather. He and his wife were getting ready to take a trip to Europe. Percy was only twenty-five. His wife was pregnant with their son. It still doesn't make sense to me. They were killed for trying to help a young boy. The boy—his name was Malcomb something. He was about nine or ten—if I remember right. He was getting beat up by a bunch of bullies. When Larry and Percy tried to stop the fight, the bullies overpowered them and snatched Larry and Percy's guns. Malcomb survived and reported what happened. The bullies were arrested and locked up in Juvy, They were too young to be tried as adults. Their parents were bullies, too. That's why they raised bullies."

Dora Lee stopped to readjust her heavy backpack. "Larry and Percy always went out of their way to help people. We still have some good cops. But the shady ones, like Nev Powers, give the others a bad name. Pisses me off."

"What do you think of Raymond Peters?" I asked.

"I like Raymond. He seems to be a good guy. I've never heard anything bad about him. He's kind of an egg-head, but I like egg-heads. They think before they act."

"I hope he'll investigate Jolene's rape properly."

"I hope so, too. He's kind of anal retentive. Goes by the rule book. I'd like to think he has the sense to know she told him the truth. Poor Jolene. I just can't imagine what she must have gone through. I've never been raped, only attacked."

"Are you referring to the time Nev tried to force himself on you?"

"Well that, too, but I was also thinking about the time this weirdo attacked me in downtown Atlanta. I was walking out of the library at Georgia State, minding my own business. Not paying attention to my surroundings. It was in broad daylight. This crazy guy comes up and says, 'Are you from out of this world?' He leaned in too close. I took one look at his glassy eyes and knew he was crazy. I told him to get lost. That's when he grabbed me and pinched my boobs. I screamed bloody murder. He ran off when I started screaming. I was so shocked. I didn't report it until I got home. The cop I reported it to asked me what I was wearing at that time, as if he thought I was to blame. I should have requested a woman cop. A woman would have understood."

"You were a victim," I said. "What you were wearing was irrelevant."

"I know. We need more women cops. I could never be one. I'm not authoritarian enough. And I hate guns." Dora Lee stretched out her right arm and pointed at an A-frame log cabin 200 feet away, barely visible in the clearing. "That must be it."

No vehicle at the cabin, only tire tracks where a vehicle had been. The cabin was isolated. No other structures nearby.

Kasandra reached in her handbag and withdrew binoculars. "We should be okay to approach."

"You're a psychic. You shouldn't need binoculars," I joked.

"I like to confirm," she said, peering through the field glasses.

"So you believe no one's in the cabin? What about security? Do you think there might be an alarm of some kind?"

"We're okay. Let King lead us."

We followed the feisty King. He kept straining against his leash. He stopped pulling when we reached the front porch. Then he took his time sniffing.

Dora Lee opened the screen door. "King has picked up a scent." She fooled with the knob to the main door. "Locked."

King sniffed his way along the wrap-around porch. We all followed him. Dora Lee let him smell the scarf again to "refresh the scent," as she called it.

King sniffed his way to a large barbeque pit in the shape of a pig. "He might be hungry and enticed by the scent of food," I said. There was a pile of coal and ashes below the grill. King pawed at the pile, digging.

Dora Lee handed me his leash. "I need to get inside." She withdrew a long metal object from her backpack. "This shouldn't take long."

Kasandra plopped down in a wrought iron chair near the grill, closed her eyes and started breathing rapidly. Perhaps envisioning the screen in her mind.

I swallowed my foul-tasting saliva and turned my attention to King. He continued to dig. In no time he'd dug a large bowl-shaped hole.

"I'm in," Dora Lee said then disappeared inside the cabin.

I watched King dig until I saw what looked like black hair. I pulled him away to get closer look. He barked in protest.

"Kasandra, look." I pointed to the hair. "What do you think?"

She squatted beside me. "We need to notify the authorities." She took King's leash from me. "King has done his job. But we can't let him disturb her body now."

I kept squatting, staring at the ground. Was this really human hair? Did it belong to Jolene? It was the texture of her hair, black, long and wavy.

As I fixated on what King had uncovered, gray clouds blanketed the day. I could feel cold drops of rain. "Don't let this be Jolene," I prayed and then puked.

Kasandra handed me a handkerchief. "Breathe, Carrie Sue. Relax."

"How could anyone relax under these circumstances, Kasandra? If this is Jolene, is it possible she might still be alive?"

"No, she's dead. She been dead for a while." Kasandra led King inside the cabin. I followed her. This place smelled nasty, musty, like the dust mites and roaches had taken over. The plantation shutters were closed, making the cabin depressingly dark.

I flicked on the switch by the door. The living room was sparsely furnished with a worn-out green couch and matching chaise. The dining room nook had a round maple table with four chairs. A serving bar with a black slate top separated the kitchen from the dining area. I searched for a phone, but couldn't find one.

King sniffed at every nook and cranny as we walked through the downstairs. "Where's Dora Lee?" I whispered. "She's not down here."

We crept up the creaking stairs, searching for her. At the top landing, I saw a flash of light. We followed it and found Dora Lee standing behind a metal desk, holding a penlight and reading from an open file. This loft was crowded with a desk, file cabinet and unmade king-sized bed. A black, white and red bedspread laid mostly on the floor. We were careful not to step on it. Above the headboard was a framed confederate flag with a picture of an eagle, its talons holding a swastika.

King barked when he saw her. Dora Lee dropped the folder she'd been holding. Papers went flying everywhere. "Scared the bejesus out of me, dog."

We shushed King and helped Dora Lee gather up the papers. "This is awful stuff about the KKK. And that's not all." She pulled out one of the drawers in the file cabinet. "Look inside, Carrie Sue." She pointed the penlight inside the drawer, spotlighting my stolen lacy panties, had to be mine. They were Victoria's Secret, pink and in my size.

"What a crazy son of a bitch. He broke into my house, bugged it and took my underwear."

Kasandra pointed to a rope tied around one of the bed posts. "This is where he tied up Jolene."

I stared at the rope then quickly turned away. "We need to call the police. Have you seen a phone anywhere, Dora Lee?"

"No, I don't think there is one. Remember I told you, I couldn't reach him on the phone, because he didn't have one in his cabin." She turned toward Kasandra. "Where is Jolene, Kasandra?"

Kasandra took several deep breaths before she answered. "She's dead. King found Jolene's gravesite under the barbeque pit."

Dora Lee blinked. "Oh, no, please no. Are you sure she's not still alive?"

I explained about the hair.

Dora Lee started to shake and sat in a desk chair, the only chair in the loft. "We need to take all of these files with us and give them to police." With a trembling hand, she pointed to the stack of files on the desk.

I shook my head. "We can't take any of this stuff, Dora Lee. We don't have a search warrant. This is private property. If we remove anything, we might be arrested for breaking and entering."

Dora Lee stood and stomped her feet, as her anger took over. "Damn, Carrie Sue. What should we do with all this stuff? We can't ignore it. He took your underwear. Proof that he broke into your house. Are you going to leave your underwear? Why don't we say we found the door open? That makes sense, doesn't it? We can say we were trying to find the phone and happened to find all of this."

"I like your idea of finding the door open, Dora Lee, in case they discover we've been inside. But we can't remove anything. It won't be admissible evidence if we do."

"I agree with Carrie Sue," Kasandra said. "We need to report this to the local police. After they find Jolene's body, they'll get a search warrant."

Dora Lee—still trembling—propped on the edge of the desk. What if we leave and someone comes in while we're gone and removes all this stuff ?"

I shivered at the thought. "You have a point, Dora Lee. Why don't I stay here, and y'all drive into Cleveland to get the police?"

Dora Lee placed the files back inside the cabinet. "I don't like the idea of leaving you here, Carrie Sue."

"I'm a little sick at my stomach. I've already puked outside. If I drive or ride in a car right now, the motion might make me sicker. I'd rather stay here. It shouldn't take y'all long to go and get back."

Dora Lee slipped her arm around me. "I'm sorry you're sick, but I don't feel right about leaving you."

"I'll be fine. Don't worry."

Dora Lee huffed. "If you think you have to stay, and I can't convince you otherwise, King should stay with you as a guard dog?"

"No, he'll want to keep digging. I don't feel like trying to stop him. Like I said, it shouldn't take y'all long to explain what King uncovered and the reason we drove up here looking for Jolene. Tell them we were trying to find her after she went missing. Tell them Jolene has accused Nev of raping her. Kasandra can explain how she had a vision. But we can't tell them we broke in and disturbed evidence."

Kasandra stroked my head, as if I were a child who needed comforting. "I agree with you, Carrie Sue. But you must be very careful and watchful." She handed me her binoculars.

Dora Lee grabbed King's leash. "Let's get the hell out of here. This place is evil."

Outside, Dora Lee glanced at what King had dug up and sobbed. I cried with her, as Kasandra kneeled on the ground, crossed her heart and bowed her head in prayer.

Dora Lee gave King another treat to keep him from barking then led him down the narrow path we'd walked before King found Jolene's body. Kasandra trailed behind.

As I watched them disappear, I shivered. The cold, damp air smelled of death.

I sipped the cold water from Dora Lee's thermos that she left with me. Through Kasandra's binoculars I saw two men fishing on the river. I could see only the back of them, not their faces.

The light drizzle became a gulley washer. I ran under the porch awning for shelter. Regret consumed me as I watched the rain pouring down, puddling the hole King had dug.

I spotted a rose bush that reminded me of the ones I'd planted near my veranda and the yellow rose I found in my kitchen after the burglary. "A warning rose," Jeff had called it.

Another wave of nausea hit me. I swallowed the bile as the sound of crunching gravel alerted me to a car driving up. I wasn't expecting Dora Lee, King and Kasandra this soon. They'd been gone less than fifteen minutes. It would take almost that long to walk to the road where our cars were parked.

I peered around the corner to the front of the cabin. A white ford pulled up and parked. I was looking for a place to hide when I saw a red umbrella pop open. "Reed Realty" was printed in white on the umbrella. On the side of the white ford was a red sign with the same insignia. A woman in furry boots hopped out of the car.

What was she doing here? Would she snoop in the back yard?

I came up with a plan to avoid suspicion. "Horrible day," I called out as I ran around the sheltered porch toward the woman.

Her red lips parted in surprise. She was tall, almost 6 feet, with short copper-colored hair. Her red suit matched her umbrella "You're right. It is a horrible day. I didn't see your car. Where're you parked?"

I pointed toward the main road. "Somewhere over there. It wasn't raining when I began my hike here. Not a good day for cabin hunting."

Her hazel-eyed questioned me. "I'm Realtor Joyce Reed. Are you in the market for a cabin?"

"I guess you could say, I'm in the hunting stage."

"I'll be happy to help you. This particular cabin isn't on the market. However, I can show you similar cabins with much better, more beautiful views. Even if it wasn't raining, we'd have to drive to see them though. This cabin here is the most isolated cabin of all the cabins I've sold." She reached inside her burgundy bag and withdrew a business card then handed it to me. "You look familiar. What's your name?"

I paused. Should I give her a fake name or real name? *"Don't lie,"* I could almost hear Dad say. I extended my hand. "I'm Carrie."

She gave my hand a firm shake. "Don't you write for the Southern Journal?" She laughed at her revelation. "I grew up in College Station. I still subscribe to your newspaper. I recognize you now. I was sure I knew you. I love your columns."

I gave her what I hoped was a sincere smile. "Thank you."

"I love everything you write. Most people might call this a coincidence. Not me. I believe there are no coincidences in life, just opportunities."

My gut quivered. How well did she know Nev Powers? Would she tell him she saw me at his cabin? "I'm happy you enjoy our newspaper."

She pulled out a ball of keys and unlocked the front door. "Lovely to finally meet you."

"Nice to meet you, too, Joyce. Do you know who owns this cabin?"

"He's with the College Station Sheriff's Department ... Detective Powers. I'm sure you must know him." She smiled brightly. "I sold him this cabin."

I followed her inside. "That's interesting. I'm not one of his favorite people. He doesn't like reporters very much. I'd appreciate it if you wouldn't tell him I was looking at his cabin. As a crime reporter, I have to remain objective. I hope you understand."

She squinted, maybe confused or suspicious. "He's not part of our rental program, but he uses our maid and repair service. He had a leak in his roof. I sent our handyman, jack of all trades, Jason, to fix it. Jason said it's fixed. Now that it's raining, I should be able to tell for sure if Jason was able to repair the leak or not. But these roof leaks are tricky."

She flicked on the lights. "I don't think he'd mind if I showed you around. But excuse the mess. You know how messy some men can be."

Joyce pointed out the exposed wooden beams and what she called "a solidly built structure." She brushed a finger over the dining table. "A little dusty. Cleaning crew is scheduled to be here Friday."

Joyce's lengthy tour and explanations made me jittery. What if the police showed up while Joyce was here? "Why don't we finish this tour at a later date. Time has gotten away from me. I need to get back to Atlanta soon. Why don't we make plans to get together when the weather is nicer?"

She frowned. "Oh, okay."

"Do you mind driving me to my car, Joyce? I'd rather not walk in the rain." I saw no other option. "How long will it take you to finish your inspection." I stood in front of the back door to keep Joyce from going in the back yard and relocking that door. We'd planned to tell the Cleveland police it was open when we arrived.

"I'll just be a minute," she said before she disappeared upstairs.

My impatience grew as I waited by the back door. "Did you find a leak," I called out.

"Looks good, no leak," she said, as she made her way down the stairs.

"I really like the sign on your car, Joyce." I walked toward the front, opened the door then pointed to the sign to distract her and draw her attention away from the back. "Very professional."

She smiled widely, no fillings in her teeth. "My son-in-law designed this logo for me and created the signs on my car and umbrellas and billboards." She fished in her purse and pulled out a business card. "*Sam's logos and signs with design,*" which included a phone number to call.

I took the card. "Thank you, Joyce. I'll pass the word. You seem to enjoy being a Realtor."

"Love it," she said. "And being your own boss has its merits. I married the broker at Reed Realty. That's how I got into the business. My husband Buford was a fantastic businessman. An even better husband. I'm a widow now. I lost Buford five years ago. He died from colon cancer."

"I'm sorry to hear that, Joyce." I walked with her out to her car and inhaled a thankful sigh. She didn't check the back door or look in the back yard.

As Joyce drove the narrow path to where I'd parked the Cadillac, she asked me questions about my life and my work. She talked about a few of my columns then asked what inspired me to write them.

When she pulled up next to the Caddy, I told her it was Mom's car. "So tragic how you lost your parents. If anyone can understand my pain from losing Buford, it's you, Carrie Sue."

She cried. I cried. She gave me a tissue to dry my eyes. She dried hers.

"It was lovely meeting you, Joyce. Sorry I'm in a rush now. Time got away from me."

"Time gets away from me every day, Carrie Sue. I completely understand."

I opened the door to escape. "Let's get together soon, Joyce."

"I'd like that. Call me whenever, or I'll call you."

I waved good-bye, jumped in the Caddy and cranked it up as if I were planning to leave. She drove off right away in a flash, then I opened my trunk to grab my tiny umbrella. I'd stashed it next to a pair of old boots I'd been meaning to give away.

In the windy downpour, my umbrella offered little protection. I was waterlogged by the time I got back to the cabin.

A few minutes later, Kasandra's Thunderbird drove up with Dora Lee and King. A City of Cleveland, Crown Vic patrol car pulled up behind them.

My body sagged with relief when I saw them. Two policemen in blue and a woman in a pin-striped, grey suit emerged. The younger cop looked to be about my age, height and coloring. He introduced himself as Charlie Bucannon.

The older cop was dark, slim and tall, with salt-and-pepper hair. He extended his hand. "Sergeant Bill Black."

The woman in the suit had short auburn hair and carried a Nikon camera around her neck. She shielded herself and her camera with a giant green umbrella, the color of her eyes. "I'm Ellen Stanley." She gripped my hand in a bone-crushing shake.

Dora Lee, King, Kasandra and I walked to the backyard. I pointed to the black hair King had uncovered. Sergeant Black squatted to take a look. "We need to secure this area."

He ushered Dora Lee, Kasandra, King, and me to the Thunderbird and asked us to wait there.

"Did you have time to get a search warrant, Sergeant?" I asked.

"We need to determine what we have first."

Dora Lee and King got in the back of the Thunderbird. Kasandra and I sat in front. King started barking and whining, as if he wanted out.

Dora Lee offered him a bone-shaped treat and patted his head. "You're a good detective, King. You did a great job today."

I watched Black open the trunk of the patrol car. He removed a large bag then carried the bag to the backyard.

While we waited, Dora Lee said, "I gave officer Black a flier with Jolene's photo and told him about the rape. And I gave him Raymond Peters' name and number. Black called Raymond. They talked."

"Did you tell him I saw Nev at the restaurant where Jolene worked the night she disappeared?"

"I explained most everything. Or at least I hope I did. He recorded our conversation. Kasandra told him about her premonition. I explained how I knew about Nev's cabin. I told him about King and his talent for finding people."

Dora Lee withdrew a roll of paper towels from her backpack and wiped King's paws. We sat quietly, watching her. After she'd finished cleaning King, she dropped the dirty towels in the trash basket stuck between the front seats.

Dora Lee then handed me a packet of saltine crackers. "These might help your sick tummy."

"Thank you, Dora Lee." I grabbed a few crackers before passing them to Kasandra.

We nervously munched and talked for an hour before Sergeant Black returned. Kasandra rolled down the window. He leaned in. His eyes looked tired and sad. "We uncovered the nude body of a light-skinned African American girl resembling the photo of Jolene Brookins. The body is intact. Medical examiner will perform an autopsy to determine the cause of death. In the meantime, we'll get a search warrant. I'm sorry."

Dora Lee, Kasandra and I cried. "Jolene's life was brutally taken before she had a chance to live out her life and fulfill her dreams," I sobbed.

About that time, EMTs pulled up in a white and red van. "They'll be transporting Jolene's body to the morgue," Black said. Two young men emerged from the van with a stretcher and followed Black to the back yard.

I stepped out of the Thunderbird when I saw the body bag. "Can I see her?" I wanted to believe this wasn't Jolene, and we'd find her somewhere alive.

He unzipped the bag. I gasped at her lovely face, soiled from being buried, but still young and sweet, as if she might wake up from this nightmare. "When are you planning to arrest Nev Powers?"

"We hope to bring him in right away."

Dora Lee gave Sergeant Black her phone number. "I have to get back to Atlanta." She turned to me. "I promised Freemont."

I nodded. "Okay, you ride back with Kasandra, and I'll stay to go over some things with the Sergeant."

She hugged me. "Call me when you can. Are you sure you're going to be okay?"

"Yes, please don't worry."

Kasandra's green eyes locked with mine. "Be watchful."

"I will."

After they drove away, Black invited me to sit in his patrol car. He asked several questions and took notes. I answered the best I could. I described Jolene's fear of Nev and the night he came into the restaurant. "That was the same night Jolene's aunt reported her missing."

As I was talking to Black, I touched my right ear. "Oh, no," I gasped. I'd lost one of Mom's good-luck earrings. How could I have been so careless. "Could this day get any worse?" I started sobbing again.

Black reached beside his seat and came up with a packet of Kleenex. I yanked out a tissue and wiped my eyes.

"You've been very helpful, Carrie Sue. But there are a few details I'd like to clarify."

He rehashed what Dora Lee and Kasandra said earlier. I verified what they'd said. Eventually I got around to mentioning my lost earring.

"Do you think you may have lost it around here?"

"I'm not sure, but these earrings are precious to me. They belonged to my Mom. Mom and Dad died in a plane crash a few years back."

"I'm very sorry. I'll keep a lookout."

"It could be anywhere, even inside the cabin. The door was open," I lied. "We went in to look for a phone, but there wasn't one."

His eyes questioned me. "Didn't you find it strange that the back door was open?"

"Yes, that is strange."

I gave Black my contact information at work and at home. In turn, he handed me his business card and said he'd drive me back to my car.

On the way, I told him about the night Freemont was shot. I explained how his security video captured the truck carrying his attackers. "Their license plate was traced to a truck owned by Nev's dad. Mr. Powers claimed his truck was stolen during the Klan march in College Station. A GBI agent, last name Godwin, interviewed Powers. I don't know Godwin's first name, but I'm thinking he could help you in your investigation."

"I heard about the Klan march and the shooting. What can you tell me about Mr. Jackson, the man who got shot?"

"He's my neighbor. He's like a brother to me. I've known him all my life. Marcus and I actually found him that night."

"Who's Marcus?"

"Marcus Handley, he's the publisher of the Southern Journal where I work. We found Freemont on the porch of his home with a gunshot wound in his chest. Freemont is still recovering from his injuries. He owns a successful laundry business, but he also attends college full time. He's a great guy. There's none better."

"Was Jackson ever able to identify the shooter?"

"They were dressed in Klan garb. Their faces were hidden. They burned a cross in Freemont's yard before they shot him. I'm sure they targeted Freemont because he's black. He also testified in court for one of the black teens indicted for shooting and killing a white teen. Freemont's testimony was persuasive and helped Tatum Brookins win his freedom."

"I followed that trial in the news, but I've forgotten the details."

"A jury found Tatum not guilty. Freemont was an eye witness for him. He was delivering laundry the night of the shooting and saw Tatum, far away from the scene of the crime. It was clear from the beginning Tatum wasn't involved. Yet, he was arrested and brought to trial. Nev Powers was the lead detective for the prosecution."

"Didn't one of those boys hang himself in jail?"

"It was alleged Calvin Newsome hung himself. He was only fourteen. His death was ruled a suicide. They found a note in his cell. That left only Tatum and Jeremy Andrews to stand trial. Jeremy was sixteen, Tatum fifteen. The attorney for Leroy Cortez accepted a plea bargain. Leroy testified for the prosecution. A jury found Jeremy guilty of malice murder." I waited for Black to finish taking notes before I continued. "Tatum's mom, Latrice Brookins, is Jolene's aunt. They all live in the same College Station housing project."

"How did you learn about her rape?"

I couldn't mention Tatum. He'd suffered enough. "Jolene told me. I have her on tape describing exactly what happened."

"That tape will be useful. I'd like to hear it. Do you think you can arrange that?"

I nodded. "Of course. I'll make you a copy."

"Is there anything else you'd like to add, Carrie Sue?"

I told him about the break-in at my house and my stolen underpants. Dora Lee had found them in Nev's cabin. This should prove helpful once Black got the search warrant. I also mentioned the threatening notes I'd received. "When will Jolene's body be transported back to Atlanta for burial? Her aunt will need to know."

"What about the decedent's mother or father?"

"Her mother lives in Alabama. The father isn't in the picture, or that's what I've been told."

He nodded. "Usually the next of kin or the person with parental authority arranges for burial or cremation through a funeral home. We'll request the name of the funeral home they plan to use. It's up to the coroner to release the body for transport."

"I'll let Latrice know. Thank you, Sergeant Black. Please keep me informed."

"Thank you. You've been a great help. Sorry for your loss."

"I'll feel better after you arrest Nev Powers," I said, as I got out of the patrol car.

Inside the sanctuary of the caddy, I sat for a few minutes, taking deep breaths to calm my shaking. I forgot to tell Black about Realtor Joyce Reed. *Damn.*

Would Joyce tell Nev Powers she'd seen me at the cabin? That question haunted me on the long drive back to my house. I didn't want to go back there, but I needed to get my mail, pay some bills, get some clean clothes and check out my updated security.

As I drove in the circular drive, I marveled at the orange sunset bleeding over the old mansion. Dad used to say this house was too big for our small family and too small to contain all the ghosts. He would have preferred a smaller, more modern, place. But Mom, decorator extraordinaire, loved the challenge of refurbishing an antebellum house. Being a southern gentleman, Dad acquiesced to Mom.

"Mom married me because I inherited this place," Dad used to joke.

"Come on, Dad, you know Mom is crazy about you," I'd say. "She'd live with you anywhere, any place."

I would often groan at their displays of affection. She'd greet him with, "Hello, handsome." He'd greet her with, "Hello, beautiful." Now I realize I was blessed to have such loving parents.

The security lights flashed on as I walked up to the veranda. Jeff had designed them to do that. He'd given me a new code and explained how to change it. Would I be able to remember after such a tragic day?

As I opened the front door and entered the foyer, I saw an envelope taped to the inside of the door. The envelope had my name on it. Fear crawled up my spine as I tore open the envelope, not knowing what I'd find inside.

I breathed a relieved sigh when I saw the note from Jeff. He gave detailed instructions on how to reset my security code, secure the door and operate the video system. He'd installed a new box for the code, he said. The box had both letters and numbers.

"Don't use anything as obvious as your birthdate," he wrote.

I punched in the first thing I thought of, "a warning rose."

After I reset the code, I watched the video screen he'd mounted on the wall, beside the door. It looked similar to Freemont's.

In the split-screen, I saw the front and back of the house, the Cadillac parked in the drive, the roses I'd planted beside the veranda, the large concrete urn, the clouds burying the full moon. I wished the security lights could illuminate the entire drive, but that damn drive is a mile long.

On the right side of the screen, which showed the backyard, I saw something move. Another possum? These marsupials have been around since the dinosaurs. They're related to the kangaroo and koala. The dinosaurs perished. The possums survived. Amazing little creatures. Like the kangaroo and koala, they carry their infants in their pouches.

I walked down the hallway to the back of the house to see if I could get a glimpse of one. On the way, I turned on every light. I could almost hear Dad say, *"Whenever you leave a room, turn off the lights."*

Sorry dad," I whispered as if he could hear me. "I need the lights on tonight."

Jeff had installed a deadbolt on the back door, similar to the one on the front. Both doors were solid, three inches thick. With the heavy-duty deadbolts and alarm system, I should have felt safe, but my gut told me I wasn't safe.

I called Freemont, but got his voice mail. I left a message for him to call.

I checked my phone messages. Marcus had called. He didn't leave a number. His message on the machine was stern, as if he'd heard about my trip to Cleveland from someone other than the woman he professed to love.

The next message came from Lisa. "We're worried about you, Carrie Sue. Please call us."

The last message surprised me. "Carrie Sue, this is Joyce Reed. It was lovely meeting you today. I look forward to getting together with you soon." She cleared her throat. "The main reason I called now is to let you know I found your earring in my car. I'm sure it's yours. Call me."

I sighed my relief and dialed her number. Her voice mail answered: "Hi, this is Joyce with Joyce Reed Realty, your key to your tranquil escape ...."

I waited for the beep. "Hi Joyce. I just got home. Thanks so much for finding my earring. Please call again and let me know when I can get it from you."

Next, I called Sergeant Black. "I'm working the night shift," he said.

I told him about Joyce Reed. "I'm sorry I didn't mention her before. But I was upset and it slipped my mind. She drove up before you got there. She came by to make sure a leak in the cabin had been properly repaired. I didn't tell her the reason I was there. I pretended I was hiking and looking to buy property. She used to live in South Atlanta and knows Nev Powers. She sold him that cabin. She also recognized me from the newspaper. She still subscribes to the *Southern Journal.* I didn't want her to know we'd contacted y'all. I certainly didn't want her to find out what we'd found in the backyard. She might alert Nev Powers if she knew."

"Did she go in the back?"

"No, but you need to call her." I gave him Joyce's number. "Have you gotten the search warrant yet?"

"We're getting it. We plan to go in there first thing tomorrow."

"Have you picked up Nev Powers yet?"

"He's hired Norris Walker to represent him. And Walker promised to bring Powers in tomorrow."

My knees buckled. I slid to the floor. Norris Walker had never lost a case. "Oh no."

"Yeah. Walk free Walker has quite the reputation in Atlanta. We sent an officer to pick Powers up. But he must have gotten word before we could get him."

"What do you mean he must have gotten word?"

"Just that. It was on the news. One of our local stations got wind of what we'd found and called us for information. Our Chief, Chief Sheppard, held a press conference."

I moaned my distress. "Why would your chief hold a press conference? What if Jolene's family haven't been notified yet? Even if they'd been notified, her aunt might be in denial. If I were Latrice, I'd refuse to believe Jolene was dead until I actually saw her."

"Chief Sheppard didn't reveal her identity. He made an announcement that a body had been found, and we were conducting an investigation. Then Walker called us and said his client would come in willingly to clear up any misunderstanding. He claimed Powers sometimes rented out his cabin."

I struggled to breathe. "Misunderstanding? That's bull. Joyce Reed said Powers wasn't on the rental program." I tried to wrap my mind around this. "Did your chief announce where the body was found?"

"No. Could be Joyce Reed told Powers."

"No, Sergeant, she came by before you got there. She didn't go in the back. I watched her."

"This is a small town. Someone could have told her or she could have stopped by later and noticed the crime tape. And if she heard the announcement about a body, she could have put two and two together."

"When I got home, I found a message from Joyce Reed. She said she found my earring in her car. She didn't mention anything about a body. Her message was cheerful. She wouldn't have been cheerful if she'd heard about a body in the backyard of a cabin she'd sold. I don't want to tell you how to do your job, Sergeant, but you need to bring Nev Powers in pronto. He needs to be stopped."

"Walker assured me he's bringing Detective Powers in."

"And you believed him? You can't even be sure it was Walker you actually spoke to, can you? What if Powers takes off and leaves the country?"

"Walker has given his word. His reputation is on the line."

My hands shook as I hung up the phone. A combination of anger and low blood sugar.

I fixed myself a peanut butter and honey sandwich and washed it down with water, before I searched through my address book for the phone number to the beach house but couldn't find it. Was it possible I'd forgotten to put the number in there? Lisa had the number, but talking to Lisa would bring more drama.

Blood drained from my head as fatigue washed over me. I unhooked the mate to the earring I'd lost, placed it in Mom's jewelry case then plopped down on the bed.

The phone rang. My right hand trembled as I reached for it. I barely had enough strength to pick up the receiver and answer.

"Are you okay?" Marcus' voice was hoarse, indicating he was exhausted or upset and probably both.

"Not really. I just got your message, but you didn't leave a number. I couldn't find the one you gave me."

He sighed into the phone and recited the number. I wrote it down on the pad I kept on the nightstand. "Jolene's dead," I blurted out.

"I know. I heard."

"Who told you?"

"Freemont."

"I tried to reach him but couldn't."

"He's with Jolene's aunt Latrice and the grandmother."

"Latrice will have to arrange for Jolene to be transferred to Atlanta for burial. I need to tell her that," I sobbed.

"Why didn't you tell me you were driving up to Cleveland, Carrie?" His voice held hurt and disappointment.

"Who told you I drove up to Cleveland?"

He exhaled a loud sigh. "What does it matter who told me? I know, and I'm just wondering why you didn't tell me."

Marcus could be obsessive about my safety. Did he have me followed? I wanted to ask him, but didn't. We were both too upset.

"It was a spur of the moment decision. I didn't want to worry you. Dora Lee suggested it after Kasandra had a vision. You were on the phone when I left and I didn't have a chance to tell you about her suggestion. The Cleveland police are planning to search Nev Power's cabin tomorrow. Powers hasn't been arrested yet. He hired Norris Walker to represent him."

"Damn. Jolene's body was found buried on his property. No way in hell will he squeak free. Why didn't they take him into custody immediately? He should have been arrested, charged him with kidnapping, murder and rape. I'll contact Godwin."

"I told Sergeant Black about Godwin. Black knows about Freemont getting shot and that we suspect Nev and his father."

"We'll nail Powers. Right now, I'm concerned about you. You're not planning to spend the night there, are you?"

"No. I just came by to pick up my clothes and my mail and check on things. When are you coming home?"

"First thing tomorrow. Meanwhile, I'll call Jeff. I want to make sure you're safe."

"How's Susan doing?"

"She's exhausted. The chemo has been rough on her. Her docs had to adjust her meds. We took her out to the beach today. She stuck her toes in the Gulf. She doesn't have the energy to stay awake for long. She sleeps most of the day."

"You sound exhausted, Marcus."

"Don't worry about me, Carrie. I want you to promise me you'll get out of that house. Go to a safer place. Go to my house or the office."

"I hate the thought of driving anywhere, Marcus. Maybe I'll go to Freemont's. I've called him, but he hasn't called back."

"He may not get home till late, Carrie. I'll ask Jeff to swing by and pick you up." His voice sounded heavy with apprehension. "I love you, baby. I want you safe."

"I love you, too."

After we said goodbye, I went to the bathroom, washed my face and brushed my teeth.

I pulled a duffle from the top shelf of my closet. I was stuffing clothes in it when the phone rang. Before I could answer it, the ringing stopped. No one left a message. I called Freemont again, thinking he'd called, but I got his voice mail.

I called Latrice. Marcus had said Freemont might be with her. But I got a busy signal. Then I dialed the number Marcus had just given me. Another busy signal.

I poured me a glass of chardonnay. As I sipped the wine, the doorbell rang.

I glanced at the video screen and saw a yellow taxi. Had Marcus called a cab for me?

I rushed out to ask the driver as the cab was driving away. I flailed my arms to get his attention, but he didn't stop.

I remembered I'd failed to get my mail. I usually drive up and grab the mail out of the box, but that night my mind wasn't functioning full throttle. The mail box is located near the curve at the end of the drive.

I heard a rustling noise as I walked. I suspected a possum or possibly a bear.

Freemont saw a black bear in his yard last April. The bird feeder attracted the bear, Freemont said. Since then, Freemont has developed a fascination with bears. He's read everything about them. They roam any time of the year if the temperature is pleasant enough to suit them, and they're easily awakened.

I turned toward the noise, expecting to see wild life of some sort. But I didn't see anything. Instead, I heard a swoop as a rope tightened around my arms and chest. I fought and kicked and tried to run but the rope pulled me back.

"Be still, you fucking bitch."

I kicked and kicked. My feet struck my assailant. He was wearing a white pointed hood.

"Shit," he said, wrestling me to the ground. "Fucking nosy bitch. You're going to die." He pounced on top of me. I struggled to breathe. The tightening rope and the weight of him crushed me. His hard shoes dug into my legs. He pinched my breasts. "I'm going to fuck you before I kill you. What do think about that?" I realized then, this was Nev Powers and I would fight him until the end.

I spit at his mask. "You're going to fry for raping and killing Jolene."

Everything went black then, and I don't know how long I was out. But when I finally awoke, I thought I was in hell. My body pulsated with pain.

"You like the way my gun fucks you."

I blacked out, probably from the pain or my brain protecting me from hell. Whatever it was, I must have been unconscious for some time, because when I awoke, I could smell my own vomit.

I still had a rope around me. My wrists were tied, but my legs were free. They cramped as I moved them. My body was bouncing around on a hard surface, each jolt brought more pain than I thought I could stand. My head throbbed. I threw up again.

I heard traffic noises, cars honking, and sirens. It was dark and I couldn't see, but eventually, my eyes adjusted.

I saw what appeared to be a pair of boots. They looked like my boots, the boots I'd been meaning to give away. Had I'd been locked inside the trunk of my own car? The vibrations, the jolts and traffic no ises to ld me we we re on the move. Where was he taking me?

I cried out to God, to Mom, to Dad, "Help me. Please help me."

I kept pleading and praying. Then I thought I heard Dad's voice say, "*Remember the trunk relea se.*" Dad had in-stalled a trunk release in this Cadillac after he'd read about a woman who'd been locked in the trunk of her own car by burglars. He didn't want us to become trapped like that. " *he poor woman would have died in the 90-degree heat if one of her neighbors hadn't heard her banging to get out,*" Dad said.

Dad wanted us to test the trunk release. Mom was claustrophobic and refused, but I eagerly volunteered. I pretended to be Houdini; the illusionist known for his ability to escape impossible situations. Could I preform the same feat with my hands tied behind my back?

I scooted my body around until I gripped the release. Would it work?

I waited for the right time to pull the lever and find out. I knew there might not be a right time. I could die in the process, but if I didn't jump, I might die at the hands of a monster.

Chapter Fourteen

Thursday, March 5

I flew through a tunnel of white light, riding a cool breeze. At the end of the tunnel, I saw Mom and Dad. They looked young, alive and happy. They waved. Their arms reached out to me. "I'm almost there," I said, calling to them. I couldn't wait to hold them and tell them how much I loved and missed them

Then I heard a woman's harsh voice, snapping me back to earth, "Can you hear me?"

Leave me alone. I tried to say the words, but I couldn't seem to move my mouth. The woman's stern voice continued to ask, "Can you hear me?" I became aware of this unbearable pain, my head exploding in agony. I wanted to go back to that heavenly place where Mom and Dad were waiting for me. There was no pain there.

Then I heard a deep, familiar voice say, "I love you, Carrie."

My eyes fluttered. I saw a blinding bright light. My head couldn't take it. My entire body ached. Please just let me go back to Mom and Dad. I waited, but my wish wasn't granted, and I had to endure this excruciating pain.

My eyes were gritty. I squinted to see, but saw only shadows in the blinding light. "Please turn that light off and stop that beeping noise. My head is killing me." I heard my voice slurring.

The light finally dimmed. "Is that better, Carrie."

"Yes. Where am I?" My voice slurred.

"In the hospital."

I opened my eyes wider and saw his giant shadow. "Is that you, Marcus?"

"Yes, baby, it's me."

"How did I get here?"

"Jeff called an ambulance. The EMTs transported you."

"How is that possible?"

"He tracked your car with an electronic device." He squeezed my hand. "I had Jeff install a tracker on your car."

"You did? Why?"

He leaned toward me. "I was worried about you. Your house had been burglarized, remember?"

I remembered but I hurt too much to talk.

"That's why I asked Jeff to install a tracking device on your car. I have one on my Jeep. I'm sorry I didn't tell you. I'm not sorry I had Jeff install it. He may not have been able to follow your car and help to save your life without it." Marcus pursed his lips. "I'm not sure what you remember, Carrie."

"Jolene's dead, and I can't stand this pain."

"We'll get you something for pain. Okay?"

The next thing I remembered was a nurse coming in and giving me a shot, which eased my head but made me groggy.

"Are you feeling any better now, Carrie?" Marcus asked.

"Yes, I think I might live." I opened my eyes wider and saw Marcus smile.

"I certainly hope so. Do you feel like talking?"

"I don't know if I'll make sense. What did you say about Jeff following me?'

"I called Jeff and asked him to pick you up and take you to a safer place."

"I was stupid. I thought you'd sent a cab."

"No, I asked Jeff to go by and pick you up."

"The cab left and I was attacked and tied up. Nev Powers was wearing a Klan mask."

"I'll check with the cab companies and try to locate the driver. What else do you remember, Carrie?"

"Nev Powers hurt me ..." I stopping talking when the flashback came. "And I'm still hurting, but not as bad."

"You don't have to talk if it's too difficult."

"Did you know, Dad had a trunk lever installed. I was able to escape?"

Marcus massaged his eyes. "Thank God. I wish Jeff had gotten to you sooner. He was headed to your house when the tracking system showed your car on the move. He caught up with you and saw Powers driving your car. Jeff didn't know you were in the trunk. Then he saw you jump out. He stopped to help you. Powers started firing. Jeff fired back. He probably hit Powers. There was blood in your car when it was recovered. Jeff didn't pursue him. His first priority was making sure you were okay. He stayed with you until the ambulance came."

"Did you get that monster?"

"No, not yet, but we will. Your car was found parked at the Atlanta airport. But we don't think Powers took a plane. He wasn't listed on any commercial aircraft."

I shivered from pain and fear. "You mean he's still out there?"

"You're safe, Carrie. There's a guard stationed at every entrance to this hospital. There's an officer stationed outside your room. Godwin and I plan to have a talk with Cain Powers. His dad must know where he is. We're also working closely with the Cleveland police. There's more than enough evidence to convict Nev Powers. If I could find him, I'd kill him."

A woman, the color of maple syrup, wearing green scrubs, entered the room. "Hello, I'm Doctor McKinsey." She smiled warmly.

Marcus turned toward her. "She's still hurting."

Freemont walked in behind the doctor. "I just wanted to see how my white sister is doing." He leaned over my hospital bed and pecked me on the cheek. "I'm glad you finally decided to wake up. But looks like you've been in a bar fight and lost."

"I need to be alone with Ms. Justice now," the doctor said. "You two can come back later for a brief visit. But make it brief. She needs her rest."

Marcus pecked me on the mouth. "I hope you feel better soon. You're more beautiful than any bar fighter I've ever seen."

Freemont smiled and waved. "I'll be back."

After Marcus and Freemont left the room, the doctor asked me to call her Doctor Mac, then examined my bandaged head and placed a stethoscope on my chest. A moment later, she looked into my eyes with a pin light. "Can you name the President of the United States?"

"Ronald Reagan."

"Correct. You should feel better soon. How are you feeling now?"

"A little better than shit."

She laughed, which I didn't appreciate. "I like your last name, Justice, what a cool last name to have. What is the origin? Do you know?"

Was she still testing my brain? "It's French, I think. But one of my ancestors was a constable in England centuries ago. He was named Justice due his occupation."

"My last name is of Irish origin. However, I have both Irish and African ancestors. The Irish slaves were sent to the West Indies, where they co-mingled with the black slaves. My husband's last name is Washington. I was tempted to change my name when I married him, but I chose to keep my maiden name."

"Why did you keep it?"

"I think society places too much pressure on a woman to take her husband's name." Doc Mac smiled. I notice the gap between her front teeth, similar to mine and Freemont's. As I listened to her, I wondered if we were related.

"My patients have become accustomed to calling me Doc Mac. So why change that?" As she was talking, she examined the boot cast on my right foot and ankle. "You sustained a Pilon fracture." She pointed at it. "End of tibia, top of the talus foot bone."

"How long will it take to heal?"

"A few more weeks, depending."

"When can I expect to leave here?"

"That's depends on how well you respond to treatment. You've suffered a serious head trauma and swelling. You're very fortunate to be alive and lucid. What is your pain level now? Let's use a scale from one to ten. Ten being the worst." Her golden eyes scrutinized mine as if she could spot a lie.

"My pain was eleven, but maybe it's an eight now. I'm not good at gauging. I'm a little woozy from the pain meds. My head throbs and my ribs hurt when I move."

"Two of your ribs are fractured."

Fatigue pushed on my eyelids. I craved sleep, thinking it would take me out of this misery. "Do you think I'll make a full recovery soon?"

"I certainly hope so."

"Be honest with me, Doc. I want to know what I'm up against."

She frowned. "I try to be honest with all my patients. If I were in your shoes, I'd demand honesty, too." She glanced at her clipboard. "Did you know you are pregnant, about six weeks along?"

Had I misunderstood her? "What did you say?"

"Your fetus is half an inch in length."

Once her words penetrated my brain, I disputed them. "That's impossible. I'm on the pill. You must have me confused with another woman."

The doc shook her head and stared at her clipboard again. "No, there's no confusion. The pill is not a hundred percent effective even if taken as directed."

"Oh, no, I can't be." I was sick the morning we drove up to Cleveland, but I blamed my nausea on trauma and tragedy. I'd forgotten to take the pill a few times. I had a period a week or so after I'd caught Kyle cheating, meaning if I were six-weeks pregnant, Marcus had to be the father. I remembered what Carol said about Susan getting pregnant. Marcus felt obligated to marry her. Then she had a miscarriage in her third trimester.

"You can and you are," Doc Mac said firmly.

"The shot I was given won't hurt her or him, will it?"

"Pain is not good for you or your pregnancy. I'd rather you be relaxed and not in pain. You've been through quite an ordeal. You've suffered genital injury, bruising of the cervix, abrasions of the labia, consistent with rape. But we found no semen present."

Tears spilled down my cheeks. "I've had flashbacks of having the barrel of a gun stuck inside me."

The doctor handed me a tissue. "I think you should talk with a psychotherapist. I can recommend a good one."

"Why do you think I need a psychotherapist?"

"Due to the trauma you've experienced. Therapy has helped me a great deal. I was a victim of date rape. For a long time after, I felt like damaged goods. Through therapy I learned I can choose to be a victor and not a victim. We're all different in how we heal. But you're a strong woman. My hope is that you'll be stronger and more confident than ever with the help of a good psychotherapist."

As I listened to the doctor, my brain went numb. "I'm so tired." I closed my eyes and sleep soon claimed me, but I didn't escape the nightmares. In one of them, I gave birth to a baby so tiny I lost her in the carpet.

Chapter Fifteen

Friday, March 6

I don't know how long I slept, but when I finally woke up, the first thing I saw was this weird hat. It was shaped like a cupcake and reminded me of the photos I'd seen of Florence Nightingale. She'd worn a similar cap. Was I dreaming or drugged out of my mind?

I was in the hospital. That I knew. I could hear the damn beeping machines. My left arm was attached to a bag of fluid.

The woman in the Florence Nightingale hat was examining the bag. Most of her hair was tucked under her cap, only a few strands had escaped. I could see she was a redhead. She wore a crisp, official-looking, nurses' uniform.

I blinked to focus on her. In the pale artificial light, her skin looked luminous, the skin of an angel. But something about her, maybe the smirk or her fierce green eyes, told me this was no angel. I knew this woman.

My heart pounded a warning. I fumbled for the emergency call button. Marcus had placed it next to my right hand to give me easy access. "Why are you here?"

She looked up, as if startled. "I'm Nurse Nipper. I'm here on orders from your doctor."

"That's a strange name." I studied her face. "You're no nurse."

I pressed the call button again.

"Relax. You don't need to get upset. I have something that should help you relax and feel better."

She withdrew three hypodermic needles out of the pocket of her nurse's uniform.

"Why do I need those?" I kept mashing the button. "Get out of here..."

She placed a finger to her mouth and shushed me. "Your doctor has prescribed this."

Then she turned my arm, the one attached to the drip. I watched in horror as she tapped the vein in the bend of my elbow joint with her left hand. On her ring finger, I saw my ring, the engagement ring Marcus had given me.

"Why are you wearing my ring?"

"You're hallucinating."

"No, I'm not. That's my ruby and diamond engagement ring on your finger. Did you steal it? Or did Nev Powers steal it and give it to you?"

I felt the prick of the needle in my arm. I slapped her hands. The hypodermics went flying. She squealed.

The next thing I knew, a nurse I'd never seen before rushed in. She had short, salt and pepper hair and a stern expression.

I pointed to Neeley Nelson, posing as Florence Nightingale. "She's trying to kill me."

Nelson shook her head. "That's ridiculous. This patient is obviously delusional."

The rescuing nurse frowned. Her I.D. badge showed her photo and name, Helen Miller CNO. She stared at Nelson, as if trying to identify her. Then she felt my pulse and inspected my monitors.

Miller asked Nelson, "What is your name? I'm the charge nurse on this floor. I don't recognize you. Do I know you? You're not wearing our hospital's standard nurses' uniform."

"I'm Mary Nipper, RN. I'm new. I work for her doctor."

"That may be, but you're upsetting this patient. I need you to step outside and provide me with your identification."

"This is ridiculous. I want to talk to your supervisor."

"I am the supervisor. I'm asking you to step outside."

"Arrest her," I said. "She tried to kill me. She even stole my ring. She's in cahoots with Nev Powers. He raped and killed a minor, and he tried to kill me. Police are looking for him now. I bet she knows where he is."

"This patient's head injury is obviously more severe than we thought," Nelson said, then stormed out.

Miller glared at me as if she thought Nelson might be right about my head injury. Then she left the room.

Soon after she left, a man in a police uniform walked in. He was about six feet, slim build, in his 40s, short black hair, brown skin. His metal badge identified him as "Ted Lewis, City of Atlanta Police." I'd never met him before, but he looked official.

"Are you suspicious of one of the nurses who came into your room?"

"Yes, she was pretending to be a nurse, but she'd not a nurse." I explained to the officer what happened. He listened, took notes then shared my information with the two-way radio he carried on his belt.

He was still with me when Miller returned. Neeley Nelson left before Miller could talk to her, she said. "I assure you no one else will be allowed in your room without authorization and identification."

I pointed to the prick in my arm. "She tried to poison me." I told Miller about the hypodermic needles. She detached my drip bag and examined the needle prick then searched for the fallen needles.

When she found the hypodermics, she left with the drip bag. A few moments later, another nurse, blonde hair in a pixie—nametag Cecelia Kepler RN—came in behind her with a new bag of fluids. Kepler looked to be in her 20s. Her blue eyes watched me with concern. Had she been told I might harm myself or her?

I watched as she attached the bag to the tube feeding into my left hand. My room had no window and no clock. "What time is it?" I asked Kepler.

She glanced at her watch. "Almost five p.m."

"What day is it?"

"Friday, March six. Is there anything I can get for you?" She smiled, and I thought she must have decided I was somewhat sane. "Your dinner should arrive shortly. Are you hungry?"

"Not really, but I'd like to watch the news."

"Televisions aren't allowed in this room, sorry."

A tall, thin man in blue scrubs brought in a tray of spaghetti and meat sauce with a salad and a roll. I had no appetite, but I didn't dare refuse the food. I was eating for two now.

Miller came in while I was force feeding myself. "You were right about that woman parading as a nurse. We found pentobarbital, pancuronium bromide and potassium chloride in those hypodermics. How she managed to get past the guard is beyond me. She had no identification. From now on, no one will be allowed in this room unless they've been approved."

She asked me to give her the names of those I'd like to see. I recited the names of my closest friends and colleagues. She wrote them down then read through the list to make sure she'd copied the names correctly. "Even these visitors will not be allowed to enter without proper identification. Some of them may have been turned away in the confusion. Better safe than sorry, I always say."

"My mom used to say the same thing. Do you know which friends may had been turned away?"

"No, I'm not privy to that information now." She left the room without further comment.

A few minutes later, another policeman came in. "I'm Larry Stephenson, your new guard."

"You remind me of my friend Freemont Jackson. He could have played offensive line for the Atlanta Falcons."

Stephenson smiled, as if pleased. "I met Freemont when he came by to see you. I told him you were resting and not to be disturbed. He had a woman with him, Dora something. And there was another woman named Lisa, that works with you, I think. She came by with her husband Thomas."

"Did you see Marcus Handley? Did he come by?"

"No, but he may have been by before my shift began."

Marcus said he and Godwin would be interviewing Cain Powers, Nev's father. But I'd lost track of the time and the days then.

"I wish I knew what was going on. There's no TV in here. I can't watch the news. I haven't even been able to see a newspaper."

"You haven't missed much," he said. "Most of the news is depressing." Stephenson seemed easy going, not what you'd expect from a guard. I liked his calm, reassuring voice.

"Could you find out if they've caught Nev Powers yet?"

He folded his arms across his chest. "Last I heard a SWAT Team was sent to his home in College Station. If I hear anything else, I'll let you know."

Chapter Sixteen

Saturday, March 7

"Carrie Sue, Carrie Sue...."

At the sound of my name being called, I woke up from my nightmare and saw Freemont standing beside my hospital bed. "Thank you for waking me. I was having a terrible dream."

"What were you dreaming?"

"Neeley Nelson was tying me up, planning to kill me. Not far from the truth. Did you hear what happened?"

Freemont shook his head. "No."

"She broke in here, disguised as a nurse." I pointed to my arm with the pinprick. "She tried to inject me with poison."

"Are you sure you didn't just dream this, Carrie Sue?"

"Yes, I'm sure. Neeley Nelson tried to kill me. That's the God's honest truth. Not only that, but she stole my engagement ring. I saw it on her finger."

He pulled a chair close to my bed and sat. "Oh, come on, Carrie Sue. That doesn't even make sense."

"You don't believe me?"

"It just sounds too crazy. You've been in a coma for days and ..."

"Ask the head nurse, Miller. She'll tell you. Neeley Nelson attempted to kill me with three hypodermics. Nurse Miller said any one of those hypodermics could have killed me. And Neeley had three. I woke up just in time. I slapped her hand. She dropped the hypodermics on the floor. I pushed the emergency for the nurse. Nurse Miller came in. Neeley ran out. Miller had all of the hypodermics tested. I'm not sure when Neeley took my ring. Powers could have taken it for all I know. He stole my underpants."

Freemont blew out a breath. "How did Neeley Nelson get in here? I had to move heaven and earth to see you."

"She masqueraded as a nurse and charmed herself in. I don't know how she did it. Nurse Miller was wondering the same thing."

"If she did that, they should have arrested her."

"She ran out before they knew what she was up to. Fortunately, I woke up and recognized her before she got a chance to kill me. The moment she pricked my arm with that first shot, I slapped her hand, and she dropped all the needles."

"You just told me that. You're repeating yourself. Are you sure you're okay?"

I studied my friend. His face and eyes looked haggard and sad. He still had his left arm in a sling. "I think I must feel better than you do, Free. You look miserable."

He rubbed his eyes. "We buried Jolene yesterday." He bowed his head. "It was a sad, sad funeral."

"I hate funerals."

"I do, too, Carrie Sue. I guess they serve their purpose. People get a chance to mourn. So many folks came out and talked about what a wonderful person Jolene was. Not a dry eye at AME Christian. Standing room only. The preacher said our loss was heaven's great gain, but I didn't find much relief in that. She had a beautiful spirit. She was a bright light to everyone who knew her. The earth lost another angel. Life's not fair." Freemont took out his handkerchief to wipe his eyes.

I cried with Freemont. "I wish I had some comforting words, but I can't even ease my own heartache and guilt. I wish I could have been able to protect her."

"Doesn't do any good to blame yourself, Carrie Sue. Do you know how long you'll be in here?"

"No, I wish I could leave now."

"How's your head?"

"It still throbs a little, but nowhere near as painful as it was. My brain scan turned out fine. I was told I have a beautiful brain."

Freemont sat stone-faced. He was too sad to joke about my beautiful brain comment. "That's encouraging."

I wanted to tell Freemont about my pregnancy, but I hesitated. Marcus didn't even know yet. If I told Freemont, he'd be burdened with keeping that secret.

Before I could decide what to do, Lisa walked in. Her eyes were red and watery, dark circles under them. She had on blue sweats and wore her blonde hair in a ponytail. Without makeup, she looked pale.

She leaned down and kissed me on the cheek. "We've been worried sick about you, Carrie Sue. Thomas and I came by several times, but couldn't get in. Lindsey said she wasn't allowed in either. Neither was Jackie, and that psychic,

Kasandra. Many, many people have been turned away. We were told you needed your rest and couldn't see anyone. I'm just so relieved to see you now. How are you feeling?"

"I'm grateful to be alive. Have you seen Marcus? He hasn't been in for a while. Do you think he got turned away, too? He said he and Godwin were planning to question Cain Powers. Then the guard outside told me a SWAT team was going over there. What's going on?"

Lisa's exchanged a sideways glance with Freemont. "Nev Powers is dead."

I exhaled a relieved sigh. "Good, he'll never hurt anyone else. I used to believe everyone deserved a fair trial, you know, innocent until proven guilty. But Nev Powers was a monster. How did he die? It's not like him to kill himself. Did the swat team kill him?"

"He was hiding under his house, Carrie Sue...and I don't know if I should tell you this..." She turned to Freemont. He shook his head.

"Tell me what? Why shouldn't you tell me?"

Lisa exhaled a loud sigh. "You're going to find out sooner or later. Marcus crawled under the house after him, and ... and ..."

My heart hammered. "Oh, no, was Marcus hurt?"

She stroked my hand. "A bullet grazed his head. That's all I know. We believe he'll be okay. I don't want you to worry, dear. Marcus wouldn't want you to worry either."

I saw a black wash as the gravity of her words sunk in. The next thing I knew, Nurse Miller was standing over me, placing a cold compress on my head. I heard screaming then realized it was me.

"Can we arrange for her to see this man?" Miller was talking to Lisa and Freemont, as if I wasn't strong enough to respond or comprehend her.

Lisa rushed toward the door. "I'll be right back."

Miller told Freemont he could stay a few more minutes. Then she turned and walked out of the room.

"Don't lie to me, Freemont. How is Marcus? Tell me the truth."

"You need to keep the faith, Carrie Sue. Marcus is tough."

"You're telling me to keep the faith, Freemont, after you told me life is unfair."

"That's why we need to keep the faith. Marcus is a hero for what he did. I don't know the whole story yet, Carrie Sue. But from what I know, he shot Powers in self-defense."

"Oh, no. He told me he'd kill him if he could find him. I should have stopped Marcus. If I'd stopped him, he'd be okay now."

"You couldn't have stopped Marcus from doing what he did."

My heart ached worse than my headache. "I need to talk to him. Where is he now?"

"Grady Hospital."

"How long will he be at Grady? And why wouldn't they bring him here instead?"

Freemont frowned. "I'm not sure."

Lisa rushed back in the room. "Thomas is with Marcus now."

"I need to see him, Lisa. Get me out of here." I started ripping off the tape holding the IV in place.

Freemont forced my hand away. "Stop acting crazy, Carrie Sue. Do you want people to think you're crazy?"

"I don't care what people think."

"Listen to me, Carrie Sue. You can't leave. You aren't out of the woods yet. Your face is purple and swollen. I don't care what they say about your beautiful brain, your brain needs to heal. Now breathe." Freemont inhaled a deep breath, as if I needed a demonstration.

Before I could protest, a dark-haired nurse, about my age, swabbed my arm, and stuck a needle in it.

Chapter Seventeen

Sunday, March 8

I *rocked a baby with two heads. Both of the heads looked like Marcus. The rocking motion made me nauseous, or was it that antiseptic smell making me sick? Someone was calling my name.*

When I opened my eyes, I saw a blurry vision of what appeared to be an angel with Marcus' face. "You're an angel."

"I've been called many things, but never an angel."

"You have a halo."

He smiled and pointed to his head. "Are you referring to this bandage?" His forehead looked blue. He shook his head. "This proves I'm no angel." He squeezed my free hand.

"What happened to you, Marcus."

His navy eyes squinted. "I'd rather not talk about it, Carrie. I'm sorry if I've caused you to worry."

I snatched my hand away. "I need to know, Marcus. Tell me what happened to you."

He huffed and paused then finally said, "I went over to the Powers' home." His eyes shifted from side to side, a signal he was measuring his words and filtering what to say. "Godwin and I were planning to meet at my office and drive over together. But Godwin got detained. In the meantime, Marilyn Weston called the *Southern Journal* to report she'd seen Nev Powers crawling under his house. Her home is directly behind his. I asked her why she called us, rather than the police. She didn't trust the police. They might protect one of their own, she said. Ms. Weston seemed intelligent and clear headed. I drove over there to check out her story. She explained again what she'd seen and where. I walked through her backyard into the Powers' yard. I left a message for Godwin to meet me over there. But I didn't wait for him. I didn't want that asshole getting away. I thought I'd be okay. I carried a flashlight and my Glock. I shouted for him to surrender. Not my smartest decision. I should have known he wouldn't give himself up. It was quiet when I crawled under the house. For a second, I thought he may have left." Marcus closed his eyes, as if picturing the scene. "I flashed my light around. That's when Powers started firing." Marcus pointed to the bruised side of his head. "He got me. It all happened so fast. I opened fire, tried to blind him with my flashlight then rolled behind a pile of junk. I heard him moan and thought I'd hit him. I didn't know for sure. I waited for a few minutes. I thought he might be pretending. By the time I felt confident enough to check, he'd bled out."

"I heard the SWAT team went to the Powers' home."

"That's right. When they arrived, they ordered everyone out of the house. Cain Powers refused to give up the fight. He was killed in the crossfire. He'd been told his son was dead. Neeley Nelson was in the house, too, and she refused to come out."

"What happened to her?"

"She was killed in the gunfight."

"She pretended to be a nurse. She came in my room and tried to poison me. She had three hypodermic needles. Each one of them was lethal, nurse Miller said."

"Jesus." He grimaced. "How did she get in here."

"Nurse Miller wondered the same thing. She was dressed as a nurse. She must have convinced the guard outside my room she was a nurse."

"Lisa always said that woman was crazy. I should have seen it. I'm sorry I didn't, Carrie."

"Not only that. But she was wearing my engagement ring."

He flashed me a look of disbelief similar to Freemont's. "The ring I gave you?"

"You're the only one I'm engaged to."

He gave me his crooked smile, the Elvis smile, I called it. "Incredible. She's dead now. So is Nev. They can't hurt you or anyone else ever again. I'll ask the morgue about the ring. But I wouldn't blame you if you refused to wear it again."

"That ring held the promise of our life together, but you gave it to me before you knew your wife was still alive."

"I gave you the ring and asked you to marry me. My feelings and intentions haven't changed, Carrie Sue."

"Even if that ring is somehow recovered, I don't know if I could ever wear it again, Marcus."

"I understand." He sat silently with his head bowed for a few minutes. I watched him, trying to read his mind.

"I've been debating whether to tell you this, Carrie..."

"Oh, no, tell me what? Does it concern us and our future?"

"No, it's concerns the ground beneath the Powers home. I smelled a sickening stench, like rotting flesh. I recommended an excavation of the area. There have been women, teens, reported missing with a connection to Powers."

"Oh, God, I'm glad he's dead. Freemont thinks you're a hero for killing him, Marcus."

"I'm no hero."

"I think you are and so does Freemont. And you killed Powers in self-defense. He was a psycho. He preyed on women. He had no conscience." I pulled on his hand to draw him closer. "What about Mrs. Powers? What happened to her? Where was she? I've never met her. She lived with her son and husband, I thought. She was paralyzed from an automobile accident. God, I hope she isn't buried under that house."

"Mrs. Powers is alive and living at Cedar Pines, a nursing, rehab facility. She's been there for a few months, I was told."

"That's interesting. Does she know her son and husband are dead?"

"Thomas talked to the administrator of Cedar Pines, and I'm sure she knows by now. From what the administrator told Thomas, Mrs. Powers is able to maneuver with the aid of a walker."

"Really? I always heard she was paralyzed and would never walk again."

"I don't know all the details, Carrie. She may have been restricted in the home. They could have been collecting disability. Or they could have gotten a big insurance settlement due to her injuries that may have been exaggerated. Regardless, I can't imagine what it must have been like living with Nev and Cain Powers." Marcus paused. "Maybe it's time we did another article on elder abuse."

"I've already written several articles on that, as you know, Marcus. But I guess it wouldn't hurt to do another article. Why not let Jackie do it? She might uncover new information on why this despicable exploitation occurs. We already know some of the reasons: violence in the home, passed on from generation to generation; disrespect for the elderly; mental illness; drug addiction; out-of-control stress and economic problems. Very depressing. I had such wonderful parents. I would never abuse them. Though I must admit, I was selfish growing up, especially in my teen years. I didn't appreciate what I had. I used to beg them for things beyond their control to give me."

He smiled. "What would you beg for?"

"I wanted a sister and accused Mom and Dad of being mean for not giving me one. I learned later Mom miscarried, trying."

I touched my tummy, longing to tell Marcus about the tiny life I carried, created out of love. But I couldn't. He was still married, and I didn't know if the life inside me would survive.

"I don't consider your desire for a sister selfish." He kissed my forehead. "Are you in any pain now?"

"Not bad. I'm feeling better. Grateful to be alive and grateful you're alive."

His eyes studied mine, as if he could read my thoughts. "Why do I get the feeling you're keeping something from me. What do the doctors say about your recovery?"

"Doc Mac says my mind is good. The X-ray tech says I have a beautiful brain."

"I have no doubt your brain is beautiful. I don't need an X-ray to verify that."

I chuckled, making my ribs ache. "How is Susan? Does she know what happened to you?"

His eyes shifted to the floor. "She's not doing well. Mom and Susan both know what happened. They know you're in the hospital recovering. They heard about the shootout at the Powers' home from watching the news. I assured them I'm okay. They'd like you to come to the beach as soon as you're well enough to travel."

"I can travel now. They can't hold me here against my will."

As I said this, Doc Mac strode into my room. She asked Marcus to step out while she examined me.

"I'd like him to stay, and I'd like a cot brought in for him to rest. He's been through quite a lot."

Marcus gave me a confused stare. I should have asked him what he wanted, but my separation anxiety had reached an all-time high. "Having him here makes me feel better."

The doctor looked puzzled. "I need to examine you in private. As to the cot, that's unlikely."

Marcus kissed my forehead. "I'll be back." As he walked out the door, I worried. When would I see him again?

Doc Mac shined a pin light in my eyes. "You look better."

"If I were home, I would recuperate faster."

She smiled. "Perhaps, in a few days, if you keep improving."

Her good news lifted my mood. I longed to tell Marcus. He should have told me when he would be back. I waited and waited, growing more anxious by the moment. An hour seemed like two.

When he finally walked in, I exhaled a relieved sigh. "I hope to be out of here soon, Marcus."

"I hope so, too, Carrie. And when your doc gives the okay, ask her if she thinks you've recovered enough to travel to the beach."

"I don't have to ask her. I know." No reason to test the doctor's good will by complicating things. "I'm sure she'll say driving is preferable to flying." I still had my fear of flying.

"Yes, I agree, Carrie. A pressurized cabin might create a problem for you."

He talked about the beach trip. We'd be staying with Carol and Susan, he said. This could be an awkward situation. I'd have to watch my words and actions. Not conducive to relaxation. "Will that house be large enough to contain all of us?"

Marcus nodded, as if unconcerned. "Yes. There's plenty of room. It'll be a short trip. Unless you wish to stay longer. It'll give you a chance to get away, visit with Susan and Mom. Susan would like to talk to you."

Chapter Eighteen

Saturday, March 14

I had a session with Dr. Roper the psychotherapist before I left the hospital. She instructed me to, "Think back to your childhood. Can you remember your first traumatic event?"

"My collie, Jill, got run over by a car when I was eight."

"Okay, rate that event on a scale from one to ten."

"It was a ten at the time. It has decreased to maybe a two. I don't let my mind think about that anymore."

"Good. You know you can control your mind, Carrie Sue. I'm sure you realize now that Jill getting run over was an accident. That accident wasn't your fault."

"Jill used to chase cars. I didn't know how to stop her."

"Regardless, Jill's death was an accident."

Dr. Roper then guided me through my life. I rated every tragedy I could think of. The death of my parents being the most tragic of all.

"How would you rate the loss of your Mom and Dad."

"That was a ten and still is."

"Yes, but you're not to blame for the plane crash that took their lives. However, I want you to know, you have abandonment issues, as a result of that crash."

"What do you mean by abandonment issues?"

"You have a fear of being abandoned."

"I don't know about that. But I have a horrible fear of flying now."

"We will work toward releasing that fear. However, today, let's concentrate on releasing your most recent trauma. You've shown great strength in surviving."

I shook my head. "I'm not ready to talk about that yet."

"I know it's difficult, Carrie Sue. However, if we don't talk about it, it will hinder your recovery." She asked me to focus on her index finger, moving back and forth. "Tell me about the night you were attacked. What did Nev Powers do to you?" How did you feel?"

I shared the horrid details as I watched her finger moving. When I came to the part where I jumped out of the trunk, I stopped talking, but her finger kept moving.

"Let go of this trauma, Carrie Sue. You don't want to be a victim. You're not a victim. You are a survivor. I understand your fear. But you can alleviate your fear by being prepared. Always have an escape route planned. Knowing that you can escape at any time will help you manage your fear and change the way you see this traumatic experience. Life is not always fair. There are crazy people in this world. There are many uncontrollable events. But you can choose to breathe, relax and rate your trauma. Observe the beauty around you. Practice living in the moment. Make a list of the things you are grateful for. Give thanks every day. The sun is shining today. You are blessed. You have a roof over your head and food to eat. Money is not an issue with you. You don't have worry about money. Those are all things to be grateful for. You are loved, be grateful. Your health is improving, be grateful."

As we finished our session, I thanked her. "I feel better already, much more centered."

"And for that I'm grateful, Carrie Sue." Her smile and face reminded me of the Mona Lisa painting.

We continued to chat until Doc Mac came in. She examined me then gave me the final okay to leave the hospital. I'd already seen Dr. Bush, my OB/GYN, the day before. The life Marcus and I had created was gestating nicely, he'd said.

I wanted to tell Marcus, but it still seemed too early. What if we lost this baby? Susan had miscarried. Mom had miscarried. Who's to say I wouldn't miscarry?

"Let's don't keep secrets from each other," Marcus kept saying, as if he suspected I was hiding something from him. Would my secret create an irreparable wedge between us?

That question nagged me as an orderly wheeled me out to the emergency entrance. Marcus was waiting there to pick me up.

He drove us to his house, where he'd prepared spaghetti and meat sauce, according to Mom's recipe. "Did you remember I fixed this very same dish the night we first made love, Marcus?"

"I do."

I thanked him for his romantic gesture. He didn't need to know I'd eaten more than enough spaghetti in the hospital. He served me a plateful, and it was good, like Mom's, but I nodded off after a few bites.

He carried me to bed like I was a breakable doll, helped me out of my clothes and into a silky, baby-blue nightgown he'd purchased. "I bought you a few things I hope you like, Carrie." He still wore the bandage around his wounded head.

"Thank you," I said, then fell into a deep sleep.

Chapter Nineteen

Sunday, March 15

When I awoke the next morning, Marcus wasn't in the bed. I smelled a delicious aroma. My stomached growled. I pulled the covers back to get up as Marcus came into the bedroom carrying a tray of coffee, orange juice, a bowl of sliced cantaloupe, a western omelet, buttered toast and honey.

He smiled as he watched me eat. I ate every morsel.

He pointed to the clock on his bedroom wall. "It's almost ten." I hope you feel rested. I've already packed a suitcase for our beach trip."

I tried to keep my face from showing disappointment. I wanted to stay at his house, rather than drive to the beach. Call me selfish. I loved the attention. I wanted to monopolize him, not share him with anyone else. But I had to face facts. He had a sick wife and a mother who expected us to show up.

"I've prepared a bed for you in the Jeep, Carrie, so you can rest on the drive down."

"Thank you for the great breakfast."

"My pleasure." He moved the tray to his desk, sat beside me on the bed and cradled my face in his hands. We kissed deeply and I could feel my desire building. A good sign. His Bermuda's winged out in front. But Dr. Bush had cautioned me not to have sex until my cervix healed.

Marcus seemed to read my mind. "I wish we didn't have to wait. But we need to. You're still healing." He kissed me again then rose to remove the tray from the room.

When he came back in, he carried me to the bathroom and sat me in a warm tub with my booted foot hanging over the rim to keep it dry. "I'm perfectly capable of bathing myself, Marcus." Did he consider me an invalid now?

"I don't want you to fall or get your boot wet. Besides, I enjoy bathing you." He hiked up the right side of his top lip in his Elvis smile. Then he washed my hair and toweled it dry. "No blow dryers, Doc Mac said."

Marcus combed my damp hair out of my face and into a ponytail. "I got you a pink, one-piece shorts outfit for the trip." He brought me the romper and helped me step into it. Marcus had always been overprotective, but at that moment, I didn't have the strength to argue with him.

"I'm exhausted, Marcus."

He carried me back to bed and I fell asleep again. When I woke up, he said, "I've already put our bags in the car." He carried me to the bathroom—for one last whizz—then to his Jeep.

He placed me on the bed he'd created in the back of the Jeep. It consisted of two sleeping bags and fluffy pillows. "This is comfortable," I said.

"I hope you feel up to talking with Susan and seeing Mom again?"

"I'm a little nervous about it."

"We'll muddle through together, baby. Weather-wise, we couldn't have picked a better day, Carrie. Sunny 60 degrees in Sea Grove."

We were barely out of his driveway when I fell back asleep. In Montgomery, he stopped for gas. I woke up. I had to go to the bathroom. He'd put my crutches in the jeep within my reach. "I can do this. I need the exercise," I told him.

He walked with me as I hobbled to the restroom. After I hobbled back to the car, I got into the passenger's seat next to him. My stomach growled, demanding food. I spotted a Piccadilly sign and asked Marcus to stop there for lunch. He agreed.

Inside the cafeteria, we ordered carrot salad, catfish, fried chicken, butterbeans, turnips, lima beans, squash casserole, cornbread and cheese cake.

"I feel like one of those koalas that eat and sleep much of the day," I said.

After we ate and got on the road again, I leaned back in the passenger's seat, closed my eyes and feel asleep before we left Montgomery. I didn't wake up until Marcus announced, "We're almost there, Carrie. Look at that sunset. Beautiful."

I marveled at the orange, yellow, mauve, and red blanketing the sky. Ten minutes later, he pulled up in the concrete driveway of the beach house he'd rented—white stone, square like a box. It didn't look large enough to house four bedrooms and three baths, as Marcus had claimed.

My heart raced with anxiety. I wasn't ready to greet his mom and Susan. I inhaled deep breaths to relax.

"You okay?" Marcus asked as he helped me out of the jeep. "Don't worry about anything. I'll get you in the house and come back for our luggage."

I hobbled inside with his assistance. The interior walls of the beach house held framed pictures of sand dollars, blue herons, palm trees, and sea shells. The designs on the chairs and sofas in the living room replicated the beach scenes.

From a picture window, I saw white sand, the green gulf and bleeding sunset. On the right side of the large window were sliding doors leading to a screened porch where Susan sat in a wheelchair, as if unaware we'd arrived. A burly, dark-skinned man, with short black hair stood beside her. He wore green scrubs.

When Marcus returned with our luggage, he helped me to the porch. Susan gasped and held out her arms to him as we entered. Marcus kissed her cheek. "I'm glad to see you're enjoying the beautiful sunset, Susan."

"I'm so happy you're finally here." She smiled then turned her attention to me. "Hi Carrie. Welcome." Her pale blue eyes were listless and her face thinner than I'd remembered. A blue blanket covered her waist and legs. She wore a peach-colored gown with long sleeves. Her pink-polished toes peeked through the blanket.

The man in the scrubs said, "I'm Leo. Maxine was scheduled to be here today, but she was a little under the weather, so I told her I'd fill in."

Marcus shook Leo's extended hand. "Thanks for helping out."

"I'm pleased to do it. Susan is a joy. Carol went to the fish market. I expect her back soon." He glanced at his watch. "I hope you don't mind if I take off now. My son has a soccer game. My wife's working the night shift at the hospital and can't take him."

Marcus nodded. "I think we can manage, Leo. You shouldn't miss your son's soccer game."

"Thanks, I appreciate it. If you need me, don't hesitate to page." He pointed to the rectangular beeper clipped to his waist. "Number's on the fridge."

Soon after Leo dashed out, Carol walked in carrying a brown sack. Marcus took the bag from her and set it on the kitchen counter.

Carol's skin looked tanner than the last time I saw her. She had on white Bermuda's and a green T-shirt, similar to Marcus' attire.

"You match," I said, nervously. "Proves you think alike."

Carol laughed. "I don't know about that, Carrie Sue."

Marcus gave her a hug. "You look great, Mom. Are you feeling okay?"

Her eyes glistened. "Thanks, and yes, I'm excited to see you ... to see...both of you. You both look wonderful." She glanced at my booted foot. "How are you doing, Carrie Sue?"

"Hobbling along, but getting stronger every day. I hope I won't have to wear this boot much longer."

She hugged me. "I hope not, too. Dinner will be ready shortly. All I have to do is steam some shrimp and corn. But if you're hungry now, I can heat up the crab soup I made for lunch."

"No rush. We ate not long ago. Are you hungry, Carrie?"

"No, I ate like a pig at lunch. Can I help you with anything, Carol?"

She frowned. "No, no, I want you to relax." She stroked Susan's hair. "Do you feel up to going out to the beach, dear?"

"I think so, Mom." *Wow, she called Carol Mom.*

Marcus motioned for me to come along as he rolled Susan out to the ramp. He had it installed for her. The beach and gulf were several yards away.

I hobbled behind them, inhaling the cool salt air. As I reached the end of the ramp, I stopped to rest. The sky had started to darken. There was a remanence of a full moon.

Marcus lifted Susan and her blanket from the wheelchair and carried her toward the Gulf. He placed her on a green lounge chair. The roaring tide soaked his sandaled feet, the feet of a Roman gladiator.

He tucked the blanket around her then ran back to me. He wrapped his arm around my waist. By then, I was exhausted and didn't reject his help.

He set me down in the chair on the right side of Susan. "The Gulf's calling me. If you two ladies don't mind, I'm going in for a quick swim."

He stripped out of his Bermuda's. He'd worn his bathing trunks underneath. I turned away to keep from staring at his hunky body.

The Gulf's choppy waves were a little rough for swimming. Mom used to warn me about the undertow and sharks. Was Marcus worried about the dangers lurking in the Gulf? Apparently not.

He dove—bandage and all—into the foamy water. I slipped the sandal from my good foot to test the temperature—too cold. I remembered how Marcus once said, *"Swimming and bathing in cold water boosts the immune system. It's a natural high, burns calories, gets the blood pumping and promotes a healthy sex life."*

"How can he swim in that?" I said.

"I don't know. Amazes me. But he's an amazing guy, don't you think?"

I nodded, but chose not to answer. "How are you feeling, Susan?"

"I'm very tired, though I love being out here on the beach."

"I remember you told me that."

"Much better than hospice." Susan coughed. I heard a rattling in her lungs.

Her use of the word hospice startled me. Had she chosen to die here? I wouldn't dare ask her, but the thought made me shiver. Susan was talking about death as Marcus battled the surf with his Australian crawl. "The beach is lovely. Can I get you anything?"

"I'd like a miracle, Carrie. But I don't think you can provide that."

I grabbed the arms of the lounger in preparation for the unknown. "I wish I could. I will continue to pray for you."

Her eyes locked with mine. "Thank you, but I'm afraid I'm at death's door. That doesn't mean I'm blind. I've seen the way Marcus looks at you and the way you look at him. You love him, don't you?"

I froze. How could I possibly answer that question? Was she saying I had no right to love him? Did she think of me as the woman who'd stolen her husband? "I want Marcus to be happy. That's the most important thing."

A tear rolled on her cheek. "I want him happy, too. He can be difficult at times, but he's oh so easy to love, isn't he?" She closed her eyes. "God, I wish I could live long enough to show him how much I love him. I would give anything to go back in time and change the events in my life that kept us apart. But I can't. It's too late for me now. But it's not too late for you, Carrie. It's not too late for him."

"If he survives the surf," I said in a nervous attempt to lighten the conversation, though I worried about his safety. The waves were fierce, slapping him around.

"I predict he'll survive." She stared out at the Gulf. "Don't you think love is more important than anything?"

"I would say so, yes, love and kindness."

"They're more important than ambition, pride and riches. Without love, you have nothing." She grimaced, as if in pain. "I envy you. I know you've lost your mom and dad. You almost lost your life, but I still envy you. Marcus loves me, but not in the same way he loves you. He was my first love. My first and my last."

I wiped my teary eyes. "I'm sure you know him much better than I do."

"I've been a part of his family for a long time. Now I'm at the end of my journey. It's finally time I go." She took a labored breath, coughed, grabbed her chest and slumped forward.

"Susan, Susan?" I kept calling her name as I stumbled up from the lounge to find her pulse. My heart pounded, but not hers. I had to force her mouth open to blow into it. In a CPR class, I'd been taught how to pump a chest. But she was extremely frail. She'd undergone a double mastectomy. I wanted to help her not hurt her.

I yelled and waved and finally caught Marcus' attention. He rose from the Gulf and ran toward us, agony on his face.

Chapter Twenty

Thursday, March 19

The Gulf of Mexico sparkled like a gazillion emeralds floated on top as Marcus steered a Sea Ray, 34-footer out to sprinkle Susan's ashes. Carol sat across from me with her arms wrapped around the blue urn containing Susan's remains. "This is what Susan wanted," Carol said. "She didn't want to be buried in the ground."

Marcus' younger sister Aliza sat beside me. She was a beautiful lady with long dark hair that blew back in the wind. She'd flown in from California with her two young sons Josh and Jonah. The boys laughed and talked, as if unaware they were attending a burial. They resembled their mom, Carol and Marcus.

Marcus and Aliza had similar full lips, navy eyes, olive complexion and high cheek bones. When I mentioned the similarities, they nodded as if they'd heard the compliment often.

I felt a splash of salt water as Josh and Jonah squealed "dolphin." I turned to see where they were pointing and saw the fins of some creature that I wanted to believe was a dolphin.

The boys begged to go swimming, but their mom refused to allow that. "The water is too cold and too deep. And I'm not completely sure that's a dolphin. Might be a shark."

Undeterred, the children continued to plead until Marcus promised to take them swimming later. "For now, calm down. There'll be no swimming if you don't show respect at your aunt's burial."

The boys promised they'd behave, though they still squirmed around all over the boat. At one point, they started to take off their life preservers. Aliza yelled, "Stop. No one is allowed on this boat without a life jacket."

"I wish Tom could have joined us," she said. "He couldn't get away. He's responsible for the care of twin babies, born prematurely." Her husband was a pediatrician.

Aliza was a pediatric nurse. She'd assisted in the delivery of the tiny twins. "They were born jaundiced with breathing problems," she said. "Their blood had an excess of bilirubin. That's a yellow pigment in red blood cells. Their little livers weren't mature enough to get rid of it," she explained.

As I listened, I held my stomach. Would I give birth to a healthy baby? It would be a miracle. Susan wished for a miracle, but she didn't get it. I swallowed my nausea to keep from puking on the boat. A tough day all around. Morning sickness and depression.

My sad mind flashed back to my last conversation with Dr. Roper. I'd called her soon after Susan passed. *"What if Susan gave up hope due to my relationship with Marcus?"*

"You have survivor's guilt, which is common," Dr. Roper sad. "But you didn't cause her death. You shouldn't shoulder the blame. None of this is your fault. You have no reason to feel

guilty. Guilt is manmade or in your case woman made. You must refuse to take it on. Think of yourself as an innocent bystander, who provided the closure she needed in order to let go of her suffering."

"I was having an affair with her husband."

"Carrie Sue, from what I know, you were engaged to a man you love very much, who thought that his wife was dead. It must have been quite a shock when you and Marcus discovered that she was still alive. Yet, despite that shock, the man who asked you to marry him and apparently loves you, did everything he could to make Susan's last days comfortable. And you agreed with his decision to tend to his wife. It's not your fault she was held in captivity during that horrible war. Life is not always fair, as I've said many times. Life hasn't always been fair to you. Life wasn't fair to Susan. But you, Carrie Sue, are still very much alive. And you can choose not to be a victim. You can choose to let go of your guilt. Enjoy your life. Be grateful for each and every moment."

As I reflected on Dr. Roper's advice, Marcus killed the motor. We floated on the choppy Gulf.

Carol stood and manage to gain her footing on the rocking boat. "You have your wings now, sweet angel. You will always be with us in spirit and in our hearts." She removed the top from the urn.

As Carol sprinkled out the ashes, I remembered Susan's last words. They still haunted me. I'd shared them with Marcus soon after she'd passed. He'd wept and said:

"I was aware Susan's cancer had spread and she might not live much longer, I wanted to make her as happy and comfortable as possible, Carrie. She lived longer than expected.

She was lucid till the end. She said she didn't want to live if she lost control of her mind."

"She must have suffered greatly, Marcus. But you were there for her. You never deserted her. You tried to relieve her suffering and make her last days happier."

He held me as he cried. "She kept apologizing for hurting me when she'd suffered much more than I had. Her decision to rescue her friend had been a brave and noble one. I tried to convince her of that. As to why she didn't share her plans with me, that was largely my fault. I tried to make her see that, too. I was stubborn and controlling. Still am, as you know. I hope I don't continue to make those same mistakes, Carrie. If you ever, ever think I don't respect your feelings and your wishes, please tell me. Never feel as if you have to hide anything from me." When he said this, I put my hand on my stomach. I'd hidden a vital secret from him.

"Dad loved Mom, Carrie, but he had a problem communicating. He was a workaholic. Mom would often ask him to sit and talk, but he'd say, 'Let's talk later. I need to work now.' I loved my dad and respected him, but in looking back, I realize he was uncomfortable with intimacy. I don't want to be like that. I know we both work hard. We share a passion for our work. But we also need to take time for each other. I love you more than I can say. The love and the passion we share is above and beyond anything I've ever known. I believe our love will endure if we communicate our feelings and don't keep secrets from each other."

Chapter Twenty-one

Friday, April 10

I finally got the nerve to tell Marcus about our pregnancy. He insisted on getting married right away. I told him we needed to wait. I was afraid Carol might consider our marriage premature. She'd sprinkled Susan ashes over the Gulf only two weeks ago.

Marcus eventually got his way. I pleaded with him not to tell his Mom that we were expecting, and thankfully, he agreed to abide by my wishes. "We'll tell her after we get back from Paris." He'd already made arrangements for our honeymoon there.

We considered having a beach wedding. Who could ask for a better setting than white sand and green gulf? But I still harbored the memory of Susan's last words, and I wanted our wedding to be convenient for our friends to attend. Freemont was swamped with work and his college studies. He couldn't find the time to get away to the beach, even for a weekend.

I agreed to have the ceremony at AME Church, which pleased Freemont. "I'm giving you away. Don't go promising that job to anyone else."

In making a list of attendees, I included Kasandra Rubin and almost called Kasandra to arrange for another reading, but I changed my mind. What if she predicted doom and gloom?.

I asked Lisa, Latrice, Carol and Freemont to send out the invitations. Several of the AME congregation had RSVP'd, already. I preferred a small gathering, but that didn't seem likely. Carol said she expected about 200 people to attend.

I still wore the boot on my foot. In another week, I expected to be free of the damn thing. Would the boot be invisible under my long wedding gown? Lisa and Carol didn't think so. They'd helped me select the gown—a sleek design of silk and lace, with tiny red roses, painted on the bodice and skirt. "Lovely," Lisa and Carol said. My stomach was beginning to swell. Would I be able to fit in the gown on my wedding day?

Marcus said he wanted me to gain more weight. He could care less about whether my gown fit or not. He was more concerned with my pregnancy. He insisted on going with me to see Dr. Bush to make sure the life we'd created was growing as expected. Dr. Bush assured us all was well. Our baby should arrive in September, he said.

The day of the rehearsal, I puked. I still suffered from morning sickness. Marcus would be picking me up from my house that afternoon. He would have preferred that I stay away from the house, but I convinced him the trip was necessary. "I have to pick up Mom's good luck earrings. I want to follow the wedding tradition of wearing *Something Old* to protect the baby to come?"

Realtor Joyce Reed had mailed the missing earring to my house, with a note that said she was still in shock about Nev Powers and the body buried behind his cabin. She apologized for telling him she'd seen me that day: "He just happened to call out of the blue. It was an innocent mistake on my part. Please forgive me."

Nev Powers had been in the news quite a bit lately, even though he was dead. During the excavation of the grounds beneath his College Station home, two bodies were found and identified through dental records as Cheryl Rodrigues, 14, and Shanna Jefferson, 15. Prior to being reported missing, they were picked up and charged for truancy. That was when Nev Powers came in contact with them. Marcus suspected there were other victims. "If I hadn't killed him, we could have forced him to identify the others and tell us where they're buried."

"No one could have forced him to do anything," I told Marcus, but he still struggled with his decision to go vigilante. The police had questioned him at length about the shooting. Eventually, they decided he'd acted in self-defense. If he hadn't killed Nev Powers, the SWAT team would have.

"I feel much safer now, knowing Nev Powers is no longer on this earth." But no matter what I said to convince him, Marcus was still overprotective. He wanted to know where I was at all times.

When I told him I planned to drive to my house to pick up my earrings and other stuff, he wanted to go along. Then Carol stepped in and said she'd drive me. I was perfectly capable of taking myself, even with the boot, but I didn't want to argue with him or Carol the day before the wedding.

On the drive over, Carol said Marcus would lighten up once he knew I'd fully recovered. But Carol didn't know I was pregnant, and of his determination to protect me and our unborn baby. If something happened to this baby—heaven forbid—he'd feel responsible.

"Your house is absolutely beautiful, Carrie Sue," Carol said as we parked in the circular drive. "It reminds me of *Gone with the Wind*."

Once inside, Carol walked through, admiring mom's talent for decorating. She'd purchased many of the furnishings and paintings from estate sales, I said.

After touring the house, Carol called to check on the wedding cake. "I need to go over to Makala's right now, Carrie Sue," she said, after she hung up from the baker. "Why don't you come with me?"

"I need to stay and gather some things, finish what I'd started."

"Okay, I won't be long. I'll call Marcus and let him know."

After she drove away in the Ford Mustang GT Marcus had rented for her, I walked out to the porch to breathe in the day. The sun beamed down from one of the bluest skies I'd ever seen. Birds chirped. Squirrels ran through the trees. It was a perfect spring day; sunny, with a nice breeze. I sat in one of the iron chairs on the porch and listened to the sounds of nature. The vegetation behind the house had grown tall and dense since Freemont and I were children. We used to roam every inch of these woods.

I could almost feel Mom and Dad in the sun and sky. I longed for their physical presence. I wanted them with me to share my happiness. They would have been awesome grandparents, the best. "I'm sorry you won't have that experience," I said, as if they could hear me. "I miss you so much."

I cried as memories flooded through me. I tried to think happy thought, but Susan's last words kept coming back.

"I'm so sorry for all of your suffering and heartache, Susan," I said as if she could hear me. "You deserved a wonderful life. I will cherish your memory as will Marcus. If only I could get a sign from you that you're at peace. I'd like your blessing before marrying Marcus tomorrow."

I studied the sky, looking for a heavenly sign. Freemont and I used to make a game out of identifying objects in the clouds. He might see an eagle. I might see an angel. But we always enjoyed cloud watching. Sometimes we'd pretend we had the power to move them, though logically we knew clouds move pretty well on their own.

I looked up and saw hearts in the clouds. A serene feeling came over me, as my guilt seemed to vanish. I kissed my right hand and threw a kiss to the clouds then hobbled back inside to gather what I needed for the wedding ceremony.

For the *Something New,* to follow the tradition, I decided my new engagement ring would suffice. Marcus had insisted on buying me a new ring, even though he'd recovered my other ring from Neeley's dead finger.

"That ring carries negative vibes," I told Marcus. "A simple wedding band is all I really want. Our love is much more than any ring could signify."

Marcus nodded in agreement, but when we went to the jewelers to select our bands, he stubbornly refused to leave until he bought a round-cut diamond solitaire set in white gold. Exquisite, but unnecessary.

For the *Something Borrowed*—which was supposed to bring good luck if the item were borrowed from another happy bride —Carol loaned me her diamond necklace. She'd worn this beautiful necklace on her wedding day, she said.

For the *Something Blue*—the color representing the sign of fidelity — I would be wearing the blue flats I'd purchased. I could only wear one, of course, with the boot. I put the left shoe on my uninjured foot and practiced walking gracefully, rather than hobbling. I was stumbling in my practice walk when the doorbell chimed.

Thinking it was Carol and I'd lost track of time, I limped down the hallway to the front of the house. In the monitor, I saw an older woman with grey hair and a pinched, stern face. She wore a blue gingham dress. She was supporting herself with a cane.

A few years back, a similar lady—though she didn't have a cane—came to visit. She turned out to be a Jehovah's Witness. I invited her in. She gave me a Bible and stayed for hours, talking and preaching the gospel. I didn't have time for that today.

I cracked the door open. The woman's thin lips trembled. She clutched a wobbling cane in her right hand. Her left hand held a large brown pocketbook. I saw no car in the driveway. Had someone dropped her off? "May I help you?"

"I'm Prudence Powers." Her voice was deep for an elderly lady. "We've never met. But you knew my deceased son, Nevil."

I stood with my month open. Was this the mother of Nev Powers? I was stunned and didn't speak for a moment. Marcus said Mrs. Powers had been transferred to Cedar Pines, a nursing, rehab facility. She could finally walk again after years of paralysis from an automobile accident. The accident had not only paralyzed her but killed Nev's twin brother.

"May I come in?"

I nodded and stepped out to help her.

She pushed my hand away. Odd. Why would she refuse my assistance? Her eyes were identical to Nev's eyes, which reminded me of the Tiger's Eye stone. The resemblance made me shiver.

"I don't plan to stay long."

I led her into the dining room. She sat across from me at the antique table Mom bought at a garage sale. "May I offer you something to drink or eat, Mrs. Powers?"

She shook her head no.

"I heard you were in rehab at Cedar Pines. You seem to be moving well. That's quite an accomplishment. It must be great to be able to move and walk again."

She stared around the room then fixed her tiger eyes on me. "I don't feel great. I'm sad. I've lost my family."

"I know what it's like to lose your family. I'm sorry for your loss."

"I don't believe you're sorry."

"Excuse me?"

"I blame you." She pointed a crooked index finger in my direction.

Had I failed to hear her correctly? Marcus had mentioned she may have been abused in the home she shared with her husband and son. How could she blame me for their deaths? "What did you say, Mrs. Powers?"

"You heard me. I blame you."

"Why do you blame me?"

"If not for you and your crew, I'd still have my son and husband."

Blood rushed to my face. I lost my temper. "Your son was a monster. He raped and killed a beautiful, teenage girl, with her whole life ahead of her. And he killed and buried at least two other girls. Their bodies were found under your house, for God's sake."

"Liar."

"And your husband and your son shot my friend Freemont." Still seeing red, I lashed out "And your son raped me with the barrel of his gun. He would have killed me if I hadn't escaped. I almost died. You should be blaming him and your husband. I thank God they won't be able to hurt anyone else."

She opened her mouth and revealed her tiny, yellow teeth. "Liar, liar, liar."

My chair fell backwards as I stood. "I think it's time for you to leave. Now."

"Not yet, dearie." She plopped her purse on the table.

I saw the flash of the gun as she withdrew it from her purse. "You're crazy. Put that away." I heard steps in the foyer.

"Carrie, you left the door open," Marcus called out.

Mrs. Powers smirked, pointing the gun at me. "Two for the price of one."

"Stay away," I yelled.

He walked into the dining room. "What's going on, Carrie?" His face mirrored confusion and horror.

Prudence Powers cocked the gun and pointed it in his direction. I leaped across the table, trying to stop her from shooting him.

As I grabbed her hand holding the pistol and tried to wrestle it from her, it fired into the ceiling. Marcus grabbed the gun away from Mrs. Powers. He stood behind her, grabbing her around the waist as she flung her arms around like a bird trying to fly. Then she closed her eyes and collapsed.

Marcus laid her down on the floor and felt her pulse. "She's still alive, but call an ambulance."

I did as he instructed, and when the paramedics arrived, Marcus said he would call the police on duty at Grady hospital, where they were taking her, and report what had happened.

Marcus wanted me to go to the hospital to make sure I and our baby were okay, but I refused. "We're fine, Marcus. I'm not in any pain, except for a little throbbing in my foot. I just need to rest."

An hour later, I packed up everything I needed for the wedding, and he drove me to the church for a short rehearsal. He didn't want me to return to my house after everything that had happened to me that day. Carol insisted that we spend the night at his house and he spend the night at the office apartment. "It's bad luck to see your soon to be bride on the day of the wedding," Carol said.

Chapter Twenty-two

January 30, 2014

Carrie Sue Justice-Handley

She turned the page of her diary to continue reading, but the pages that followed were blank. Why hadn't she written anything in her diary about her wedding? No doubt she was zoned out that day, but she still had her photo album, filled with wedding pictures, to refresh her memory. She'd thumbed through that album yesterday.

She closed her diary and pushed herself up from the pillows stacked near the fireplace—the burning wood smelled of pine sap, a bittersweet reminder. Her injured right leg, stiff as an oak, ached worse than usual, due to the cold weather and lack of exercise. She'd lain in one position for too long.

A crashing sound startled her as she turned toward the picture window. What was that? Her heart hammered as she listened and watched the falling snow—glistening like diamond dust. Would she regret escaping to this old house? Perhaps, but she was determined to face her fears, not run from them.

Disaster casters had predicted a blizzard. Their dire forecasts had caused most of the Atlanta area to shut down.

Not unusual for an old house to make eerie sounds when the wind is howling outside. As a child, she'd jump in bed with her mom and dad when a storm hit. Her dad would have preferred a smaller, more modern space, but this house had been in his family since the early 1800s. It had even survived Sherman's torching of Atlanta during the Civil War. Her mom, an interior decorator, refused to live anywhere else. She loved the antebellum architecture and enjoyed the challenge of making it into a livable home.

Her life in this house had been mostly happy until it turned tragic and made her more hypervigilant. Her employees at the Southern Journal had cautioned her not to return to the house where she'd been attacked. As a way of explaining why, she said she needed to sort through all the memorabilia. She'd been thinking of donating this place to the Atlanta Historical Society.

Carrie Sue grabbed a lantern and began inspecting each room—downstairs and up—but not the attic. She refused to enter that haunted space. One of her ancestor's hung herself up there.

The closets held clothes she needed to pack and give away. Nothing surprising or frightening.

She rechecked the doors leading outside—all locked. The security system didn't work, due to the power outage, but the doors were locked, and she'd seen nothing suspicious on her walkthrough.

In the kitchen, she found a bottle of Sweet Blackberry Wine—a Christmas gift from Jackie Steiner, a longtime

Southern Journal employee. She poured a glass and sipped. Tasted like blackberry cobbler, even though the label boasts 14 percent alcohol.

As she poured a second glass, her cellphone rang. The iPhone screen identified the caller as "Free."

"Hi Freemont, let me call you back. I need to go out in my car and charge my cell phone before it goes dead. The storm has knocked out the power in this old house."

"Okay, but hurry, I've got great news. Call me back pronto."

The cold chilled her to the bone as she dashed out in her housecoat and Long Johns to crank up her new Cadillac—a Christmas gift to herself. She turned up the heat in the car then attached the charger to her phone and called Freemont back.

He answered on the first ring. "Are you ready to hear some great news."

"Yes, I could use some great news."

"I'm about to meet with a famous movie director. Can you believe that, Carrie Sue?"

She laughed, as she often did when they talked. He was still her best friend after all these years. "Are you going to be a movie star now?"

"Could be. I'm in LA, the land where dreams come true. Remember I told you Dora Lee and I were flying here with Martin. He has a scholarship at UCLA."

"I know. That's wonderful. I'm sure he's excited."

"Yeah. I think we've finally got him settled in. He loves it here, and I do, too. It's warm and beautiful."

"Don't rub it in."

"You sound a little puny."

"I'm okay, just trying to stay warm. I've gathered enough firewood to keep the downstairs fairly toasty, and I found three lanterns that still work. So, I can't complain."

"You sound hoarse. What's goin' on?"

I haven't talked much today. I've been too busy reading my diary. I found it locked up in an old cedar chest. I've spent most of the day traveling back in time. I only wish I could change the horrible stuff and keep the good."

"I didn't even know you kept a diary, Carrie Sue, but that's beside the point. You need to let go of the past and practice living in the moment."

"Easy for you to say, Free. Your moments are lovely and you probably don't need to make peace with the past, but I do. I can't believe I didn't write anything about my wedding, but I wrote about Prudence Powers coming here. Remember her?"

"She was one crazy old lady. The apple sure didn't fall far from the tree in that family. She was lucky they shipped her off to Milledgeville. She should have been arrested and jailed. But let's change the subject, shall we? How long do you expect to stay in that house?"

"I don't know. I'm not ready to leave yet. I have too much memorabilia to sort out and go through."

"It's been rough on you, I know. It's only been a year since you lost Marcus, and everyone grieves differently. Eventually you'll get to where you can focus on the good memories. You and Marcus were extremely blessed to have each other for as long as you did. You were sweethearts till the end. There was nothing he wouldn't do for you. Nothing you wouldn't do for him. You made three beautiful children. Bridget is a miracle baby. She survived everything you went through. She's a lot like her dad. She worries about you."

"I wish she'd focus on her own life and not mother me. I'm not ready for a reversal of roles. I still can't believe she's all grown up. It seems like yesterday she was born."

"Yeah, they grow up too fast. Dora Lee and I were just saying the same thing. We were looking at old pictures the other day. We have some great photos of you and Marcus at your wedding. And you're right. It does seem like yesterday, but it's been decades. When we were kids, it took forever for Christmas and then summer. Now in the blink of an eye a decade passes."

"I've been looking at old photos, too. Tiffany was the cutest flower girl I've ever seen. She was so tiny then. I can't believe she's now an M.D."

"I can't believe it either. I may not be her natural father, but I claim Tiffany as my daughter. I always thought Martin would be a lawyer. Dora Lee and I would be covered then. But Martin's set on an acting career. I've done everything on God's green earth to try to talk him out of it."

"He definitely has the talent and passion to be an actor. He writes well, too. Who knows? He might become a famous director one day. Ah, to be that young again. I used to have a burning passion for journalism."

"Oh, come on, Carrie Sue. You still have that passion. You run a successful newspaper business and everyone loves the columns you write."

"I appreciate the encouragement, Free, but I feel like I'm just going through the motions nowadays. I miss Marcus so much. I don't sleep well. I keep having nightmares of the day Marcus died. I blame myself."

"There was nothing you could have done, Carrie Sue. You know what the doctors said. He died from a ruptured brain aneurism."

"I should have seen the warning signs. He'd been having headaches. It wasn't like him to have headaches. I should have made him get a physical, but he thought going for a run would make him feel better. If I'd forced him to see a doctor, he might be alive today."

"You need to let this go, Carrie Sue. You and Marcus had more than thirty great years together. You two were blessed. He's with you in spirit. My mama passed decades ago. But I still feel her with me. Same thing with your mama and daddy. Our loved ones are with us. And they live on in our children. Speaking of kids, have you heard from the twins? They should be in the Holy Land by now."

"Yes. Seth and Ben both love Israel. They Face Timed me two days ago. They'd travel all the time if they could."

"Have they decided what they're majoring in yet?"

"No, not yet. A counselor at UGA has been advising them. I'm not trying to influence them one way or the other. They're only freshmen. They have plenty of time to decide. I thought they might go into political science. They were both excited about signing up for a Political Parties course. But they may have thought the class involved partying."

Freemont laughed. "They're a party in and of themselves."

"Yes, they're definitely happy-go-lucky, the complete opposite of Bridget."

"Yeah, she has always been an over-achiever. Being the oldest and on the serious side, she'd already taken the over-achiever identity, so the twins picked the fun-loving identity."

"Wise observation. You're probably right, Free."

"All in all, Carrie Sue, you've got some great kids. They love you. They depend on you. You need to stay healthy and up for them and for you. You're always making lists of what you need to do. Why not make a list of everything you're grateful for?"

"I know I should be grateful."

"Hold on a minute, Carrie Sue. James Marcellus just walked in."

She heard the two men greet each other before Freemont returned to the phone, "James and I met this morning, Carrie Sue. His daughter Jo is enrolled at UCLA, too. She and Martin are the same age. And, guess what? I found out he's gettin' ready to do another movie. He'd like to film it in the south. And he's looking for a haunted, antebellum house, like the one you have. I even told him about the girl who hung herself in your attic. I know that was ages ago, way before you and I were born, but I believe the story. Don't you? Your grandmother wouldn't have written about it in her journal if it wasn't true. Okay, that's the scoop. I'm passing the phone to James."

"Wait a sec, Free, don't..."

"Hello Carrie Sue." The deep voice reminded her of Marcus. She'd seen an interview with James Marcellus on *Entertainment Tonight*. He was an Oscar-winning director. His wife had died from colon cancer a couple of years ago.

"Hello, Mr. Marcellus."

"Please call me James or JM. I don't answer to Mr. Marcellus. I see you're having snow in Atlanta. How are you fairing?"

"I've never quite mastered the skill of driving in snow, so I'm staying in."

"Living in California, I certainly have no desire to master that skill. If the Weather Channel is accurate, you'll have warmer weather soon. I hope so. I'm flying into Atlanta next Friday. Freemont has piqued my interest. I'd love to see your ancestral home. I'm searching for a house like yours for my next project."

She hesitated, not knowing what to say. She didn't feel ready to receive a guest and certainly not one she didn't know well. "This house is a mess right now and disorganized. I've been going through all sort of memorabilia lately."

"I'm not *Southern Living.* I mainly want to get a sense of your home's setting, and see if we can come to an agreement. No pressure. I'm looking forward to meeting you."

Before she could object, Freemont said, "Okeydokey, Carrie Sue. James and I are goin' to get a bite to eat and chew the fat. I'll call you later. Meanwhile, keep the faith. Love you."

After they clicked off, she called Bridget to share what Freemont and James Marcellus said. "Wow, Mom, that's exciting. That house would be perfect. It's incredibly spooky."

Bridget and Carrie Sue chatted for several minutes—long enough for the fire in the living room to burn down to embers.

She shivered from the lack of warmth and threw four logs in the hearth, then wrapped up in an afghan. As she watched the flames, she drifted off to sleep and dreamed of her wedding day.

Marcus was wearing a tailored tux, his dark hair slicked back. His navy eyes shined as he said, "I'll always love you, baby, in this life and beyond. You're my soulmate forever."

About the Author

Sandy Semerad earned a journalism degree from Georgia State University in Atlanta, where *Carrie Sue's Diary* is set. Similar to protagonist, Carrie Sue Justice, Sandy worked as a newspaper reporter in Atlanta for many years. She grew up in Geneva, Alabama, near the Florida line, and now makes her home in Seagrove Beach with husband Larry and their Shih Poo Elvis. Sandy has two daughters, Rene and Andrea, and a granddaughter, Cody. For more information, visit her website sandysemerad.com and connect with her on Facebook and Twitter.

Read more at www.sandysemerad.com.

Other novels by Sandy Semerad:

Sex, Love & Murder

Hurricane House

A Message in the Roses

Made in the USA
Monee, IL
20 October 2023

44882349R00174